# Slay
# in Character

## Also by Lynn Cahoon

# SLAY
# IN CHARACTER

## LYNN CAHOON

**KENSINGTON BOOKS**
www.kensingtonbooks.com

KENSINGTON BOOKS are published by

Kensington Publishing Corp.
119 West 40th Street
New York, NY 10018

All Kensington titles, imprints, and distributed lines are available at special quantity discounts for bulk purchases for sales promotion, premiums, fund-raising, educational, or institutional use.

Special book excerpts or customized printings can also be created to fit specific needs. For details, write or phone the office of the Kensington Sales Manager: Attn.: Sales Department. Kensington Publishing Corp., 119 West 40th Street, New York, NY 10018. Phone: 1-800-221-2647.

Kensington and the K logo Reg. U.S. Pat. & TM Off.

First Printing: December 2018
ISBN-13: 978-1-4967-1681-1
ISBN-10: 1-4967-1681-7

eISBN-13: 978-1-4967-1682-8
eISBN-10: 1-4967-1682-5

10 9 8 7 6 5 4 3 2 1

Printed in the United States of America

To my friend, Laura Bradford, who is always there to listen, to plot, or to help rein in the bright and shiny ideas.

# Acknowledgments

The more books I write, the longer I'm an author, the more I realize what I don't know. There's always something new to learn in the book-writing world. But there is one thing that keeps me going: readers who tell me they love my characters as much as I do. I've been putting Cat, Seth, and Shauna through the wringer now for four stories. And I love the process more and more each time. My mother-in-law told me what needed to happen in this book after reading *Of Murder and Men*. And although I didn't take all her suggestions, one did stick. I think you'll agree, it was for the best.

# CHAPTER 1

How did the saying go? History repeats itself, or to forget our past is to relive it in our future? She was probably mixing a few different sayings. Cat Latimer played with the quote in her head as she helped Seth unload the five writers from the SUV. The day trip to Outlaw, a local ghost town, was a new retreat adventure add-on, and all five writers had signed up for the extra day for the June retreat. Even the Covington College student attendee, Jessi Ball, had paid the extra fee to visit Outlaw with the group.

The dust from the parking lot settled around them, and Cat wiped it from her face. The air here was thinner, as they were nestled high in the mountains. Outlaw had originally been an old mining town. In the high valley, the sun seemed even closer and brighter. She adjusted her sunglasses and took in the entrance. The pine smell from the trees filled her senses and reminded her of a camping trip she and Seth had taken the summer after senior year. The last campout before he'd joined the army and left for his new future. She could taste the s'mores they'd made before they'd lain out on the air mattress he'd set up next to the fire pit. She pulled herself from the memory and looked over at him as he helped the last guest out of the vehicle.

Feeling the heat from the memory and the Colorado summer day, Cat handed each writer a small backpack she'd had made up with *Warm Springs Writers' Retreat* on the front along with a black-and-white picture of a Victorian-era house. "Inside you'll find a water bottle, a disposable camera, a notepad for inspiration, two pens, and a few bakery items from Shauna, our resident chef, to keep your brain cells firing."

"When do we meet for lunch?" Connie McDonald slipped on her sunglasses as she glanced around the parking lot.

"We'll be eating at the saloon, so meet us there at high noon." Cat smiled. The group, except for Jessi, were all historical romance authors and were all from the same writers' group in Connecticut. They'd booked the retreat as soon as Cat had put up a note about the added visit to the Colorado ghost town. After that, Cat had had several inquiries from romance groups wanting to book the entire house. She'd have to work out the arrangements with Shauna, but if they could pull it off, the retreat could probably host two or three of these special events a year at full occupancy.

"Does anyone want my camera? I'll be using my phone, and besides, I can get pictures anytime."

Jessi held up the camera and Kelly Adams snatched it from her hand. Kelly was a striking brunette whose emerald green eyes seemed to bore right though you when she talked.

Kelly tucked the camera into her bag, then looked around at the group, who were all staring at her. "Oh, yeah, please and thank you."

"Kelly doesn't get out much," Cora Sanders fake-whispered to Cat. The woman was in her fifties, but with her blond hair loose around her shoulders, she looked younger. "She's been under continuous deadlines for the last two years since her book sales went crazy through the roof."

"My sales aren't that crazy," Kelly muttered, a flush on her cheeks, "but my contracts are keeping me busy. I'll admit that."

"She's a contract collector," Lisa Freeman teased. "The rest of us are lucky to have one contract at a time, and our friend Kelly here has three."

Kelly's face turned beet red. "Four, counting the novella contract I just signed last week."

The group exploded into laughter.

"Frankly, I'm not sure why we keep her around." Cora took Kelly's arm in hers. "Let's go step into the Old West and get some ideas for our next best sellers."

Seth Howard leaned against the vehicle and watched the women leave. They'd included Jessi in the group quickly. "Your retreats are never boring. I guess I always thought writers would be the type to stay in the library reading until they turned into a book or something."

"You're stereotyping. Writers are fun people. We want to experience life so we can write about it in our books later." Cat put her backpack on. "I put your water and cookies in with mine so I wouldn't lose you here."

"Where do you think I'm going to go? Ride out on the range to drive in the cattle? Or maybe wander about in the mountains to stake a mining claim?" He shut the doors and remote locked the car.

"Either one sounds exactly like where I might have found you one hundred years ago. Your ancestors helped build Covington, didn't they?" Cat took his hand as they walked toward Main Street and the action. She enjoyed being home in Colorado. More, she enjoyed reviving her relationship with Seth Howard, her high school sweetheart. Her mom even asked about Seth during their weekly calls.

"Howards were some of Covington's founding fathers. Just wait until we have your group do my hiking day. You'll learn all about my mad mountain man skills." Seth pointed to the horses tied up at the end of town near the blacksmith's shop. "Looks like they're getting ready for the trail ride. Next time we schedule this, we'll have to do the weekend so we can actually get out into the mountains."

Cat thought about the women who'd signed up for the Outlaw retreat. Of the five, only Jessi seemed like the type who'd brave getting on a horse and riding through the wilderness. Cat could just see her insurance agent's eyes widening as she explained the additional activity. "Maybe. I'll have to talk to Henry about a bigger umbrella policy."

Seth chuckled. "I always forget about the business

side of things. Maybe we should just stay with visiting Outlaw. I'm planning on playing a few hands of blackjack while we're here, though. I hear they let visitors win."

"With play money." Cat smiled at the childlike grin that covered Seth's face. Between that and a slight scruff of beard, the guy looked like he could step into one of many roles actors played in the tourist town. All he needed was a cowboy hat and a button-down shirt to replace the *I Heart Rock* T-shirt he currently sported. And some cowboy boots to replace his Nikes. "I wish this had been open while we were going to high school. I would have jumped at the chance to spend my summer working here."

"They hire a lot of the drama kids from Covington. I guess their folks would rather they stay here and work than go back east to the bigger cities." Seth pulled her onto the wooden sidewalks attached to the buildings and out of the dirt of the main street. "Speaking of Covington, have you seen your friend Dante lately?"

Cat winced. She knew Seth didn't like the guy. She had to admit, Dante was a little scary, mostly due to his belonging to a large Mob family. Seth was watching her. "No, I haven't seen or talked to Dante lately. Why? Have you seen him in town?"

"I did some work for his butler over at that huge house down the street from yours last month. Did you know he has signed copies of your books in his library? I think they are the only paperbacks he has in the entire collection." They paused at the Olde Tyme Photo Shop, where the writers had stopped to get pictures of themselves in Western garb. "Thought it was a little strange, that's all."

"I have a fan." Cat leaned into him. "Stop being so overprotective. I know Dante isn't the type of man you want me to be friends with."

"Your uncle agrees with me." Seth didn't look at her as he spoke.

"I know the guy's bad news. I'm not going to do anything to put myself in any danger." She felt like she was being lectured like a child.

Seth put an arm around her and pulled her close. "Now, that, my love, is an utter falsehood. Trouble finds you like a dog with a buried bone."

Cat had to grudgingly agree. Sometimes she did seem to be in the wrong place at the wrong time. But it wasn't her fault. "I don't do it on purpose."

Seth was about to speak when Cora came out in a saloon girl outfit and pulled them both into the shop.

"You two have to be in the picture as well." She pointed to the racks of clothes. "Go get changed, we'll wait."

Cat sent Seth a what-can-you-do smile and headed off to the side of the room where the women's clothes were located. She was relieved the conversation had been interrupted. She'd wanted it ended before she had to admit that she'd actually been in Dante's study signing the books for him. Seth wouldn't understand, even if it didn't have a thing to do with their relationship.

She chose a dress in a soft blue and walked toward the changing room.

"Oh, no, that won't do at all." Jessi traded the dress Cat had chosen for a sexy saloon girl dress. "We're all being bad girls. You have to join us. And Seth can be our bouncer."

"I think they were called protectors back then, dear." Kelly adjusted a headband with a long pink feather.

"Whatever, it will be a cool picture." Jessi hung the more conservative dress out of Cat's reach. "And you are going to look hot. That's one reason I love working here. I look smoking in these costumes."

"You always think you look hot." Another girl giggled next to Jessi.

"Because I do." Jessi grinned and hugged the girl. "Cat, this is my roommate, Danielle. She and I have been friends since freshman year, and now we're both working this summer here at Outlaw."

"Hey." Danielle held up a hand in greeting. "My shift starts in a little bit, I probably better be going."

"It was nice to meet you." Cat glanced at the dress Jessi had shoved into her hands.

"You too." Danielle turned to Jessi. "Don't worry, I'll handle your shifts this week. I could use the extra money. Some of us are putting *ourselves* through graduate school."

"I can't help it if my mom is insisting on a second degree for me. If she wants me to get it, she's footing the bill." She hugged Danielle. "I left my keys to the BMW on top of my desk. Use it tonight. I don't want you trying to catch a ride from any of these losers."

"You didn't call them losers when you were dating them." Danielle held up a hand. "No time to discuss, I'm going to be late."

"She seems nice." Cat tried to reach for the more conservative outfit while distracting Jessi.

"She's too nice. I guess she's naïve. She doesn't realize that there are bad people out there. I learned that lesson early, but Danielle? She was raised in Idaho. Nothing bad ever happens in Idaho." Jessi stared sadly in the direction her friend had left. Then she caught Cat's movement out of the corner of her eye. "No way. You aren't looking like a nun with that hot man next to you."

"You work at the saloon?" Cat hadn't known Jessi was actually one of the summer employees. She stopped trying to get the outfit she'd picked out and went inside the dressing room and slipped out of her clothes and into the dress Jessi had given her. Or what appeared to be a dress. The bodice was a corset and the dress was hiked up and sewn to show off the wearer's legs. "I didn't know that. It's nice of you to come with us."

"Oh, I love being here, especially when I'm not working. It's like a playland. I get to play dress-up every day and they pay me." Jessi swished her skirts. "Besides, I really wanted to meet the other attendees. I love talking to real writers. Come on out and I'll fix your corset. It's a pain to do by yourself."

Cat adjusted herself, then folded her clothes into a neat pile by the bench. Glancing at her image in the mirror, she thought she looked like Hollywood's idea of a saloon girl. The neckline dipped low and the shoulders of the dress hung to the side, so there was no way she could wear a bra with the getup. She took one last look in the mirror and exited the dressing area.

"Turn around and I'll get you laced in." Jessi leaned close as she did up the back of the dress.

"You look totally mag. Your man is going to want a copy of this for his private collection."

Cat felt her cheeks heat. What was it with romance writers that they always wanted to chime in on her relationship with Seth? He glanced over and gave her a wink. The guy didn't look half bad himself.

Cora called out to the group. "Okay, everyone, come and get set. It's time for us to go back in time. Think of the last heroine you wrote and pretend you're her."

Lisa moved toward the stage and snorted. "My last character was a schoolteacher. If she'd have been caught in a dress like this, she would have been run out of town."

The woman laughed as the photographer adjusted them into a pose. After taking several shots, he checked his camera and nodded. "I think you all will be happy with this. Anyone want some individual or couple shots?"

"Yeah, get one of me and the ball and chain." Seth grabbed Cat by the waist and spun her around. "We've got some dancing to do later."

By the time they left the photo shop, several of the women had gotten individual shots taken. As they returned to the street in their normal clothing, Seth leaned close. "You know he's got to be making a mint off those."

Jessi overheard his comment. "Oh, he's just an employee like the rest of us. The entire town is owned by a corporation. We all work for one man, a guy out of Denver. Of course, we never see him, but the kids call him Mr. McDuck, like that rich guy in the old cartoons?"

Cat glanced around the street. She could see how this town could be the brainchild of one person. It all fit seamlessly. The next shop was a general store where you could buy period reproduction clothes and, to her surprise, snacks.

"Chocolate? Or salty?" Seth looked at her. "I have to buy my favorite girl a treat."

"You are taking this courting thing way too seriously." Cat pointed to what looked like fudge in the glass case. "I'll take a hunk of that. It looks yummy."

Kelly stopped near her. "I have to say, I'm enjoying today. I told the others I'd come to the retreat but all I was going to do was work, not play around. I've got a deadline at the end of the month and two more by end of year. I didn't have time for the travel and to take a day for this."

"Sometimes taking a real break is just what you need to jump-start your creativity." Cat looked at the woman. "Did you really just sign a fourth contract, or were you teasing back there?"

"I have four contracts and, now, three different publishers. I don't know if I'm coming or going, but I love writing these series. And then, wham, a bright and shiny idea hits, and I'm talking to my editor, and before you know it, I have an offer. On a book that was just an idea. Who would turn that down?" Kelly stretched out her arms. "So if you don't see me after today, just know I'm upstairs in my room writing."

"You're going to shame me into writing this week." Cat fingered the fabric on what appeared to be a leather vest. Glancing at the price tag, she knew it was a real leather vest. "I have been trying to take retreat week off from word count days."

"This is working. You're running this retreat. That can't be easy." Kelly picked up a leather journal. "Now, this is cute. I'm going to get one for each of my sisters. Add a nice pen and my Christmas shopping is done."

Cat watched as she scooped up ten of the journals and went to the cash register to pay. When she came back, Cat reached for the sack. "Let me take this back to the car so you don't have to carry it all day."

Jessi popped into the conversation. "I'll do it. I need to make sure I hit my steps today anyway." She held up her wrist and showed them her Apple watch. "I love this thing. My mom sent it to me at the beginning of term last year."

"Nice computer on your arm." Seth handed Cat the fudge. As she reached for it, he held on for just a second longer. "Don't think you're not sharing that."

"Give Jessi the keys, she's going to take Kelly's package back to the SUV." Cat took a bite of the chocolate treat.

He glanced at his own watch. "It's almost time for the big shoot-out on the street. You sure you don't want to stay and watch? I can take the bag back so you can enjoy the day."

Jessi laughed and held out her hand for the keys. "It's the guy in the black hat. It's always the guy in the black hat that dies. Do you know how many times I see Bradley killed during a summer? I think I can miss one show."

"Okay, but it's going to be cool. I hear they use fake blood and everything." He dropped the keys into Jessi's hand and put his arm around Cat. "Just don't go for a joyride. I know what the mileage is on the car."

"You're not such a trusting guy, are you?" Jessi headed to the door, Kelly's bag swinging in her hand. "I'll meet you guys at lunch."

Cat got the group moving out onto the street so they could watch the staged gunfight. Before the show started, a white cat with black patches ran across the dirt road and jumped up on the railing where residents could tie up their horses. Or at least they could back in the day. The cat blinked its green eyes at her as if to say, You know you want to pet me.

"What a beautiful cat." Cora stood next to Cat and stroked the long fur. "Do you think she lives here?"

"I don't know." Cat reached out her hand, and as she scratched under the feline chin, she felt a tag. She leaned down and read the name engraved on the heart-shaped tag. "Looks like Angelica belongs to someone. There's a vet clinic name here too, Dr. Simon. Maybe I should call them and see if the cat's been reported missing."

As if she'd heard them discussing her, Angelica gave Cat one last rub with her head, then jumped down and ran across the road again. Cat started to go after her, but Seth held her arm.

"The shoot-out is starting." He pointed toward the men strolling down the street toward each other.

Cat searched the other side of the street, but the cat had disappeared. She'd have to be content in calling this vet and letting them know where they could find the wandering Angelica—if she was lost, that is.

She leaned into Seth's side and prepared to watch the show.

As Jessi had predicted, the tall, lanky cowboy in the black hat did a great job of dying on cue. A funeral director's wagon pulled up to retrieve the body, blocking the crowd's view, and someone from the saloon called out from the swinging doors. "Grub's being served. Come eat now or don't. Not my problem."

"What a welcoming invitation," Cora remarked as the group made their way to the dining area where they would be eating lunch. "Customer service must not be high on their list of values here at Outlaw."

"You get the immersion experience. I'm sure our version of customer service isn't what the Old West was built on." Seth held the swinging door open. "It was more of a live or die experience, right?"

"With a love story under every quilt." Lisa agreed as they gathered around the table with a Reserved sign announcing *Warm Springs Resort.* "I'm so excited to be here. I've always wanted to write an American Western historical. If I have to write another duke I'm going to stab someone with my favorite pen."

"A violent group of outlaws we have visiting our fair town." The waiter grinned as he put mugs of water on the table. "We're pulling out all the stops for you all. The cook even chipped ice to cool this water we got from the creek."

Laughter filled the room as they got settled, but Jessi's chair was still empty when the first course of country beef stew was served. The soup was thick with rustic cut vegetables, but Cat couldn't eat. She was worried about Jessi.

Seth sensed her unease and leaned close. "I was kidding about the joyride, but maybe I should go see if the car is still in the parking lot."

Cat glanced at her watch, then at the crowded room. "Give her a few more minutes, then go check on her. She might have met up with one of her friends."

As if on cue, Jessi burst into the saloon and scanned the room. Cat held up a hand and the girl started making her way to the table.

"Sorry I'm late. The parking lot was crazy busy." Jessi put her head down and started eating.

Cat and Seth glanced at each other. Jessi's excuse had sounded false. Seth leaned close. "We may want to watch that one during the retreat."

# CHAPTER 2

Shauna had set out sandwiches and snacks in the dining room when they arrived back at the house. Seth and Cat were already sitting at the table drinking a beer when she came back into the kitchen. She looked from one to another. "Bad day?"

Cat shrugged. "I'd call it a weird day." She went on to tell Shauna about Jessi's disappearing and reappearing act. Then the rest of the afternoon, the girl had seemed distracted. "She went from the life of the party and perfect hostess to withdrawn, moody, and antsy."

"Maybe she ran into someone in the parking lot." Seth nodded, thinking about the day. "She looked a little upset when she got back."

"With college kids, who knows. I remember my years at Ohio State, I was always flitting around about some guy." Shauna set out four bowls from the cupboard. "I made Italian veggie soup for dinner along with some grilled cheese and ham sandwiches. Or I could make something else?"

"This isn't a restaurant. Whatever you made will be fine." Cat pulled out her planner and opened it to the current week. "Anything we need to discuss for the retreat?"

"The group has your regular appointment at the library tomorrow at ten. Professor Turner is coming on Tuesday. You're scheduled for the Life of a Working Author session on Wednesday, and the bookseller is coming in on Friday." Shauna rattled off the schedule as she set the soup on the table. She went back and got out plates and silverware and gave them to Seth, who took his and set the other two near the soup bowls. She scanned the table. "What did I miss?"

"For the week? Nothing but our traditional Saturday-night dinner." Cat tapped her pen. "No issues with air-conditioning up in the attic?"

"I went up this morning before we left and it seems fine. But I'll check it midday tomorrow, just in case." Seth took a sip of his soup. "This is amazing, Shauna."

Grabbing a platter from the oven, she put a pair of tongs on the top and set the sandwiches within reach of everyone. "Glad you like it."

The back door opened and Uncle Pete strode in. He wore his police chief uniform and he set the wide-brimmed hat on the bench by the back door. "Am I late?"

Shauna jumped up and filled the last bowl and set his usual place at the table. "I wasn't sure you were going to make it."

"And miss one of your soups? I'd be crazy." Uncle

Pete stopped by Cat's chair and kissed her on the cheek before sitting down.

"I didn't know you were coming for dinner." Cat studied her uncle. He looked happy. Well, as happy as a small-town police chief could get. She loved how he'd started coming by more often. They were the only family they had in Aspen Hills, since her parents had moved to Florida.

"Your friend called this morning and invited me over. I think Shauna was just missing me." Uncle Pete reached a hand over to shake with Seth. "I haven't seen you in days. How's the fishing down at the creek?"

"Rainbows are hitting hard." Seth grinned. "You need to get down there this week before they stop."

"I'm knee-deep in paperwork. Who'd have thought me taking a week off could cause such a problem?" He sipped his soup. "Tasty. Shirley sends her best, by the way."

Uncle Pete had a new girlfriend. Shirley Mann had been a guest at one of the writers' retreats last winter. She also was a retired cop, so she and Uncle Pete had a lot to talk about. Now they were doing the long-distance relationship thing, and he'd spent the last week in Alaska on her turf.

"How's her book coming?" Cat took a sandwich from the pile.

"We didn't really talk about her book." A flush came on his cheeks. "Speaking of fishing, Shirley took me out on a charter, and we brought in a boatload of salmon. I sent a few filets home in dry ice. I'll bring some over later this week."

"Hmmm, fresh salmon. I'm pretty sure I can make something amazing with that." Shauna put her hand over the top of Uncle Pete's. "I'm glad you're back. I was missing seeing you at the table."

After dinner, Cat went to the living room to spend time with the guests. Kelly and Jessi were gone, but the other three sat and chatted. Cora saw her in the doorway and waved her in. "I hope you don't mind, but we thought we'd talk for a while here."

"The house is yours for the week. Third floor is off-limits and second-floor rooms are by invite only, but other than that, treat the house like your home. There's a study on this floor as well as a large writing area in the attic. Plenty of spots for you to tuck in and get some words in." Cat sat in one of the wingback chairs. "We'll have our group sessions in here, just because it's the largest room."

Connie kicked off her flip-flops and pulled her feet underneath her on the couch. "I just love everything about this house. Was it passed down in your family?"

Cat shook her head. "Actually, my ex-husband and I bought it when we were both teaching at Covington. I loved doing the renovating. When we divorced, he stayed here and I went to California. After he died, I inherited the house from his estate."

"Good for you. I don't think I've ever heard a story quite like that. Typically, the wife gets the shaft and doesn't recover financially for years in divorces." Lisa sat her wineglass down on the table.

The women around her broke out into laughter.

Lisa looked around, confused. "What? That's what

happened to every woman in my family who got divorced."

Cora grinned. "In my family, that's how the women get rich, is by marrying and divorcing well."

"And that's why I write romance, to heal the wounds of the past." Connie yawned and stood. "I don't know about you guys, but I'm beat. I'll see you all in the morning at breakfast."

As she left the room, Cora sighed. "I guess it's too early still."

Lisa nodded, seeming to understand.

"Did I miss something?" Cat looked from woman to woman.

Cora leaned closer. "Connie lost her husband last year. They were high school sweethearts and they adored each other. We used to call them the perfect couple. Then he got sick. It broke her heart."

"She doesn't like talking about people giving up on relationships. She gave me a stern lecture about being happy for what I had when I was griping about my husband and his inability to put his socks in the hamper." Lisa smiled. "She's become our chapter matchmaker. She believes in love."

The next morning, Cat went downstairs to grab some coffee before heading to her office. She'd decided she'd spend the first hour of the day with her new manuscript. Then she could deal with retreat business. That way, Tori and her high school friends that populated Cat's series wouldn't be far from her mind when she went back to writing next week.

The first thing Cat saw when she came into the kitchen was Shauna sitting at the table. Cat watched as Shauna ran her hands over her face, apparently trying to hide the fact she'd been crying. Kevin had been gone for six months, and she was still grieving for her lost love. Maybe Cat could ask Connie to talk to Shauna. Cat had suggested a grief group several times, but Shauna had pushed the idea away.

"Good morning. Sorry if I disturbed you." Cat avoided looking at her as she walked to the coffeepot to fill a large travel mug with coffee. "I'll be in and out. I'm writing this morning for a while."

"I'm glad. I worry when you take too much time away from the stories." Shauna walked over to the stove and took a pan of muffins out of the oven. "You get grumpy."

Cat spun on her heel. "I do not get grumpy."

Seth walked into the kitchen. "What? Is Cat not writing again?"

"Is that what you think too? That I get grumpy when I'm not writing?" Cat took one of the muffins and wrapped it in a napkin. Then she changed her mind and took a second one. The peanut butter and walnut aroma was enticing.

"Wait, how did I become the bad guy? I just asked what we were talking about." He poured himself a cup of coffee. "I'm really glad Pete's back and I'm not the only guy around."

Shauna finished putting the muffins into a basket and set it on the table. "I need to check the laundry."

After she left, Seth sank into a chair. "She's still hurting, isn't she?"

Cat put her hand on Seth's shoulder. "Yeah, she's missing Kevin this morning. Hopefully having a full house will help her keep busy and her mind off him."

"I hope so. I really like Shauna. She's like my little sister. I hate seeing her hurting." He ran his hand through his hair.

"Me too." Cat took a muffin and put it on a napkin in front of him. "Eat. You'll feel better. I'm going to my office."

He reached up and pulled her down into a kiss. When he let her go, he grinned at her. "You're a good friend, and honestly, you are never, ever grumpy."

"Keep it up and you'll be in the running for boyfriend of the year." Cat took her muffins and coffee and headed up to her office to write.

At nine thirty, she'd gotten in more than an hour of writing and was pleasantly surprised at the progress. These new characters were going to be a great addition to the series. A knock pulled her out of her thoughts, and she turned around to see Shauna standing in her office.

"Sorry, I should have waited, but you know me." Shauna smiled and glanced out the window. "I bet you don't even notice the gorgeous view you have of the mountain range from this window."

"Every now and then I stop and look out and realize how lucky I am. What brings you to my tower?" Cat shut down her computer. She was back on retreat time. More words would wait until tomorrow.

"Just checking in to see if you're taking them to the library or if Jessi is taking them. She's a chatty one. Did you know she's from Boston?" Shauna straightened a pile of books Cat had left on the coffee table in front of the couch where she'd been reading last week.

Again, she hadn't had the investigator run the Covington student's background. She'd felt foolish enough when all the historical romance writers had come back squeaky clean. What had she expected? Maybe she needed to talk to Uncle Pete about stopping the process. "Uncle Pete might know more about her family history. After I take the group to the library, I'll stop to see him on my way back."

"I'll make up a treat bag for you to take to him. He looks like he's lost a little weight." Shauna started to go through the doorway, then stopped. "I'm sorry I'm a witch right now. It will get better."

"You miss Kevin." Cat stepped closer to her and put her hand on Shauna's shoulder.

Shauna barked out a laugh. "Yes and no. I just realized I haven't been riding since his death, and you know Snow is just standing around in that stall. No one in that family likes her, probably because she was mine."

"Maybe Paul would sell her to you?"

"And where would I keep a horse, the backyard?" Shauna laughed. "I'll get over it."

"Actually, the backyard is bigger than it looks. But yeah, Mrs. Rice would have a cow if you stabled a horse here." There had to be a place to board horses somewhere in town. Cat decided she'd talk to Uncle Pete about that too. Maybe having her horse around to ride and care for might pull Shauna out of this funk.

As she made her way down to the lobby, she made a mental to-do list for the day. Everyone was in the lobby except two. "Where's Kelly?"

"She's still working." Cora shrugged. "I tried to get her to take a break, but the woman is like a machine. She's determined to finish that book by the end of the week. I don't think we'll see much of her."

"I wish she'd take advantage of some of the perks we have set up for you. Like access to the Covington Library." Cat knew the joy of researching at the library since she'd gone to college here. Besides, sometimes a good research session filled in a hole you didn't know you had.

Cora glanced around at the other ladies. "I don't know. Kelly can get pretty set when she's writing. We tried to do a writing camp with her last month, and she stomped out because Lisa mentioned we might want to break for lunch. Kelly is insane about her process sometimes."

"Well, I'll drop her library card off with a carafe of coffee and a few muffins when I get back. I don't want her starving herself while she's here." Cat glanced up the stairs. "What about Jessi? Is she coming?"

Lisa shook her head. "She said she had to meet up with her roommate today. They had something that she needed to deal with."

"Danielle? I hoped Jessi would be able to separate herself from her normal life this week." Cat sighed. She'd been worried that the girl wasn't taking the week seriously. She nodded to the front door. "I guess we're ready, then."

Dropping the group off with Miss Applebome

took all of three seconds once they reached the library. The librarian still hadn't completely forgiven Cat for taking a book without checking it out a few months ago. It wasn't like Cat would have kept the stupid thing, but Miss Applebome still tried to peek into any bag Cat brought into the library.

By the time she got to the police station, she wanted coffee and sugar. She glanced at the bag she held in her hand. Maybe Uncle Pete would share. She could smell Shauna's fudge brownies through the paper bag and the plastic wrap. Or maybe it was her imagination, but her stomach was rumbling.

Katie sat at the front desk, reading a book. Apparently, crime in Aspen Hills was quiet for at least the morning. When she saw Cat, she flushed and pushed the book into a drawer. "Hey, Cat, your uncle isn't here. He was called out to Outlaw."

"Outlaw? That's funny, we were just there." She pointed to the drawer. "What are you reading?"

"I don't understand." Her face lost all color.

"Seriously? I saw you reading when I came in. I'm only asking because I'm curious. So, what are you reading?"

Katie's gaze darted back and forth. When she determined the empty front office was truly empty, she leaned closer to Cat and slipped the book out of the drawer. "I'm reading your book. I can't believe you wrote this. It's so good. I know it's not really meant for women my age, but I love reading Young Adult. Tammy at the bookstore is always ordering in a book or two for me."

"Glad you're enjoying Tori and the gang." Cat

held up the bag. "Mind if I put this on Uncle Pete's desk?"

"Only if you do me a favor." She handed Cat the book and a pen. "Sign it *To Katie, my best friend in the world,* and then your name. When you're rich I'll sell it on the black market."

Cat signed the book and then moved it back toward Katie. "I'm heading into Uncle Pete's office. I'll be right out."

She waved her through.

When Cat reached her uncle's office, she slipped through the door and set the bag on his desk. She glanced through the contents of the bag and realized Shauna had only sent one brownie. Cat sighed. She would have to wait. About to leave, she noticed a new picture on the bookshelf. There, next to the photo of her taken in front of the house was a picture of Shirley and Uncle Pete on what looked like a charter boat. He had his arm around her and they both looked happy.

Cat picked up the frame and studied the picture. Uncle Pete had been widowed for years. Was Shirley going to change his status from single to part of a couple again? And would that also mean a move to Shirley's Alaska, or would she move here? So many questions, and all of them weren't any of her business, but selfishly, she hoped her uncle would stay around Covington. Her parents had made the move to Florida, running away from the bitter winter season. If Uncle Pete left, she wouldn't have any family here. Well, except for Seth and Shauna, who if they weren't related by blood or legal decree were just as much her family as the blood relatives.

She smiled as she made her way back to the front of the station. Seth and Shauna were a lot more like family than some of her cousins that she never saw or talked to anymore.

As she stepped out onto the street, Uncle Pete pulled his car into his parking slot in front of the building. She waited for him to get out and onto the sidewalk. "Hey, I heard you got called into Outlaw. Anything wrong?"

"Someone tried to break in last night, so they of course are blaming the school for the young hooligans we're harboring." Uncle Pete gave Cat a quick hug. "What are you doing here?"

"Shauna wanted me to drop off some snacks. And I had a question, speaking of the college." Cat pointed to a bench. "Sit down, I won't take up much of your time."

"This doesn't sound good." But he followed her to the bench and sat, turning toward her with an arm draped along the back of the bench. "What do you want to know?"

"What do you know about Jessi Ball?"

Uncle Pete eyed her curiously. "I thought you were doing background checks."

"I was, but I don't do them on the Covington kids, but maybe I should with the look you're giving me." Cat rubbed her neck. "Go ahead, tell me the worst."

"Jessi comes from a wealthy family. Before you ask, no, she's not connected. I've heard her mother was friends with Dante and Michael." Uncle Pete took off his hat and ran a hand through his hair. "Don't look so shocked. Aspen Hills is a small town.

And legacies like sending their kids here mostly because they know it's safe."

"Speaking of safe, are there houses around Outlaw?"

"Weird question, but no. The town shuts down when the doors lock. None of the staff live on-site. In fact, once the snow falls, the place will be unreachable until first melt. Why?" He studied her, concern showing in his face.

"I saw a cat up there. I'm not sure if it was just lost or if it lived there, but if there aren't any homes nearby, I'm going to assume it's lost." She keyed in a note into her phone. "I'll call the vet clinic and see if anyone's reported a cat missing."

"It won't last long up there. We've been having problems with coyotes taking down small animals near town. In Outlaw, the cat wouldn't survive a winter."

Walking home, she thought about life in a small town. No matter what you did or who you wanted to be, the past was always there to remind you about who you were before. Sometimes she missed the anonymity she had in California. She'd been just one of the crowd then.

Here, she wasn't just an author, or even the retreat owner, she was also the police chief's niece, and with that came a responsibility to make sure Aspen Hills stayed safe, and that included seeing if she could bring home a lost cat.

# CHAPTER 3

The group wasn't back from the library yet. It was after four. Cat glanced at Shauna. "Are you sure they said they could find their way back?"

"When Cora called, she said they were doing lunch in town, then heading back to the library. She wanted me to give Kelly the message in case she wanted to go into town and eat with them at Reno's." Shauna glanced at the board. "I've set up the after-lunch snacks, but I don't think Kelly's left her room, and Jessi's not back from wherever she disappeared to."

"This retreat is so different than any others we've had. Typically we can't get rid of the guests. Now they don't want to come back to the house." Cat decided to change the subject. She leaned over the table, closer to Shauna. "So I found a picture of Shirley in Uncle Pete's office."

"A sexy picture?"

"Eww, no. Not a sexy picture, but one of him

and her out on the fishing boat. They both were grinning like fools." Cat grabbed a brownie from the pan on the counter. "I think they are serious."

"What does that mean? They're going steady? Or he gave her his class ring?" Shauna shook her head. "I think it's different with older folks. I read an article that said people who date in their advanced years seem to know what they want, so they get serious faster than younger people because they don't have to worry about spending the rest of their life with this one person."

Seth came in from the backyard. He'd been working on a project near the old oak tree out in what she called the pasture. Cat had tried to get him to tell her what it was going to be, but he was keeping the final product a secret. He'd sworn them both to stay away from that part of the yard until he finished. "Uh-oh, did I come in at a bad time?"

"We're talking about Uncle Pete and Shirley. And I don't want to talk about it anymore. It's kind of freaking me out." Cat watched as Seth washed up at the kitchen sink. "How's the secret project going? Please tell me it's an indoor swimming pool. I'd love to be able to do laps in the morning."

"If I answer all the what it's not questions, you'll be able to guess what it is, so, I'm not answering that question either." He dried his hands on a towel and glanced at the clock. "Do you mind if I eat with you this week? I'm a little strapped for cash."

"Of course. It's part of your amazing benefit package as our part-time houseboy." Shauna considered him as he walked across the kitchen. "Although we may need to get you a better uniform. Houseboys don't typically wear dirty jeans and a T-shirt."

"That's good, because I'm not a houseboy. I'm a domestic engineer." He grinned at her. "Or something like that. What are we eating?"

"I'm making chicken tacos and Spanish rice unless someone objects." Shauna turned the page on the magazine she'd been skimming for recipes.

"Sounds great to me." He gave Cat a squeeze as he went by. "I'm running upstairs to make sure the air-conditioning is working in the attic. I set up a little workstation for me up there for my laptop during retreat weeks, if that's all right."

"I'm not sure why you're being so polite and charming right now, but I kind of like it." Cat waved him off. Seth had started the renovation on the other wing, but Cat liked the feel of the smaller retreat groups. "I'm surprised you don't set up a room just for your office somewhere. We have enough rooms we aren't using."

"I don't want to impose." And with that, he disappeared from the kitchen.

Cat looked at Shauna. "Is it just me or is Seth being weird?"

"He's always been a bit off." Shauna opened the fridge. "Do you think Pete will be joining us for dinner?"

"He didn't say anything. Hey, you're not still mad at Seth, are you? You know he feels bad about everything that happened." Cat watched for Shauna's reaction.

"Sometimes things can't be just taken back. I

wish he would have talked to me about it, but instead, he went to you." Shauna started chopping vegetables for dinner. "I'll get over it. It's just going to take some time."

Cat wished Shauna had never met Kevin, not for the pain he'd caused her friend. But if wishes were horses . . . She wondered if Paul was around this week. Maybe Cat would just have to make a drive out to the ranch and see if she could get him to sell the horse. It was a small thing, but Shauna would be so much happier.

"Look, I'm going to go check on our guests and see who is back. Do you want me to refresh the snack center in the dining room?"

"Just let me know if it needs anything. I don't think it's been touched since I set it up this morning. This is a totally different group." Shauna smiled, and for the first time in a long time, Cat thought the action touched her eyes. "I may need to slow down on my baking this week. I might even find time to start reading again."

As Cat made her way through the house, it felt empty. Shauna was in the kitchen, Seth was up in the attic, and apparently Kelly was holed up in her room, but other than those three, Cat had the house to herself. She breezed through the lower-level rooms, adjusting a chair or a pillow here and there, but mostly, the house was ready. Now the retreat guests just had to come back.

Cat chose a book from the bookshelves and settled into one of the wing chairs in the living room. That's where she was when Jessi came into the room almost an hour later.

Jessi had a bottle of water and a cookie from the

dining room. She plopped down into a chair next to Cat. "Where is everyone? I ran back from Outlaw so I wouldn't miss dinner at Reno's."

"They haven't come back from the library yet." Cat glanced at her watch—almost six. "I'm sure they'll be back soon. You know how absorbing researching can be."

"I guess I'll give Cora a call." She stood and started to leave the room.

"Hey, hold on a moment. I thought you weren't working this week?" Cat set the book down on the table. "You know you have to make time to write. It doesn't just happen."

"I know. I don't know what happened. Danielle was there for the first couple hours of the shift, then she poofed. I'm going to give her a piece of my mind when I see her. She lost all of my shifts because the manager doesn't trust her now." Jessi smiled and held up her hand with the cookie. "I've dealt with the rest of the week. And I told my manager I couldn't work anymore until next Sunday. So I'm clear. And I promise, I'm taking this very seriously."

"I'm not your keeper, but I want you to have a good experience."

Jessi started to say something, then the room filled with the other women who had arrived back from the library.

"Sorry we're late. We'll just run upstairs and change and then we'll be ready to head to town for dinner." Cora shook her backpack. "You won't believe how much work I got done today. The library is a gold mine of historical recordings. You are so lucky to live here."

"I'm not much into that old stuff. I want to write a serious story about life and loss." Jessi stood and joined her group. They strolled out of the room, leaving Cat alone with her book again.

"They come, they go. It's kind of like having kids," Cat said to the empty room. Shauna would have dinner ready at six and the three of them would eat in the kitchen. Hopefully, she'd get some conversation going at dinner.

Cat was wrong. Shauna was lost in thought, pushing her food around her plate. And as soon as Seth wolfed down his food, he turned to Cat. "Hey, I'm going to go back to the apartment for a few hours. I want to get my stuff ready for the fishing trip next week."

"It's just you and the boys, what do you need to get ready? I'm sure you can buy beer anywhere on the way there." Cat grinned. Seth and several of his high school friends had been going on this June trip for years. Or at least since Seth had come back from his time in the service. A week in the wilderness with a bunch of men and no shower? Cat wouldn't go if Seth begged her. Besides, she had a deadline coming up, and she had to be seriously writing next week, once this retreat was in the books.

"You'd be surprised. I have to go through my lures and make sure I have the right ones for rainbow trout. And those suckers keep changing their minds on what they like to bite on." He took his plate to the sink and stopped to kiss Cat. "Thanks for dinner, Shauna. If you need me before I get back, just call and I'll come right back."

As he went to the door to leave, Uncle Pete came

inside. He looked at Seth and his keys. "Going somewhere?"

"I was." Seth tossed his keys in the air. "Getting ready for the guys' trip. You still thinking about coming with us?"

"I believe that's off the table now." Uncle Pete closed the door. "If you wouldn't mind staying around for a while, I need to talk to you all."

"Uh-oh, that doesn't sound good." Cat took her plate to the sink. "Can I dish you up some dinner while we chat?"

"I don't think so, but if you'd put some aside, maybe I can take it with me. I need to go up to Outlaw again." He took his hat off and ran a hand through his thinning hair. "Sometimes I think retirement wouldn't be such a bad thing."

"I'll make you a couple of sandwiches and pack a bag for you so you can eat and drive." Shauna stood and went to the fridge. "Unless you can't eat in the car."

"Brenden's going with me, so he can drive while I eat. Tuck another meal in there for him, if you don't mind. I think it's going to be a long night." Uncle Pete poured himself a cup of coffee. "So if you all are in here, I suppose your guests are out to dinner?"

Cat glanced at the clock. "They left about an hour ago. I would expect them back in a few, but with this group, who knows. I've hardly seen them today."

"Including Jessi? Or is she here?" Uncle Pete pulled out his little notebook and set a pen next to it.

"No, she's with the group." Now Cat started to

feel a little nervous about her uncle's arrival. "Why are you asking? Does this have something to do with her working at Outlaw?"

"Maybe. I need to talk to her. Has she said anything about her roommate?"

"Danielle? I met her Sunday. She seems like a normal kid. Don't tell me she's in trouble." Cat relaxed a little. At least Uncle Pete's visit wasn't about the retreat guests.

"Actually, she's missing. She left her station today and never showed back up after lunch." Uncle Pete sipped his coffee.

"I know." Cat shook her head when Uncle Pete choked on the sip he'd just taken. "I mean, Jessi told me that she got called in to work because Danielle was supposed to take her shift and then bailed. Why on earth would they call the police over a girl skipping out on work?"

"There's a witness who says she saw Danielle getting into a black car. She says she told her manager about it, but he thought she was making up stories to keep Danielle from getting into trouble. I guess the witness isn't the most trustworthy employee they have." He paused and took another sip of coffee.

"Wait, there was a witness to a kidnapping and they thought she was just telling stories? Who are these people?" Shauna paused in wrapping several cookies and stared at Pete.

"She didn't say Danielle was forced, she just got into a car. The girl said she thought she was meeting a guy on her break and then got sidetracked. They're kids. They don't make the best decisions."

"Why do they think something has happened now?" Seth had poured his own coffee and sat next to Uncle Pete.

"Her folks called in a missing person report. She was supposed to have dinner with them tonight and she didn't show. When they called her supervisor at Outlaw, he'd told them she took off around ten." Uncle Pete sighed. "They are swearing that their daughter wouldn't leave work like that. Of course, that's what all parents say. Except this time, I believe them."

"So you're going to start a search party? If she got into a car, she could be anywhere." Cat glanced at the clock. "And she's been gone almost ten hours. They could get a long way from here in that amount of time."

"We have to start at the beginning. Figure out if she's really still not at Outlaw. Some of those buildings are pretty destroyed. She might have gone into one of them and fallen through the rotted wood." Uncle Pete looked up as Shauna set a bag and a travel mug of coffee in front of him. "Thanks."

As he stood, Cat stood as well. "Do you need help? We can come up too."

"No, but tell Jessi I need to talk to her as soon as she gets in. She can call me on my cell, no matter what time it is. I'd go run her down in town, but I need to get going." He paused, looking at Seth. "I'd like you to hang out here this week while the retreat is in session."

"Why?" Cat glanced from Seth to Uncle Pete. "Danielle's possible disappearance isn't related to the retreat. Why does Seth need to hang close?"

Uncle Pete paused in front of her. "Because

Danielle is friends with Jessi. I don't know what this is about, but I don't want you taking any chances."

Seth nodded. "I don't have to be anywhere else. I can be here."

"I think you're overreacting," Cat said, but her uncle just waved her off.

"Thanks again for the meal, Shauna." He kissed Cat on the cheek. "I'll talk to you later. Make sure that girl calls me as soon as she comes back."

Seth sat back down at the table. "Well, there's one thing you can say about Aspen Hills."

"What's that?" Cat didn't want Seth to have to change his plans just because her uncle was feeling overprotective, but she wasn't going to be able to change his mind.

"It's never boring."

Cat went back into the living room, and she was trying to read but mostly thinking about Danielle and hoping she was just screwing off when she heard the front door open. She put the book down and went to the lobby to catch Jessi.

Cora saw her first. "This is such a fun little town. After we left Reno's, we went to the bar and sang karaoke. I haven't done that in years."

"I should have come back to write, but I have to admit, I do an amazing 'Total Eclipse of the Heart' rendition." Kelly grinned. "Besides, I'm ahead of schedule for my word count thanks to today's session."

"You're a machine," Lisa shouted. Then she weaved. "Oops, I'm a little deaf from the music."

"You're also a little drunk, my dear." Cora held her up. "I'm putting this one to bed. Then I'm coming back down for some coffee and cookies. Anyone joining me?"

"I'll be here waiting." Kelly headed to the dining room. Connie followed, but before Jessi could fall in line, Cat grabbed her arm.

"Come into the study for a minute, we need to talk."

Jessi followed her into the bookshelf-lined room. Cat nodded toward one of the big reading chairs she'd added after cleaning out Michael's stuff from the room. It almost felt like a study versus her ex-husband's home office. Almost.

"Look, if this is about me disappearing today, I swear, I've got that situation handled. I'm still steamed at Danielle for taking off like that, and you can be sure I'm going to give her a piece of my mind when she comes back, but Tara and I are cool. Tara, that's my boss. I bet Danielle is somewhere with Keith. I guess he has the week off too." She gave Cat a winning smile. "I promise, writing has my entire attention for the next week."

"Jessi, it's not that." Cat told her about Uncle Pete's visit. "So her parents think this might be serious. I'm sure you're right, she just took off with this guy, but just in case, my uncle wants to make sure she's not in any danger. Will you talk to him?"

"Of course." Jessi's face had turned chalk white. Worse, for the first time since Cat had met her, Jessi's youth showed in her eyes, along with a healthy dose of fear. "I'll do anything. Has he tried to call Keith?"

"I don't know if he knew Danielle was dating him. Here, you can use my phone." She paused before dialing the number. "Are you okay to talk? Do you need some water or something?"

"Maybe a beer. But no, really, I'm okay. I want to help." She gave Cat a small smile. "I'm tougher than I look."

Cat nodded, then dialed her uncle's number. "She's here. I'm putting her on the phone."

"Hold on a minute, Cat. Don't let her know, but we found Danielle. She was in the upstairs bedroom over the saloon. She's been strangled."

# CHAPTER 4

Somehow Cat had kept her face composed as she listened to her uncle. Then she handed the phone to Jessi. She put her hand on the girl's shoulder. "I'm going to get us some coffee."

In the kitchen, Cat filled Shauna and Seth in on Uncle Pete's news as she filled two cups with coffee.

Shauna fell back in her chair. "I can't believe it. That poor girl. Who would want to do that to such a young thing?"

"I've heard rumors that there has been some Peeping Tom hanging out at the college. Maybe he followed Danielle and caught her at the wrong time?" Seth stood and pointed to his coffee cup. "Don't wash that. I'll be right back. I want to check the doors and make sure everything's locked up tight."

"No wonder Pete wanted you to stay over. Why

didn't you tell us about this?" Shauna put a hand on his arm, stopping his movement.

He turned toward Shauna. "They're just rumors. Nothing that has been proven. I talked to Pete when I heard them. He said he figured it was one of the frat houses doing initiation pranks. They were looking at expanding the video security around the dorms."

"We don't know if that has anything to do with Danielle's death. Uncle Pete was called up yesterday because of some break-ins at Outlaw. Maybe she was just at the wrong place and saw something." Cat tried to shake the vision of Danielle that had come into her head. "No matter. We can *maybe* an answer all night long. But I've got to get back to Jessi before she finishes with Uncle Pete. Seth, thank you for checking the doors. And, Shauna, it's going to be okay."

She didn't stay around to hear the fallout from her words. She had some comforting to do, and as soon as she opened the door, she could tell Jessi knew about Danielle. Cat set the coffee on the desk by Jessi and grabbed a box of tissues off the bookcase. Listening to Jessi's side of the conversation, she knew they were almost done talking. The girl was a wreck. Finally, she handed the phone to Cat.

"I can't believe she's gone. I was all, I'm going to kick her butt, when really, she was already dead. Maybe I should have gone looking for her. I should have known she wouldn't just bail on me." Jessi picked up the coffee cup, took a sip, then stared at it like she didn't know where it had come from.

"I know this is a shock. If you want to leave the retreat, I'll refund Covington the money and you could come back anytime." Cat took the cup from Jessi's shaking hands. "What do you want to do?"

The girl looked up at Cat, her eyes filled with tears. "I want to talk to Danielle. I want to tease her about her OCD. I want my friend back."

Then she burst into sobs.


The next morning, when Cat came downstairs, Jessi was sitting in the lobby with her laptop. Her red-rimmed eyes were dry, but Cat guessed she had been crying most of the night. Jessi set the laptop down.

"Hey, how are you this morning?" Cat sat next to her.

She took a deep breath before answering. "I'm good. Sad, but I don't want to go back to the dorm, and besides, your uncle said my room was a no-go zone until they find Danielle's killer. I may have to relocate next week when I go back to school."

"Sorry about that." Cat glanced at the laptop. "Are you sure you want to write? You could just stay here. You don't have to participate in the sessions."

"No, I want to write. I need to keep my mind off Danielle." She glanced up the stairs. "All the others came to my room last night and we talked for a long time. They're so insightful. I felt like I was home with a bunch of my aunts. Except, of course, my aunts are always shopping and talking about what they bought. They're not very supportive."

"Well, you're more than welcome to stay. I just want you to know, if you need anything, we're here for you." Cat stood. "Including coffee. I'm going to fill up my travel mug now. You want some?"

Jessi held a cup up from the spot on the floor where it had been hidden. "I'm already taken care of in that area. Now to work out this reveal scene. I want it to be emotional, you know?"

"The hardest scenes to write are the ones where they rip your heart out." Cat paused. "We have a Hemingway professor coming in to talk later this morning. You might enjoy listening to his session."

"Oh, Professor Turner's coming? I love him. I took every class he offered. He's so interesting." A small smile curved Jessi's lips and made Cat smile as well.

She'd never heard Turner called interesting. In fact, a lot of the groups tended to zone out while he spoke. But not everyone loves everything. "I'm glad to hear you'll enjoy the session. I'll check on you later."

In the kitchen, Shauna sat at the table reading something on her tablet. She didn't look up as Cat passed by. "Good morning to you. What has you so intense?"

"I'm looking for new muffin recipes. I want to try a few out with this group so I can taste-test them before I put them in the cookbook." She paused and looked at Cat. "How's Jessi this morning?"

"She's dealing." Cat didn't know what else to say.

Shauna stood and took her cup to be refilled. "It's hard especially at first. Nothing seems real."

Cat's phone buzzed with a text. She glanced at the phone, then slipped it back into her pocket. "Where's Seth this morning? Still sleeping?"

"Hardly. He took off to his apartment at first light. I guess he thinks we'll only be attacked by raving murderous mobs in the nighttime. I tried to feed him breakfast, but he turned me down." Shauna turned her attention back to the tablet. Then looked back up. "You don't want breakfast now, do you?"

"No, I'm fine. I'm going to run an errand really quick. I should be back by ten at the latest for Professor Turner's session. Jessi's one of his fangirls." She screwed the coffee lid on tight. She was going to regret this, but she knew if she ignored the text, his next step would be to show up at the house. And with Seth around, that might not end well. "See you soon."

"Okay." Shauna didn't even look up as Cat left the room. She slipped on her tennis shoes that she kept downstairs in a closet, and after waving to the madly typing Jessi, she slipped out of the house.

She'd almost made it past Mrs. Rice's when her neighbor came around the house from the side flower beds. "Catherine. I haven't seen you out and about for days. What's going on with your retreat this week? I saw your uncle's police car sitting in front of your house yesterday. You don't have any troublemakers this time, do you?"

"No, I don't think so. Uncle Pete was just there to pick up a dinner Shauna had made him. I swear, if she was a few years older, he'd sweep her up and I'd be looking for a new cook." The lie came easily, but as soon as it left her mouth, she knew she'd made a critical mistake. "Not that it would ever happen. Shauna's happy right now."

"Well, as happy as she can be after that unfortunate accident with her last boyfriend. You girls sure live interesting lives." She bent to pull a weed from the front bed where the fence divided her yard from the sidewalk. "You remember if you ever need someone to help out, I'm just a few steps from your door. I make a mean apple tart."

"Yes, ma'am, I'll remember." She glanced at her watch. "Anyway, I need to get going."

"Wait, did you hear about the poor girl who was killed up at Outlaw? That place is cursed. Always has been. You can't count the number of people who have been killed up there."

"There's been other murders?" Cat hadn't thought to look into the history of the old Western town.

"Some girl disappeared in 1965 or '66, I can't remember which year, but they found her body up above the saloon. All dressed up like one of those girls who used to work the bar, if you know what I mean." Mrs. Rice winked. "And another one in 1973. I know that's right because that was the year Mr. Rice went to Texas to work. I was on my own here with a murderer running around."

"Wow, I've never heard of any of this." She was going to have to get the full story from Uncle Pete.

"You know the college sweeps a lot of these things under the rug. They don't like any controversy around this town, not at all. Of course, you know all about that since your poor Michael's death was one of the dirty little secrets the college didn't want found out." Mrs. Rice glanced toward her house. Somewhere a phone was ringing so loud, Cat could hear it from her place on the sidewalk. "I better go. That's probably Doris with some more news. You let me know if you hear anything, okay?"

Cat watched Mrs. Rice hurry back inside her too-large-for-one-person house. She hadn't known Mr. Rice, as he'd died when Cat was a kid, but her mom had played bridge with Mrs. Rice for years. Or at least until she and Cat's dad had moved to Florida. Now they played backgammon with their friends.

She glanced at her watch and hurried along to her destination. A large black limo sat running in the driveway, the driver leaning against the side of the car smoking a cigarette. He smiled as Cat came up the walk. "Well, if it isn't the local author. My daughter loves your books. She's certain she'll come into her powers as soon as she hits high school. I think she's going to be a little disappointed."

Cat smiled. She'd heard this a lot. Her main character, Tori, was a witch out of water. Her folks had raised her in the land of normal until they couldn't deny her supernatural talent anymore. That's when she went away to the private boarding school for the special. "Tell her I appreciate her reading, and I'm doing a signing at the local bookstore when the next book releases. I'd love to meet her."

"That's mighty kind of you." He grinned as he nodded to the door. "I won't keep you. I know Mr. Dante is expecting you."

Cat climbed the stone steps like she was going to the principal's office. She liked Dante. Well, kind of. He was interesting and charming and felt a tad bit dangerous. Cat had never been attracted to bad-boy types. Until now. And she couldn't be attracted to Dante because she was dating Seth. No wonder he didn't like her even talking to Dante. He must feel her confusion as much as she did.

The door opened and a woman in a maid's outfit held it open. The woman wore pants instead of the skirt she'd seen on Halloween costumes, but it was definitely designed to broadcast to everyone she met her status in the household. "Miss Latimer, Mr. Cornelio is expecting you. Follow me, please."

How did everyone know she was coming when Dante had just texted her less than ten minutes ago? She hadn't spent that long talking to Mrs. Rice. Pushing the question away, she followed the woman into the library. Dante sat in a leather wingback chair reading.

He glanced up when the footsteps echoed across the tile floor. "Good, I'm so glad you could make time for me." He crossed the floor and leaned down to kiss her cheek.

Cat stepped back, avoiding the contact. "I don't have a lot of time. What do you want, Dante?"

"I see we are still at that stage." He pointed to a chair next to his. "Please sit down. I need to ask you a favor."

Cat moved to the chair and perched on the edge. "Your driver has your car running out front. Planning on making a quick exit?"

"I must fly back to Boston as soon as we conclude our discussion." He winced. "Family business."

"Oh." Cat didn't really want to know family business. She decided she'd have to ask the question again. "So what do you want?"

"Jessi Ball's mother is a close friend." He paused, looking at her face. "But I see you already know that. Interesting."

"What do you want me to do with Jessi? Kick her out of the retreat? She seems to be interested in actually writing something."

Dante stood up and paced to the window, glanced out, then back to the chair. This time he didn't sit, he leaned over the back and crossed his arms. "Catherine, I want you to protect her."

"From what?" Now Cat felt lost, like she'd stepped out of a movie and then back in, only to find she'd missed the key clues.

"Her friend Danielle was recently killed." His eyes seemed to burn into hers. He was looking for a signal or a spark, or maybe he just liked intense eye contact. Cat couldn't tell.

"Yeah, I know that. I was the shoulder Jessi cried on last night when she found out. What exactly do you want from me?" Cat felt the anger and help-lessness sweep over her.

"Like I said, I want you to protect Jessi." He looked at Cat like she was a slow learner. "Isn't that obvious?"

"Who do you want me to protect her from?" Cat stared at him, understanding finally putting the pieces together for her. "The fact her friend was killed has no bearing on Jessi, does it?"

He finally sat in the chair and put a hand to his brow. "I believe they got the wrong girl. I suspect they were trying to kill Jessi."

The driver stepped into the room. "I'm sorry, sir, but if we are going to arrive in Boston in time for your meeting, we have to leave now."

Dante stood and reached for Cat's hand. "Walk me to the car."

She followed. "Are you going to explain what you just said?"

"It's simple," I told Elizabeth I'd watch out for Jessi while she was here. You just have to keep her safe until I get back." He paused at the top step just outside the door. "Can I count on you, Catherine?"

"I won't let anything happen to her." She paused. "Are you sure she's safe here?"

He climbed into the car and looked back at her with sad eyes. "No, no, I'm not."

Cat watched him drive away, then walked down the sidewalk and headed home. She needed to talk to Uncle Pete. If Dante's suspicions were valid, Jessi might be in danger. And if someone was targeting one of her retreat guests, they would have to come through her.

She didn't see Seth's truck parked across the street. He sat in the driver's seat and watched her leave Dante's and head back to the house.

# CHAPTER 5

Uncle Pete sat at the kitchen table when she arrived back at the house. Shauna had a plate of eggs, bacon, and toast in front of him along with orange juice and coffee. Cat knew her friend liked feeding people. It made her feel like she was helping. He wiped his mouth and pointed to a chair. "I've been waiting on you. I wanted to talk to you about Danielle."

Cat poured a cup of coffee and sat. "I really don't know much."

"That's not what I'm hearing." He pulled out a notebook. "Three of your guests remember you and Jessi talking to Danielle at the photography shop on Sunday."

"I told you about that. She was hanging out with Jessi when we went in to get our picture done. They made me into a saloon girl." Cat thought about the lighthearted conversation. "Danielle said she was covering Jessi's shifts because she had student loans.

But that's about all I got out of the conversation. Danielle was a broke graduate student and Jessi's costs were covered by family."

"I was afraid it was nothing." He pushed his empty plate away. "The manager at Outlaw is saying the girl was killed by some crazed Covington student. Covington's saying it must deal with Outlaw and their people. Of course, a lot of the staff at Outlaw are Covington graduates, so they could both be right. And I've got nothing."

"Seth told us there was a stalker at the college this year." Shauna set a full plate in front of Cat and took the empty one from Uncle Pete to the sink. Then she filled her own cup and sat with the pair. "Is that true?"

"We've had some incidents of what we used to call Peeping Toms, but I haven't been able to pin that on anyone. I'm pretty sure it's the boys from the frat houses. They seem to want to push the edge with their initiation rites every year." He shook his head. "I'm getting too old for this petty crap."

Cat stared at the eggs on the plate in front of her. She took a couple of bites, then set her fork down. "Do you think Jessi's in danger too?"

"That's kind of a leap. Yes, the girls were roommates, but I'm afraid the killer probably has more to do with Danielle's life than anyone else's. Why do you ask?" Her uncle leaned forward. "Did she say something to you that you're not telling me?"

"Yeah, Cat, why are you so concerned about Jessi all of a sudden?" Seth strolled into the kitchen and leaned against the counter.

"I was just wondering, that's all." Cat didn't look

up, afraid Seth would see the lie in her face. The guy could read her better than anyone she'd ever met, including the man she'd married.

Seth took a chair and turned it around, sitting backward and leaning his arms across the back. "Is it just curiosity or did your discussion with Dante this morning lead you to that question?"

"Dante's in town?" Uncle Pete was glaring at her now too. "Why didn't you tell me?"

"I am not Dante's social secretary, and from what I know, he was in town this morning but he just left to go back to Boston a while ago." She glared at Seth. "How did you know I talked to Dante? Were you following me?"

"No, I was just driving back from my apartment when I saw you go into that house. I parked and waited for you to come back out. I've told you before, I don't trust the guy."

Cat took her mostly uneaten breakfast and scraped it into the trash. She suddenly didn't have an appetite. "You should trust me more."

"I trust you. I don't trust him." The intensity in their conversation seemed to have everyone else disappearing from view.

"Stop fighting." Shauna slapped her hand on the table. "It's not worth it. People need to be kind to each other when they still can. So Cat, tell us what Dante wanted. I've never known the guy to show up without a piece of information."

Cat sipped her coffee and willed herself to calm down. Seth worried about her, especially when Dante was involved. And maybe he had a perfect right to do it. "Okay, I got a text asking me to meet him at his house this morning."

"So naturally, you just go right into the lion's den."

"Seth, let her tell the story. You can nag her later." Uncle Pete's voice had an edge to it, and Cat thought Seth wouldn't be the only one nagging her later.

"Anyway, he thinks they may have mistaken Danielle for Jessi for some reason. And now he's worried that Jessi will be next. I think he's overre-acting, but who knows?" Cat saw the look of con-cern that passed between the two men sitting at her kitchen table. "I'm more interested in the his-tory of the Outlaw killer that Mrs. Rice was telling me about. Is it true that there have been two mur-ders of young women dressed in a saloon girl cos-tume is strangled in one of the rooms above the saloon?"

"What? And you guys went there for a day of fun? What kind of place is this?" Shauna's hand shook a little as she sipped her coffee.

"Your neighbor is spreading old wives' tales. We haven't had a murder up there since the current owners turned the place from a true ghost town to a tourist attraction. More than likely, it was just an easy place to kill someone since it was deserted. No one used to go up there except kids to party where their folks couldn't find them." Uncle Pete patted Shauna's hands. "Don't worry, dear. This really isn't the Old West with gunfights and short life spans. We're civilized now."

"Except a girl was killed this week in the room above the saloon." Cat decided she was going to start researching Outlaw's history as soon as Uncle Pete left. There might be a connection, although a serial killer who waited a decade between killings didn't seem like a logical conclusion. But it was a place to start. She glanced at the clock. "Ten to ten? Crap, Professor Turner should be here by now for the seminar."

"I restocked the dining room after breakfast, but I'll refresh the coffeepots now. The guests are going to need caffeine to stay awake in his lecture. That man is in love with all the Hemingway lore." Shauna stood and went to the coffee machine to start a new pot. "Pete? Do you want a cup to go? Or are you hanging around?"

"I've got a crime to solve, I can't just sit here jawing all day." He stood as well and put his cup in the sink. "But I will take a cup of that coffee to go, if you don't mind."

Seth glanced at his watch. "I'm doing a walk through the house every couple of hours when the doors are open, just to be safe. If you don't see me in twenty minutes, call the cops, and stay out of the basement."

Cat paused at the door. "I feel like I'm living one of those slasher movies. The killer is always hiding in the basement."

As she walked through the lobby, she realized that most of the group was already in the dining room, getting refreshments for the session. She didn't pause there but instead went right to the living room where Professor Turner stood, adjusting the podium. He glanced up as she entered the room.

"There you are." He glanced around the room. "I hope you don't mind but I let myself in. I came in a little early to set up. Last month there was a set of chairs to the side where I'm sure people couldn't see the slides very well."

Cat followed his gaze. He had moved the comfortable living room furniture that she and Shauna had set up in little conversation groups all around the room into a mini classroom. The couch served as the back row, and the other chairs were in rows in front of it. He had definitely made himself at home. "Let me grab the screen and projector for you. Sorry I'm a little late on getting you set up."

"No worries, Catherine. A good orator can work under any conditions. Have I ever told you about the time I had to teach class in the middle of a blizzard? Only one poor student made it across campus to attend, but even when the audience is small, the show must go on." He set his laptop on the podium and laid out the cords for Cat to hook to the projector. "Hemingway is a national treasure, and we must spread the gospel."

As she finished setting up the audiovisual equipment, she noticed Cora at the doorway. Her eyes went wide as she took in the rearranged room. "Come on in, we're just finishing up."

"You all are serious about your seminars." Cora had her Warm Springs Writers' Retreat mug in one hand and a small laptop in another. "I'll put this on a chair to save my spot and go back for a couple of cookies."

Cat paused by Professor Turner. "If you're ready, I'll go round up the troops. I think you'll recognize one of our guests."

And as if that had been her stage cue, Jessi walked into the room. She ran up to Professor Turner and gave him a tight hug. "I'm so happy to see you. I haven't seen anyone since classes released in May. What have you been doing?"

As the professor went into what Cat knew would be a detailed outline of his whereabouts and actions since he'd last seen Jessi, Cat snuck out the door. Everyone, including Kelly, was in the dining room, getting ready for the seminar. The plates of cookies Shauna had put out earlier were almost empty. Cat snagged a peanut butter cookie as she walked into the room.

"Everyone to the living room. Covington College's expert on Hemingway and curator of the Hemingway papers at the library is ready to start." She took a bite of the cookie, then after brushing crumbs off her shirt, she added, "Professor Turner is a little obsessed with Hemingway, so he'd love to field any questions after the formal lecture has concluded."

"So you're saying that we should be nice to the guy and not make him uncomfortable," Connie translated. "Check. I'm good at keeping a man's pride façade intact."

The group moved out of the dining room and into the living room. Cat stayed behind. "Not quite what I said, but I guess they got the meaning." She turned toward the door and stopped.

Seth stood there, watching her.

"Look, if you're going to yell at me, let's just hold off the fight until Sunday after the guests leave. I'd rather not air our dirty laundry in front of paying customers." She pushed back the tears she knew would come if they really did fight. She hated fighting.

To her surprise, he walked over and pulled her into a hug. "I am so sorry. I shouldn't be this jealous. I guess I'm reacting to the Michael thing." He tilted her head up and kissed her. "Tell me I'm an idiot."

"You're an idiot," she repeated, then she kissed him. "And Dante's nothing like Michael."

"No? He's rich, successful, and can give you the world." He didn't break eye contact. "That day when you got married as I stood in the back of the church, all I wanted to do was trade places with him. I wanted to be the person you made those vows with. And I knew I'd screwed up big-time by losing you."

"I can't change the past. I thought I was in love with Michael. He was all the things you weren't." Cat felt a stone in her throat. They'd never talked about this before.

"Like Dante and his huge library."

"Maybe. Book smart, intelligent, working with ideas instead of his hands." She saw a flash of pain in his eyes. "I thought that was what I wanted, but I was wrong. I want you. And if that means we can't discuss high literature in the study over tea at night, so be it."

"I'd talk genre fiction over a few beers." Seth grinned and squeezed her. "I'll never freak out about you talking to Dante or anyone again."

"Yes, you will. You're just that type of guy. But when you do, remember that I chose you. I chose us."

She saw a movement out of the corner of her eye and realized Shauna was in the doorway, watching them.

"You two are made for each other." Shauna set down the tray of brownies and gathered up the empty plates. "Now, do you two lovebirds think you can pry yourselves apart long enough to help me re-stock in here while the guests are occupied? These women like their treats."

They set up the dining room and then con-verged in the kitchen. Cat kept an eye on the clock so she could go out and thank Professor Turner when the lecture ended. When she went out at eleven, he was already in the lobby areas and head-ing to the door.

"Oh, I guess the time got away from me. I didn't realize you were already done." Cat glanced at the clock: 11:05. That had to be a record. Typically, Turner's lectures went at least fifteen minutes over the hour he was contracted to teach.

He didn't even slow his pace. "Sorry, I've got an appointment back at the university. A reporter is coming in from Denver to interview me about the Hemingway collection. I'm so nervous, I can hardly think straight. Good afternoon, Catherine."

Seth stood beside her and watched Professor Turner's hasty exit. "Man, he's in a hurry."

"Yeah, and the weird thing was, he didn't men-tion this at all when I talked to him before the ses-sion. He's not the type to act all cool about something like this." She narrowed her eyes and glanced toward the living room. "Let's go see if the guests know anything about this interview."

When she went into the room, the chairs had all been moved back and the group huddled over near the fireplace. Cora looked up and poked Jessi.

"Ouch, what was that for?" Jessi narrowed her eyes, then followed Cora's gaze toward Cat and Seth. "Oh, hey, we were just making lunch plans."

For some reason, Cat doubted that was really what the women had been talking about, but she let it go. "When did Professor Turner find out about this interview?"

Jessi's face went bright red, and the other four pretended to be focusing on something else.

"Jessi, do you have something you need to say?"

She shrugged. "I snuck out and had one of my friends call and pretend they were a reporter. We used to do it all the time when we'd have a Friday-afternoon class with him. You would think he'd start to question it when no one shows up, but it's worked more times than not."

"That wasn't very nice. Maybe one of the other guests wanted to learn more about Hemingway." She could hear Seth's chuckle behind her.

Cora spoke up. "Actually, since he didn't write in our genre or in the time period we're all passionate about, the rest of us were all just being nice to him."

Cat surrendered. "It's your retreat. You can do what you want. So are you going to the Diner for lunch?"

Jessi broke in. "Actually, no. I've called a car to come and get us. We're going into Denver, so we'll probably be late."

"Oh." Cat glanced at Kelly. There was no way the woman would want to leave her work-in-progress that long. "Are you going too? Or do you want Shauna to make you a lunch?"

"No, I'm tagging along. What is the saying, *All work and no fun makes Jack a dull boy*?" Kelly asked Cora.

"Exactly right." Cora glanced at Cat. "Kelly sometimes gets sayings mixed up."

Jessi's phone beeped. "There's our driver. Let's go everyone."

Cat watched as the group dashed out of the living room. She heard footsteps running upstairs to grab a jacket or a purse. She straightened a chair and glanced at Seth when the women had left and the lobby area was quiet. "You buy that line she was selling?"

"Not even a little. So where would our writers be going on a Tuesday that they didn't want us to know about?"

Two hours later, she got the call from Uncle Pete. She set down the book she'd been reading and picked up the phone. "Hey. Are you calling to say you'll come for dinner tonight? Shauna says we're eating at six."

"No, that's not why I'm calling. Will you send Seth and the car up to Outlaw to pick up your retreat guests?"

"What are they doing in Outlaw? They said they were going to Denver." She stood and paced through the conversation.

"They keep saying they are here for research, but the place is supposed to be closed up tighter than a drum, and yet they were all sitting in the saloon, chatting when my deputy arrived. An alarm had gone off and alerted us that someone had broken in." He lowered his voice. "I'm probably not going to get the manager to agree to charge them, especially with Jessi Ball as one of the gang, but I'd sure like to scare them a little."

"I'll go find Seth. He'll be up there as soon as possible." She paused before asking the one question that made sense. "Were they looking into Danielle's death?"

"They deny it, but that's the only reason I can come up with that they came here today. They all are sticking to their story, so I have to let them go." He sighed. "Your guests are always challenging."

"Not always." Cat corrected him. There had been at least a few retreats where nothing bad like this had happened. "I'll talk to them when they get back about staying out of your investigation. Maybe they'll listen to me."

"Or maybe not." Her uncle hung up before she could ask what he meant.

Seth was in the attic, on his laptop. When she came in, he leaned back in his chair and grinned. "I'm on top of the world, Ma."

"Your driving services are needed." She sat down on a window seat next to the desk where he'd set up and told him about the phone call from Uncle Pete.

"What are they looking for? Ghosts or killers?" He closed his laptop and stood, grabbing his keys from the table. "This group is going to be a handful, aren't they?"

"Maybe both. I just hope they don't get themselves into trouble." Cat shivered even though the room was warm. Dante's warning about keeping Jessi safe echoed in her head. She didn't want anything to happen to the bright, happy girl who was staying at the retreat.

# CHAPTER 6

They were all in the living room, waiting for her. When Seth had dropped them at the front door, he'd told them to wait, as Cat wanted to talk to the group. Now, as she paused at the doorway, she wondered what she could say to keep them safe. She didn't care if they wanted to investigate Danielle's murder, but she didn't want them to get hurt. Besides, Uncle Pete did care if they were messing up his investigation. And Dante didn't think Jessi, at least, was safe. And Seth, he worried about everyone.

Why couldn't these retreats be just about the writing? She glanced at the two dozen roses on the table by the entry. Linda Cook sent them at the start of every retreat. At first Cat had thought it was as a joke, because of her overzealous admirer at the first retreat. But now she realized the flowers were a symbol of hope. Of success and protection for the new guests and for the house that welcomed them each month. Writers were a different lot. Each had their own idiosyncrasies, and each retreat would be different because of that. She took a breath and entered the room.

The murmuring stopped as soon as she walked into the room.

Jessi stood. "I'm so sorry, Cat. This is my fault. Please don't blame the others."

Cat waved Jessi back down into her chair and glanced around the circle before pulling up a chair to join them. "What is your fault, exactly?"

Cora started to speak, but Jessi shook her head. Cat waited in the silence.

"Okay, so I got to thinking about Danielle and how she was killed at Outlaw. I thought maybe we might find some clues that the police didn't know to look for." Now that the floodgates were open, Jessi talked like she was on a timer and needed to get everything said before the bell rang. "So I hired a car to take us up there. Except when we got there, he ran my card and my money manager had put a hold on my account. I used my school card, and he watches that like a hawk. He steps in when he thinks I'm spending too much. It's my money, I can spend it any way I want. Anyway, the car left while we were in the saloon. I was trying to get it back when your uncle showed up. I guess we tripped some security system thing I didn't know about."

"That explains how you got there, but what happened once you were at Outlaw? What exactly were you looking for?" Cat wondered just how tight a leash the family had on Jessi and her activities. She knew she was going to talk to Dante about this manager guy stranding her in a ghost town. That couldn't be safe either.

"Clues. You know, like on that show *Murder, She Wrote*?" Kelly leaned forward. "We broke off into two groups and searched the upstairs for anything that shouldn't be there."

"And what did you find?" In for a penny, Cat thought.

Cora glanced around, and all the woman shook their heads in a silent *go ahead*. Then she pulled her Warm Springs Writers' Retreat bag out and dumped it on the table. Pieces of paper, cigarette butts, and a broken silver chain lay in front of them. The piece that caught Cat's eye was an old decorated hair comb. Cora checked her bag for any remaining items before she spoke. "This is what we found. All of these were in the room where Danielle was found. And the police didn't take them into evidence."

"And now you've broken the chain of evidence, so if any of these things are clues, they can't be used in a trial setting." Cat grabbed a tissue and picked up the hair comb. "This looks old."

"It is. It's mine." Jessi spoke quietly. "I bought it last year when I started playing Kate the saloon girl at Outlaw. I found it in an antique shop in town. Darryl had a fit when he got the bill. That was probably when he started turning off my cards. I've complained to Mom, but she's backing Darryl on the money front."

Poor little rich girl, Cat thought, and she wondered if Danielle had thought the same thing. "Had you been in that room before?"

Jessi shook her head. "Not since first year. One

of the girls took a guy up there after we closed up one night for a quickie and he fell through the floor. Those boards are old and can't hold a lot of weight."

"Which is another reason you shouldn't have been up there." Cat stared at the comb. "When was the last time you saw this?"

"Last week. After my Saturday shift, I put it in my jewelry box in my room. Danielle must have gotten it out when she got ready for her shift. She was always borrowing my things without telling me." Tears filled Jessi's eyes, but she wiped them away. "We fought about it, a lot."

Cat set the comb down and picked up the first sheet of paper. It was a charge slip like the kind you got for gas and was dated earlier that year. She frowned and checked the date on all the slips. Most of them were just like the first, but all were dated within the last six months. A couple were for snacks and alcohol purchases, again, within the last six months.

"Well, someone had been using that room for a while." Cat looked at the cigarette butts. "And these are all the same brand."

"Yeah, we saw that, but before we could look closely, the police car lights came into the saloon, so I tucked everything into my bag." Cora stared at the items gathered on the table. "It means something, doesn't it?"

"It means you all are in trouble for obstruction of justice. What were you thinking?" Uncle Pete's voice came from behind Cat and even made her jump, and she hadn't been the one his wrath was aimed at this time. He walked over and glanced at the table. Then, surprisingly, he sank into the empty chair that completed the circle. "I'm glad I stopped by this evening. Do you all want to tell me the rest of the story you forgot to mention when I found you in Outlaw?"

Cora went through everything they'd just told Cat. Then she sighed. "Don't blame the rest of them. Hiding this from you was my decision. And I'm prepared to take the punishment."

"No, Cora, this whole stupid idea was mine. I should be held responsible." Jessi swallowed and looked at Uncle Pete, her face calm and determined. "I'm ready to go."

"I'm not taking you," he glanced around the room, "or any of you anywhere. I would like to strongly suggest you refrain from your Nancy Drew habits and stay out of my investigation." He gathered the items, put them into an evidence bag, and sealed it.

"So we're not going to jail?" Cora's eyes widened.

Uncle Pete smiled, but the emotion didn't light up his eyes. "Not today."

Glancing at the clock, Cat realized it was already six. "If you are going to find someplace to eat, you better get going. I take it you didn't have lunch."

"No, we were going to go and grab takeout once we got done at Outlaw, but, well, you know what happened then." Kelly stood and stretched. "I could go for pizza again. I'm starving."

Cora paused by the door. "We saw that cat again. The black and white one? Does the caretaker live up there? She must be his."

"I don't think they have an on-site caretaker." Jessi frowned as she made her way out of the room with the other women.

As they filed out, Cat started to stand, but Uncle Pete put a hand on her arm and held her back. "I need to talk to you."

Cat held up a finger, then went to the pocket doors separating the lobby from the living room. She slid them closed and then returned to sit by her uncle. "What's up?"

"I called and talked to Jessi's driver, and he said when he called in the charge, he was told the credit card was stolen. That's why he left them there, thinking it paid them back for using someone else's card." He leaned back into the chair.

"But it wasn't stolen, it was Jessi's card, right?" Cat felt confused.

"It was. I called her financial manager and got his side of it. Apparently, he's been concerned with her overspending, so he's monitoring all her purchases. When he saw that limo charge, he called the card in as stolen." Uncle Pete shook his head. "To protect her. I told him that instead, he'd put her and her guests into a dangerous situation. If we hadn't gone up there to check on the break-in, your guests would have been spending the night and I would have been looking for them in Denver."

"Did he realize what he was doing?"

Uncle Pete glanced toward the door. "Honestly, he seemed upset that he'd put her in a dangerous situation. Something felt off about his reaction, though. I may just be tired. Anyway, I can't believe I'm going to ask this, but I have two favors I'd like to ask of you."

"Shoot." It was apparently her week for granting favors.

"I want you to take Jessi to her dorm room tomorrow and see if there's anything missing or unusual. I've gone through it, but it's a typical girls' dorm room. Messy with clothes all over." He smiled at her. "Like your room used to be as a teenager. I remember your mom used to rail at you all the time about cleaning it up."

"I knew where everything was." Cat smiled at the memory and made a mental note to call her mother on Sunday after the guests had left. It had been a few weeks since she'd talked to her. "Are we looking for something specific?"

He glanced at the clear packet with the items from the saloon that Jessi and Cora had found after his police officers had scanned the room. "I think she'll know it when she sees it. I'd send one of my female officers with you, but Katie has the day off and Irene is doing a seminar at the college on safety for the new freshmen coming in."

"I'll take her over first thing in the morning." She thought about the retreat schedule. "I think I'm giving the seminar tomorrow, but it's not until ten. We'll have time."

"Great. I appreciate it. And if you find anything," he handed her a clear bag, "bring it by the station. I think it's more likely Jessi will notice something gone than evidence of the killer being in their room. The graduate dorms have much better security than undergrad ones since they are newer. I don't think anyone could get inside undetected."

"Not a problem." She took the bag and put it in

her pocket. "What's the other favor? Keeping an eye on the guests?"

"No. And I can't believe I'm asking this, but would you call your friend Dante and ask him about Jessi's fund manager?" He watched her face.

"Sure, but why don't you call?"

He shrugged. "I kind of read him the riot act a few months ago about leaving you alone. I told him you were trying to get over this whole thing with Michael and didn't need him messing with your new life. Anyway, I'm not his favorite person right now."

"He's concerned about Jessi. He wouldn't hold that against you." Cat shook her head. "Like I don't stay mad about your sticking your nose into my business when it was totally uncalled for. Uncles can be overprotective."

"I hear what you're saying, but I know what these people are like. And sometimes, well, you can be a little naïve." He blushed as she stared at him. "Well, it's true. You have a good thing going with Seth. I'd hate to see you mess it up."

"Again. You wanted to add *again*." What was with Uncle Pete was treating her like a teenager? "I'm a grown woman who can make her own decisions and mistakes, thank you very much. And besides, if it's any of your business, I don't see Dante that way."

"Now I've ticked you off too." He put his hand on hers. "I'm sorry, Cat. I'll try to be a little less involved in your life."

"Involved I can deal with, as long as you realize it is my life." She let out a deep breath. She had lied to her uncle just a tiny bit. She found Dante exciting and handsome, but she knew she had a good thing with Seth. She wasn't going to mess it up over a fling with a totally impossible life choice. "Don't worry, I'll call Dante and keep myself in check while I try to find out about Jessi's money guy. But if I run off with him to the Bahamas and chuck this life, you only have yourself to blame. I can't be held responsible for my feminine hormones."

"Point taken. Just call me when you find out something." He glanced at his watch. "Does the invitation to supper still stand? Or are you too mad at me to share a meal?"

"You're always invited for supper, you know that." She stood, and as he followed, she hugged him. "I should be mad at you, but I understand."

The front door had just closed and Cat watched through the window as the five women made their way to the sidewalk. "I know they were friends before they came, but they have taken Jessi into their group seamlessly. Maybe that's why they're already in trouble on day three of the retreat."

"Strangers take some time to warm up to each other. They don't have time to plan B-and-Es so early in the week." Uncle Pete put a hand on her back. "Let's go eat and not think about murder for at least an hour. I could use the break."

When they entered the room, Seth was sitting at the table, reading something on his phone. Shauna was at the other side, reading on her laptop.

"I've got to make a call to Dr. Simon's clinic before it closes." Cat smiled at the peaceful scene and then called out to the room. "Look who is joining us for dinner!"

Cat grabbed her phone and stood near the edge of the room to make her call. When she got the office voice mail, she looked at the clock. The offices were already closed. She left a quick message and then put her phone in her pocket.

While she was on the phone, Shauna had closed her laptop and set it on the kitchen desk. Now she was bubbling to Uncle Pete. "I'm so glad you came. You must have had a horrible day. I didn't know who would be here and when for dinner, so I made a batch of lasagna. Garlic bread is warming in the oven and I have a fresh green salad in the fridge. Will that work?"

"I'm so hungry, I could eat a box of Pop-Tarts and probably eat the box too." Seth set his phone down and waved Pete closer. "Come over here and check out this area we're looking at backpacking into. I'm looking at it in Google Maps and it looks a little different than I remember."

As Uncle Pete and Seth talked about the upcoming fishing trip, Cat went over to get plates and salad bowls out of the cabinet. She glanced at Shauna. "You okay?"

"I'm just been thinking about that poor girl. Do you think her killer was the guy causing problems over at the school? Women just aren't safe anywhere anymore." She got the bread out of the oven, put the steaming loaf into a basket, and covered it with a towel. "I thought getting out of the city, we'd have less of this."

"One, we don't know if we have a problem

here." Cat didn't like where the conversation was going. Not at all.

"We have a dead girl. That's a problem." Shauna glared at her as she grabbed the pan out of the oven. When it banged on the stovetop, Cat winced.

"You're right. I'm sorry, I didn't mean to diminish Danielle's death. But, Shauna, you didn't even know her. Why are you so upset?" Cat put a hand on her friend's arm. "Seriously, tell me what's going on."

"I think it's just so soon after Kevin." Shauna glanced at Uncle Pete and Seth, who had stopped talking and were looking toward her and Cat. "Look, I don't want to ruin your dinner. I've just had a bad day. Can you finish this up? I'm going to my room."

"Aren't you hungry?" Cat put a hand on Shauna's arm. "I want to help."

"Let me go to my room. If I get hungry, I know where the leftovers will be." Taking off her apron and putting it into the hamper in the pantry, Shauna left the room.

Seth grabbed the plates. "Is she okay?"

"I think so." Cat got the salad out of the refrigerator along with an assortment of dressings. As her hand paused over Shauna's favorite, she sent up a shower of love to her friend, hoping her thoughts might make at least a little difference. As they sat down to eat, her thoughts were racing with concern for Shauna and Jessi. Both women were hurting, and that made her heart ache a little too.

After dinner, Seth helped her clean up the kitchen as Uncle Pete was heading back to the station to work. She sighed as she watched him leave.

"I'm worried about all the time he's putting in lately. He's not as young as he used to be."

"Wow. Don't tell him that. Your uncle is the most active man I know. Did you know he started working out at the gym a few months ago? My trainer, Matt, he's been seeing him twice a week, and he says Pete's really shaping up." Seth leaned closer. "You think it's got something to do with a certain ex-officer in Alaska?"

Cat rinsed the last plate, holding it under the warm water. "I do. And I have to be honest, I have mixed emotions about that. I thought this thing with Shirley would be good for him. Open him up to dating someone who lived in Colorado. Not at the edge of the world."

"You know Shirley's not unwilling to move here, if they get serious. She loves Aspen Hills." He studied her. "So what's got you worried?"

"I guess I'm being silly. I'm always worried about change. I've always been Uncle Pete's girl. If he gets married and moves, well, I'm not even going to think about it." She dried her hands and started up the dishwasher. She turned and smiled at Seth. "You're thinking I'm overreacting, right? Maybe I hold on to the present too tightly."

He pulled her into his arms. "I think you hold on just tight enough."

# CHAPTER 7

Jessi was already in the dining room eating break-fast when Cat came down. Cat had had a restless night, thinking about Uncle Pete and Shirley. Today, she'd decided, would be a happy day. She could check off Uncle Pete's chores this morning, then set herself and Shauna up for a mani-pedi as soon as the retreat was over. Getting your nails done didn't solve all the world's problems, but at least you looked great while you were doing it.

Cat grabbed a cup of coffee and paused at Jessi's side. "Hey, we've got an assignment from Uncle Pete we need to do this morning. What are your plans for the day?"

"I was planning on writing, attending the seminar, going to lunch and dinner, and just basically staying out of trouble." Jessi grinned. "No outside field trip planning for this girl."

"At least not today," Cora added, laughing.

Kelly stood and grabbed her coffee cup. "Good. I'm behind on my word count, but I didn't want to miss out on any of the shenanigans."

"Don't worry, we'll come get you before we go heist the bank," Connie deadpanned.

"You are kidding, right?" Kelly glanced at the women sitting around the table. "Tell me she's kidding."

"She's kidding. Go write." Cora patted her arm as she walked to the sideboard for another muffin. "We'll let you know when we're gathering in the living room for the seminar. Then we'll go to lunch and discuss the bank robbery."

"You guys are awful. No wonder you're my friends." Kelly grabbed a couple of cookies and left the room.

Jessi turned back to Cat. "I'll be ready to go as soon as I finish breakfast. Will that work?"

"Let's say eight. That way I can get a few words in before my day implodes." Cat patted her on the shoulder. "Are you feeling better?"

"Still sad. I guess that doesn't just go away."

Shauna had come into the room with a fresh pitcher of orange juice. "No, it doesn't just go away."

Everyone in the room looked up at her. They, like Cat, had heard the pain in her voice.

Shauna met their gaze and smiled at the group. "But it does get better. With time and some good friends."

Cat followed her out of the dining room. "Are you okay? I was worried about you last night."

"I'm fine. I think I've passed a turning point. I'm sure I'll have days, but from this day forward,

I'm going to try to be me again. I only needed one last cry. But last night, while I was thinking about Kevin, I realized I was sad for Danielle's family and Jessi too. It's not just all about me anymore, at least not in my heart." Shauna paused at the fridge. "I heard you talking to Jessi. What does your uncle have you doing now?"

Cat explained her assignment as she sipped her coffee. Shauna pushed a plate of peanut butter cookies toward her.

"Breakfast of champions." Cat grinned as she held the cookie aloft. "It has protein, dairy, fat, and grain. Almost all the food groups."

"You'll burn through that fast, but at least you won't be starving at lunch. Let me know if you want a real breakfast." Shauna was glancing through a cooking magazine. "I really need to work up some new recipes. That always makes me feel better. Anyway, what exactly does Pete think you'll find?"

Cat paused. "I have no idea."

"Hey, I meant to tell you. Toni at the vet clinic called early this morning about the cat. She looked in their files and they don't have any record of a cat like that being reported lost, but she talked to the vet tech and he remembers Angelica. He says she belonged to an older woman who used to live outside Aspen Hills on Lookout Road. Her name is Mary Davis. According to the records, she missed her last annual checkup for the cat."

"Did they call the owner?" Cat hadn't realized until now how worried she'd been about the feline running around Outlaw. Maybe she'd go up and catch the cat and bring it down to this Mary lady.

"They tried, but her number's disconnected. I called the police station and left a message for Katie. She doesn't come in until nine, but you know she knows everything. I could have called Mrs. Rice, but that's my last resort." Shauna picked up her own cookie. "I wasn't feeling that strong this morning."

Laughing, Cat went upstairs to write for an hour before going with Jessi to the dorms. Shauna was definitely feeling better.

Now, an hour into searching through Jessi and Danielle's room, Cat really had no clue what they were looking for. Jessi had found several articles of clothing that her friend had borrowed without asking and hung in her own closet.

"And this sweater. I'd thought I'd lost it. I even asked her if she'd taken it, but she said no. And I believed her." Jessi shook her head. "I guess I didn't really know Danielle as well as I thought. The chick lied to me."

"Maybe she forgot she'd borrowed it." Cat opened the final desk drawer she hadn't look through. This time, her uncle's instinct had been off. Way off. Danielle seemed like a normal young woman with too much makeup, too many clothes, including the ones Jessi was reappropriating, and too many shoes. Cat assumed Jessi would be pulling some of those as well, since several pair looked too high-dollar for a scholarship kid.

"I don't think so. If she was taking my clothes, what else did she take?" Jessi sank down on Danielle's bed and rubbed the silk comforter on the top. "And as mad as I am, I still wish she was alive. I'd yell at her, then we'd make up and go have a spa day. We fought a lot, but we always knew how to make up. Friends are like that, you know."

Cat was reading in a journal she'd found in the bottom drawer. She barely heard Jessi's words. Finally, she looked up. "Jessi? Who's Max?"

"He's my boyfriend. We're on a break right now. He's going back east in the fall for law school, and he wanted to focus this summer on a few classes he's taking to prep. He didn't really get serious about school until last year. Then his folks gave him the beatdown. Get his grades up or he would have to work in their restaurant instead of going to law school." She had lain down on Danielle's bed and now she sat straight up. "Wait, how did you know about Max?"

"I think you're going to be mad at Danielle again." Cat held up the diary. "Apparently, they'd been seeing each other for over a year."

By the time they got back to the house, Jessi had left no fewer than fifteen messages on Max Trandor's voice mail. Most of them were not repeatable, and Cat had to give her credit for using words she didn't think a hardened lifer at the Denver prison could use without blushing. The girl was mad.

Walking through the door, Cat took her arm. "I know you're upset. Do you want to take the day?"

She nodded. "I'm going for a run. It always calms me. But if I go too far, can I call and get a ride back? Apparently, my limo service is not accepting my calls."

Cat gave the girl a hug. "Are you sure you don't want company? Seth loves to run."

"No, I won't go far." Jessi sighed. "I really just need to be alone for a while."

Watching her go upstairs to change, Cat hurried into the study and locked the door. No need for anyone to overhear this conversation. "Uncle Pete, it's me. What do you know about a Max Trandor?"

As her uncle ran the kid's name in his system, she told him what they'd found. That Danielle had a habit of taking Jessi's stuff. And apparently, that habit included her boyfriend.

"Are you sure Jessi didn't know?" Uncle Pete's question surprised her.

She stopped paging through the diary. "Of course she didn't know. The girl was devastated. And she called this guy and let him know she's done with him."

"You let her call him?"

"And how was I supposed to stop her?" Cat responded but then realized she was talking to dead air. Her uncle had hung up on her, probably to track down Max to check his alibi. Maybe he had gotten tired of Danielle and wanted to break it off. She could have threatened to tell Jessi. Apparently, faithfulness was one of her requirements in a life partner. Max had blown that relationship up as soon as he slept with Danielle the first time.

Cat started reading the diary, then, checking the clock, thought she had just enough time for one more call. She set the journal down and picked up her phone. Her call was answered on the first ring.

"Well, Catherine, I'm glad to hear from you, but I'm hoping this isn't bad news." Dante's voice was warm and comforting.

Cat shook off the glow from his tone. "Look, I wanted to ask you about Jessi's money manager. What do you know about him?"

"Darryl? He's been handling the kid's fund for years. He's very involved with Jessi's family and has several of their trust funds under his care. Why?"

Cat went on to tell him about the car service and Jessi being stranded. The more she talked, the quieter it got on the other side of the line.

"I'm not going to ask how she actually got out of the house without you knowing."

Cat interrupted him before he could go further. "Hold on, buddy. She told me they were going to Denver for lunch. That's not unusual. And she was with four other adults. I never thought they would go to Outlaw to investigate Danielle's murder."

"Okay, I understand. But this stranding her, I'm going to have a talk with Darryl. And I'll get back with you if I find anything unusual. He's such a nice man. This must have been some sort of a mistake."

The line went dead before Cat could ask how Dante was going to look into the man's financials, but she thought it was probably for the best. The less she actually knew, the better off she was.

And with that favor done, she locked the diary in Michael's desk and slipped the key into her pocket. She'd give it to her uncle as soon as possible. There was no way she wanted Jessi to read even half of what it said. Danielle was a horrible person. Or had been a horrible person and a worse friend. She'd used her friendship with Jessi for all of the perks she could get and then laughed at her behind her back. No wonder the kid needed to run to blow off steam.

She grabbed her notes for the talk and went into the kitchen to fill up her coffee cup. No one was there. Not Seth, not Shauna. She really wanted this week to be over. She ran a hand over a picture of a smiling Shauna on the back of her horse that Kevin had taken last summer. The look of pure joy on her face made Cat smile. Shauna was strong. She'd get through this.

Everyone sat in the living room chatting. Cora, Connie, Lisa, and even Kelly were already there. The only guest missing was Jessi. Cat glanced at her watch. She should have been back by now. She tried to keep her voice casual as she asked, "Anyone heard from Jessi?"

"I saw her leaving about forty-five minutes ago for a run. She said she'd be back for the session." Cora looked worried now. "Should I call her?"

"Yeah, give her a jingle. We'll hold off starting if she's on her way back." Cat didn't want to worry. She felt like all she'd done since the retreat had started was worry.

Cora hung up her phone and shook her head. "It went straight to voice mail. But my phone does that if I'm playing music and I put it on do not disturb. I'm sure she'll be back shortly."

"I'm going to grab a quick sandwich before I start. I didn't have breakfast." Cat left the room and was just starting to dial Uncle Pete's cell when Jessi burst into the lobby. Relief filled her body as she watched the young girl hurry toward her.

"Sorry, I know I'm late. I had a call from my mom." Jessi wrapped her ear buds around her phone. "I'm drenched from the run back. Do I have time for a quick shower?"

"If you make it quick. Everyone's waiting on us." Cat gave her a reassuring smile.

"No more than ten, I promise." She started toward the stairs, but paused at the bottom. "Tell everyone I'm sorry for being late, and first round at Bernie's tonight is on me."

Cat slipped her cell phone back into her pocket. She was jumping at ghosts. Between Dante's cryptic warning and Uncle Pete's scare tactics, she was on her last nerve. The guests wouldn't be the only ones having a few adult beverages tonight. She moved toward the kitchen to grab a soda and met Seth in the hallway.

"I thought you had a thing." He held one hand behind his back.

"You mean a session with the group? I do, we're just waiting for Jessi to get cleaned up after her run." She tried peeking around him. "What do you have behind your back?"

"If I wanted you to know, I would have shown you." He held the kitchen door open for her. "Go on, get in there. I'm heading down to the basement, and I'd appreciate it if you didn't follow me."

"Why would I want to follow you? I've got work to do." She moved toward the doorway.

He leaned in and kissed her. "Thanks for not questioning me."

As the door closed after her, she shook her head. "Everyone is stark raving mad around here."

"Maybe it's the lead pipes." Shauna came out of the pantry with an arm full of canned hominy. "They say old houses like this have bad piping. Isn't that why Lizzie Borden went all hacky?"

"Lead poisoning? I've never heard that theory. Besides, she was . . ."

"Back east, I know." Shauna sat the cans on the counter and checked her recipe. "I just can't stop making soups. Every time I think I can move on, another soup pops in my head. I'm doing pozole tonight, if that's all right."

"I don't care. Soup's fine for dinner. Especially if we have those dinner rolls you made up last week." Cat grabbed a soda out of the fridge. "I guess I better go entertain the others while we wait on Jessi."

"Cornbread. I think we'll have green chili cornbread with the soup." Shauna turned and went back into the pantry.

As Cat left the kitchen, she was beginning to wonder if Shauna's lead poisoning theory wasn't spot-on.

In the living room, there was a rousing discussion on the use of boning in petticoats. Cora was shaking her head. "Seriously, Kelly, how would someone ride with that kind of crap surrounding her? The women out here were more rugged, more basic. I think what you've read was for woman back east or maybe in European cities."

"I'm sure I've read that frontier woman wore the exact same dresses." Kelly tapped her finger on the table. "I'm willing to go ten on it."

"I'll take that action." Connie tapped the table as well.

Cora blew out a breath. "You could have waited to see if I was going to take her challenge."

"Why? I know she's wrong. It's an easy ten bucks for me. You don't need the money, you have a contract." Connie shrugged. "So how are we going to verify?"

"You could check in with our librarian. Miss Applebome knows everything about this area, especially during the Old West time frame." Cat glanced around at the group. "Were you all betting on a fashion accessory?"

"Last time it was on the estimated annual amount of snowfall Denver got in 1860." Lisa shook her head. "Welcome to our world."

"What? It keeps research interesting. Thanks for the idea about your librarian, Cat, but the challenger has to prove her point. So now Kelly's going to have to go to the library and find three sources that prove her challenge. She may not get any more writing done this week. She's kind of stubborn and won't just accept defeat." Cora patted her friend on the shoulder. "We'll drop you off at the library after lunch. No need for you to go into this with an empty stomach. You never know when you might eat again."

"Man, you guys take your research seriously." Jessi strode into the room. Her hair was still wet, but her makeup was touched up and her clothes looked brand new. "Sorry I'm late."

"We were entertaining ourselves." Cat motioned toward an empty chair. "What do you want to talk about?"

After a few minutes of brainstorming, Cat glanced

at the paper in front of her where she'd been taking notes. "Okay then, we'll start with these, and if we have time, we'll do a second brainstorming session for any additional items."

As usual, Cat started the story at the beginning. How a frustrated English professor had sent off a novel that would never get her tenure to an agent her new husband had met once. "Michael wasn't happy with my choice of proposals. He wanted something more literary, but this was what I liked to read and what I wanted to write. So I sent it in to her."

"Literary snobs. That's what we call those types when we're alone and wanting to make ourselves feel better." Cora nodded her approval at Cat's younger self's actions. "She loved it, right?"

"Surprisingly, yes. It was just what she was looking for." The agent had signed her that day, then took her outside where she could show her joy without letting anyone else know. She had a signed contract in hand before she even mentioned the sale to Michael. Even longer before she'd admitted to herself that she was a published author. By the time she had claimed the word, she was going through a divorce, and what her professor husband thought about her career wasn't any of her business.

They broke up the session just before noon so the retreat guests could get to the Diner before the rush. Which was really anytime during the summer. Cat stayed at the lobby desk long after they had left as she started thinking about Danielle and her demise. Who had wanted her dead? Did it have anything to do with Jessi? Or was it simply a lovers' quarrel gone bad? She glanced at her phone and wondered if her uncle had found anything out about Max.

The bell over the front door jingled and a tall man in a suit walked into the lobby. The man looked like he'd be better off in a polo shirt and Dockers. She realized with a start that he looked like her fifth-grade teacher, Mr. Stewart. She'd loved the guy, especially since his class schedule included an hour of reading every day. Maybe he was the reason she'd fallen in love with stories.

"Can I help you with something?" She leaned on the desk as she appraised him. The suit he wore was expensive, and the cuff links sparkled like there were real diamonds attached. So not like Mr. Stewart. He turned toward her, and Cat was surprised to see the man was probably in his fifties, a touch of gray on his temples giving his age away.

"Yes, thank you. I'm here to see Jessi Ball." His deep baritone made her smile. Now he really reminded her of her teacher.

"Sorry, Jessi just left for lunch. Anything I can do to help you?" She frowned, wishing she hadn't spoken so quickly "How did you know she was even here in the first place? Who are you?"

The man reached in his pocket, and instinctively, Cat tensed. Feeling stupid when he pulled out a small metal case, she took the business card he offered her.

"Sorry, I should have introduced myself. Darryl Taylor. I'm her money manager. I came to apologize for the mix-up earlier this week. I can't believe I put that sweet girl in danger."

"Well, you stranded her and four other women

with your action." Cat knew it was petty. The guy was here to apologize, and she was making it worse.

"I know. The police officer who called told me the implications of my actions. That's why I flew out here specifically to apologize to Miss Ball. She's been working really hard on advancing herself, and I can't believe what happened." He looked around the lobby. "This is a really nice home. The retreat must be costly. I wonder, if you could tell me, is she paying for this week?"

"Actually, the school pays for the room for the Covington student that is chosen to attend. It's quite an honor." She tucked the card into her notebook and quickly shut the cover. "Jessi seems to be making the most of it, even with the circumstances around the death of her friend."

"I heard about Danielle's death. So tragic. Do the police know why she was killed? I never met the girl, but Miss Ball always talked about her in such glowing terms. I am so terribly upset at the confusion my actions caused. I've had to be strict with Jessi as she has a habit of being quite the spendthrift, and her mother is concerned about her spending habits. If I had known the trip was halfway over by the time the driver called in the card, I never would have declined the charge."

Uncle Pete's description of his conversation came back into her mind. The words he was saying were all correct, but somehow, they had a different meaning. "I'm confused. Why exactly did you need to know who was paying for the retreat?"

He looked like he was pained at Cat's question.

"I don't really want to air Miss Ball's dirty laundry, especially to a stranger, but let's just say I'm concerned that her money might be used to support a habit that she's recently broken. Her mother would be quite upset if the girl slid back into her old ways."

# CHAPTER 8

"He said what?" Shauna poured another cup of coffee as Cat told her about the conversation. "Is he trying to imply she's a drug addict? Or maybe has a drinking problem? Or maybe the habit he was so upset about is shopping. I could see Jessi having a mad shopping habit. But the others? I haven't seen any signs, and believe me, I had my share of druggies in the bar when I was bartending. It's a little hard to hide, especially long-term use."

"I don't know. The whole conversation was weird. He was super nice, but there was just something." Cat thought about Jessi. She was a runner. She was energetic. She wore tank tops and short sleeves. "Do you think he's trying to cause trouble for her? If he gets me to think she's a drug user, I kick her out of the program. If I'm really upset, I whine to the college. She gets a bad rap there too."

"He's her money manager. From what I know

about these guys, they are like a locked vault with your information. That's the only way they can keep the trust of their clients. Why would he want her to have a bad reputation?" Shauna shook her head. "It doesn't make sense to me. Besides, this is what I don't understand about rich people. They have so many layers in between them and the actual action, you can never figure out what really is the issue. You know, I've tried to call Paul ten times in the last month to see if I could just go visit with Snow. The horse has to be lonely. I tried to get Kevin to buy a second one just to keep her company, but, well, we never got there."

"Why don't you just go out to the farm and see her?" Cat sipped her coffee.

"Yeah, right. I thought of that, but Dwayne, the guard, stares through me like he's never seen me before in his life. I went to the hospital and gave his wife a present when she had their son last year. Now I'm a stranger?" Shauna's voice had been getting louder and louder. "Of all the things I miss about Kevin, and believe me, there are a lot, losing that horse has been the worst."

The will was still in probate. Cat wondered if Shauna's ex-boyfriend-slash-fiancé had really taken the time to make sure she was protected. "Have you called your lawyer?"

Now the wind seemed to leak out of her sails. "Yeah, she says to hold on. That the will should be probated soon. Kevin left me something. I know that. I just don't understand why it would take this long."

Cat hoped that Kevin's inheritance included the

horse, or Shauna would be more upset than she was now. "Why haven't they done a reading yet?"

"Jade keeps putting it off. The boys have school or activities or are at camp." Shauna sipped her coffee. "She can't play this game forever. My lawyer's working on it. I've just got to trust the process. Remember? It's happy day. I'm going up to my room for a while. I'll see you at dinner."

Cat watched her leave the room. Seth was outside working on his secret project, and the writers were still at lunch. She was alone, and if she was going to go, this was the best time. She put her plate in the sink. Outlaw had a gift shop in town. Maybe the employees there had some gossip about Danielle's death. And if she hurried, she could stop by the gym where Jessi's now-ex-boyfriend worked and talk to him. Uncle Pete couldn't cover every angle.

She wrote a vague note on the board about walking into town. She'd stop at the bookstore and make sure Tammy was ready for her talk on Friday. At least that way, she'd have plausible deniability if anyone questioned her about snooping. It wasn't her fault people wanted to talk to her.

As Cat left the house, she thought she heard her conscience laughing at her. The bookstore stop was quick, and so she went down the block and into the Outlaw store. A lot of the items she'd seen at the ghost town were also available here, including the leather journals. Cat wondered how costly it would be to put the Warm Springs Writers' Retreat logo on them and give them out to the guests. She'd have to talk to Shauna about that since she typically dealt with the marketing and promotion part of the business.

"Aren't those lovely? You could use one for writing down recipes or even as a journal. I've kept a diary since I could write, but now I call it journaling." A young woman in the outfit Cat had wanted to wear for pictures stood next to her. Her non-time-period name tag identified her as *Your Experience Hostess—Janelle.* She picked up one of the notebooks and smoothed its leather cover. "It's luscious."

"Yes, it is. I'd be interested in a bulk sale. Do you know if you do wholesale pricing?"

The girl's eyes widened. "No, I don't, sorry. And Tad, he's the manager, he's out talking to the attorneys." She looked around the empty shop. "I don't know if you heard, a girl was murdered out at the property."

Bingo, Cat thought. Janelle liked to talk. She put on what she hoped passed as a look of shock. "No. What happened?"

"She went to work, then she disappeared. When they finally found her, she was dead upstairs in one of the bedrooms." Janelle shivered. "That saloon has always given me the creeps. I hate working shifts out there, even if the girls are paid more at the actual site. I'd rather stay here where it's safe."

"How did she die?" Cat wondered if the only gossip she was going to get was about the creepiness of the Old West town. "In one of those gunfights? I thought they were all for show?"

"Oh, no, she was strangled. The guy I know who saw them bringing her out said she was still dressed in the costume. Headdress plume and all." Janelle shook her head. "I knew Danielle. She told me last week her boyfriend was ready to propose. She was so ready to be done with this life and this town. I guess he's from Boston. A lot of the kids at Covington have family in Boston. It's kind of weird."

"Are you a townie?" When Cat was in high school, they called themselves by the moniker, like it was a club. Or more likely, a gang. She could tell by the smile on Janelle's face that she'd also grown up in Aspen Hills.

"For sure. I thought I recognized you. You're that author that runs the writers' thing." She twirled her hair. "I really like your witchcraft books, even if they are for younger kids."

"Thank you. I enjoy writing them." Cat wondered what *younger* meant to this girl who was probably all of seventeen or eighteen. She tried to steer the conversation back to Danielle. "So she was about to be engaged? That's so sad. Did you know the guy?"

"No, I never met him." Janelle frowned, clearly thinking about the times she'd been with Danielle. "And I never saw anyone with her. She seemed to always be with Jessi Ball. She works for Outlaw too. But a lot of the girls are dating someone from out of town. It makes classes easier to prioritize if you don't have a guy hanging around all the time. Especially since the management frowns on us dating other employees."

"Oh, there's a rule?"

Janelle shrugged. "Not exactly a rule, more like a suggestion. They just don't want us running off into the empty houses and getting friendly, if you know what I mean. Although I would think that would add to the realism of the experience for the tourists."

Janelle didn't have any more information on what happened to Danielle, but Cat felt like the trip hadn't been completely wasted. Danielle had thought Max was going to propose. Jessi thought she and Max were just on a break due to his high stress load. It was time to find out what exactly Max *had* thought about the two girls. Cat bought a notebook to show Shauna and started to leave the shop.

"Oh, there was one weird thing."

Cat paused at the counter. "What?"

"Danielle was complaining about someone taking her clothes. I guess she had borrowed something from her roommate and put it in her work locker, but it was gone when her shift was over. No, it wasn't clothes, what was it?" Janelle tapped a finger over her lips as she thought. "Oh, it was earrings. I guess she borrowed some really expensive hoops, and of course, we can't wear them in costume, so she put them in her locker. And poof, they disappeared."

Cat thought she knew the answer but had to ask anyway. "Do you know who she borrowed the earrings from?"

"Jessi Ball. That's Danielle's roommate." The bell over the door rang and Janelle looked that way. "Sorry, real tourists. I've got a role to play. I'll be sure to stop by next time you have a book signing."

Cat moved her way through the Old West replicas and thought about the role Danielle was play-

ing. Could it have been as simple as someone tak-
ing the fantasy too far? Or was the answer in this
Max and his two-timing ways? She'd have to ask
Jessi about the earrings too.

She tucked the bag with the journal into her
tote and crossed the street to head toward the
gym. If Jessi was right about his summer schedule,
Max should be in the weight room, pumping iron.
She hadn't seen a need to join the Aspen Hills Fit-
ness Club since she still had privileges at Covington College, which meant she could swim or use
any of the equipment for free. And by the end of
summer, Seth promised to have a small gym set up
in the basement of the house. Right now, it had a
treadmill and a bike, but as soon as this retreat session was over, Seth was starting the remodel.

Cindy, one of her students from her time at Covington, sat at the front desk. "Hey, Mrs. L. What
are you doing here?"

"I need to talk to someone. Is Max Trandor
here?" She glanced around the rows of equipment. A few treadmills were in use by several men
and women, none of whom looked young enough
to be Max.

"Wow, he's popular today. Yeah, he's in the weight
room." Cindy stood and pointed around the corner.
"Just go left at the water fountain and past the—"

She didn't get a chance to finish her directions
when they heard raised voices coming from the
area. Cat shook her head. From the heated words
she heard, the fight could only be between two
people, Max and Jessi. She hurried in the direction of the noise with Cindy at her side.

"Crap, and my boss just stepped out. Do you

think I should call the police? I've never dealt with a fight before. Well, except that time Mrs. Rice pushed that girl off her treadmill because she wanted to use it. Seriously, there were fifty others, but you know Mrs. Rice. She's a creature of habit."

Cat had a few other descriptors for the woman, but she didn't have the time to gossip about her. "Hold off calling. Maybe I can defuse the situation."

As they walked into the room, Max and Jessi stood in the middle. Three men were standing by the mirror, free weights in their hands, watching the ruckus. On the other side of the room stood Cora, Connie, and Lisa. Cora shrugged when Cat caught her gaze. Before she could ask what the heck was going on, Jessi went off again.

"How could you sleep with her? Behind my back," Jessi screamed at the red-faced man who must have been Max.

"Look, she came on to me. I didn't go shopping. Besides, you were too busy with playing dress-up for your stupid job. Do you think I can just wait for when you have time? A man has needs." He reached out to her. "Besides, baby, it didn't mean anything. She was just someone to pass the time with. You know we're soul mates."

"We aren't soul mates if you can just stick yourself into any woman who lets you. How could I ever trust you again? What would happen if you felt left out because I went on a work trip or went to visit family?" Jessi's eyes swam with tears. "No, Max, we're done. I just wanted to know why you'd betray me in such a manner. And I'm keeping the ring."

She swung around to leave and stopped abruptly

when she saw Cat. Now the tears were starting to fall. She turned her anger on Cindy. "Look, I said what I needed to say, and I'm leaving. You didn't have to call my babysitter."

"I'm not your babysitter, and Cindy didn't call me. I was here to ask Max a few questions, but it looks like a bad time. Why don't we all go back to the house and calm down." Cat put her arm around Jessi and started to lead her out of the room. She glanced over her shoulder and caught Cora's gaze. "Let's go."

Sometimes she *felt* like a babysitter. What had Jessi been thinking? If Max had been angry enough and killed Danielle in a fit of passion, did she think he was just going to sit there when she told him they were through? Man, she wanted a drink. Or chocolate. Or maybe both. She realized they were next to Bernie's. Midafternoon, the place was dead. She decided to have a spur-of-the-moment come to Jesus meeting. And maybe she could talk some sense into the justice brigade.

"Who wants a beer?" Cat nodded to the bar. "I'll buy first round."

Connie eyed her suspiciously. "In the middle of the day? Maybe we should just go back to the house and write."

"I *want* a drink." Jessi swiped at her cheeks with her hands. "No way I'm wasting good tears on *that* guy anymore."

"I'll drink to that." Cora took Jessi's arm and shot a look at Connie. "You don't have to come if you don't want to. Kelly's back at the house writing."

"I'm game. I haven't had a drink during the day

since college. Of course, we were way too young anyway, so we didn't make the best decisions, but it was fun." Lisa put her hand on Connie's back. "Come on, loosen up a little. Who was it that said write drunk, edit sober?"

"Hemingway," Cat answered. "We don't have to stay long, but I really want to talk to you all about your little adventures."

"Uh-oh, we're in trouble." Lisa grinned, then the smile faded as she took in Cat's expression. "Seriously? We're in trouble?"

"You're not in trouble. I just want to have a conversation about this whole thing." Cat opened the door and waved them inside the gloomy interior. The smell of stale beer and cigarette smoke engulfed them as soon as they stepped into the small building. Even though legally, smoking anything in a bar or restaurant had been banned for years, she guessed the old-timers didn't quite worry about technicalities, as she saw ashtrays stacked up on the bar edge.

Bernie was sipping on something in a coffee cup and raised his eyebrows in surprise as they walked in. "Well, I'll be. This is a surprise. Cat Latimer in my bar with a group of lovely women in tow to boot. Jessi, I know your poison, but what can I get for the rest of you?"

Jessi shrugged as the group turned toward her. "What? It's a small town and this is the best bar around."

The women called out their orders and Cat gathered them around one of the larger round tables in the back. She gave Bernie her credit card and told him to keep the tab open. This conversa-

tion might take a while. Cat waited for the drinks
to arrive. Finally, after Bernie had dropped off the
last beer, Cora sighed.

"Go ahead. I know you've got something you
want to say. I can feel the judgment coming off you
in waves." Cora sipped from her bottle.

"I'm not here to judge. But I do feel responsible
for you while you're part of the retreat." Cat paused,
picking at the beer label. "It's not as safe here as it
appears. Aspen Hills has some secrets that if you
run into them, you could get hurt."

"Like freak snowstorms or floods? It's June, what
could happen?" Connie laughed and held up her
bottle. "We promise to stay out of the sun, Mom."

She told the group about the uniqueness of the
student population at Covington. Cora leaned
back and whistled. "So Danielle? That's why she
was killed?"

"No." Jessi shot out the word. "Or, I guess, I
don't know. Danielle was a scholarship kid. The
college likes to admit normal kids to the campus
too. My mom went here, so she wanted me to attend. She said it was the safest campus in the
States. I guess she was wrong."

"Knowing this about Aspen Hills only makes
your little town more interesting." Cora glanced
around the table thoughtfully. "I don't believe that
the sins of the father should affect the children."

"My parents were closet drinkers." Lisa shrugged.
"We all have crosses to bear."

"Cat's right, though. We should leave the investigation to the professionals. Especially here. I
can't believe I've dragged you into this twice al-

ready." Jessi looked at each one of the women in turn, and when she was done, tears filled her eyes. "You should hate me."

"We could never hate you, Jessi. Each one of us made our own choice to go back to Outlaw and to support you while you told off your creep of a boyfriend. You are so much better off without that guy, by the way." Connie sipped her beer. "Unfortunately for you, you've been adopted into our little writing world. So don't think you're going to get away with not staying in touch after the retreat. We will hunt you down."

Jessi leaned back in her chair. "This was not the reaction I expected."

"Me neither, but there's one thing you all aren't taking into account." Cat paused as she made sure she had everyone's attention. "Danielle's killer is still out there. So you shouldn't go off playing detective and stirring up trouble."

"Way to put a buzzkill on the party," Cora said. Everyone turned toward her and then laughed at her pouty face. "We'll stop the face-to-face accusations. But this is an interesting situation. Can we talk about who could have killed Danielle? This is just like living through one of those old *Hart to Hart* shows."

"Who?" Confusion filled Jessi's face.

Cora shook her head. "Never mind, child. I keep forgetting you are at least twenty years younger than the rest of us."

"Speak for yourself," Lisa said. "I'm thinking I'm more like Jessi's older sister."

"Whatever." Connie jumped into the teasing.

And with that, Cat realized that Jessi had been adopted by the group. They wouldn't let her history change how they felt about her. She'd been admitted into their club. Cat took out a notebook and started writing down the ideas that the retreat guests were bringing to the table.

# CHAPTER 9

"**Y**ou did what?" Uncle Pete sat at the kitchen table glaring at Cat. He'd been in the same spot when Cat and the retreat guests had returned from their outing around three. During the walk back, they'd helped Connie brainstorm her new book. They'd had two rounds of drinks and had listed off all the possible reasons they could think of that would have gotten Danielle killed. Of course, some of them were less than practical. But Cat thought her uncle might want to at least look at the list before he started to lecture her.

"We brainstormed reasons for Danielle to have been killed. What's wrong with that?"

He held out a beefy hand. "Do you want me to list just the top ten? First of all, you were in Bernie's, and we know he's connected. You're lucky he didn't pick up the phone and call in one of the family members to handle you. They don't like people 'brainstorming' the reasons behind a kill."

"You really think the family is responsible for Danielle's death? Isn't strangulation a little too personal for a hit murder?" She didn't blink as she stared at him.

Uncle Pete, on the other hand, squirmed in his chair. Apparently, she did have him on the ropes, if just for a little bit. "Anyone could have come into the bar and overheard you. Like the killer, for example."

"No one came into the bar. So that's off the list." She grabbed a loaf of bread and the jar of peanut butter and brought them back to the table. "I'm starving."

"You're drunk." His tone was flat like his eyes as he watched her.

Cat shrugged. "Tipsy, not drunk. Besides, last I looked at my driver's license, I'm legal to drink nowadays."

"Not the brightest thing to do when you have a retreat group in and there's a killer on the loose." Uncle Pete's eyes bored into her.

"You have Seth watching out for me. It was daytime." Cat spread a thick layer of peanut butter on the bread slice, folded it in half, and took a huge bite. "Peanut butter is a gift from the gods."

"I could always tell when you'd been out drinking as a kid. The kitchen would be ransacked and all the bread would be gone." Uncle Pete smiled. "Hand it over, I want one too."

She did as she was instructed, and for a minute, neither one of them spoke, enjoying the shared moment. Then she stood and poured herself a cup of coffee. "Humor me and look at the list. I'd hate to know we nailed the suspect with our little brain-storming session but he got away because you were afraid that he might try something bigger than what we imagined."

He glanced down at the list Cat handed him. "I'll check some of these out. Can I assume your group is done investigating?"

She thought about the scene at the gym. "God, I hope so."

Uncle Pete burst out laughing. After a few minutes, he wiped the tears from his eyes and shook his head. "Now you know how I feel every time you go off on a hunt for a killer."

She pointed her butter knife at him. "Just to be fair, I typically try to figure out what's going on, I don't go looking for killers. They just seem to find me. That's not my fault."

"If you didn't go around asking questions—" His phone buzzed and he pulled it out of its holder. "Never mind, I'll save the lecture for another day. Chief Edmond here."

She put away the bread and peanut butter and pulled out Shauna's calendar for next month's retreat. The booking was full. Cat wasn't sure how long she'd be able to keep a full house of writers each month, but for now, the side business was doing well. And the money had almost paid for all the house renovations. Life was good. Well, except the fact Danielle had been killed. She wondered what theories her uncle was already exploring in the case. She glanced up as he put his phone away. "You have to go?"

"Yes. There's been another incident at the

school. I'm beginning to think this doesn't have anything to do with the fraternities. We might have a real problem on our hands." He tucked the paper into his pocket. "Do me a favor and keep the group in control, at least for the next day or so. I'd hate to lose someone just because they went snooping up the wrong tree."

"Sounds like a plan." Cat was beginning to sober up but thought maybe she should just go up to her room and watch one of her shows she had recorded.

He slipped his hat on. "Tell Shauna and Seth hello. It's weird not seeing them here in the kitchen. Did they leave for something?"

"Actually, Seth's out working in the back." Cat glanced at the empty whiteboard. "Shauna must be up in her room. She didn't check out on the board."

"I'm glad you're finally doing something with that old pasture. I'm sure if you clean it up some, you'd be able to sell the lot to a builder. People are always looking for land in this area." Uncle Pete paused at the door.

"Seth's doing something. I don't know what. Besides, I'm not really anxious about selling. I'd rather keep a hold of it just in case there's a rainy day later on." After Uncle Pete left, Cat stared out the window onto the backyard. The back lot was shaded from view by a row of trees that lined the official backyard of the house. Michael had said the extra lot they owned behind the house had originally been for the household animals, and there was a barn on the edge of the property. The place was interesting with lots of history, which was one of the reasons she'd campaigned to purchase the house, although it had needed a lot of work then and even more now. "What are you doing out there, Seth Howard?"

As if she'd conjured him by calling his name, he appeared at the end of the tree line. She watched as he came toward her, and about halfway across the yard, he looked right into her eyes. The smile on his face widened. He'd definitely seen her inside the window, watching him.

He came in the back door and paused at the sink to wash his hands. "What are you doing today?"

"Trying to keep the guests from playing detective." She held up the coffeepot. "Want some?"

"Actually, I'm going to have some iced tea. It's a little warm out there today." He grabbed a glass out of the cabinet and paused. "Can I pour you a glass?"

"Sure." She put her empty coffee cup in the sink and sat down at the table. "What exactly *are* you doing out in the extra lot?"

Seth set the tea in front of her and then sat next to her. "I've told you, it's a secret."

"I'm not sure I can deal with more secrets. It's been a little crazy around here since I moved back." Cat leaned her head on her arm and watched him.

He glanced around the empty room. "You can't tell Shauna, but . . ."

The door to the kitchen banged and Shauna strolled in, carrying a basket of towels to fold. "What can't she tell me?"

Seth straightened and looked at his watch.

"Crap, I told Bernie I'd come by today and give him an estimate on building a patio behind the bar. I've got to run."

Cat and Shauna watched as he bolted out of the house and jumped into his pickup parked by the house. Shauna dumped the clean towels on the table and started folding. "So that was weird. What's up with your boyfriend?"

"I have no idea." Cat helped Shauna with the laundry, then excused herself to go upstairs to her office. Maybe she could find some information on this Max guy who had been cheating on Jessi with Danielle. She still needed to talk to him, but today, she was heeding her own advice and staying out of the investigation. *At least, the in-person interviewing part,* she amended the statement as she powered up her computer.

Two hours later, she stood and stretched. Max Trandor was as straight as a rod, at least in his on-line persona. No weird Facebook posts. No over-the-top antics at Covington. Basically, the kid had been an average student in a few clubs. Not the type to get into Harvard on his works, but maybe for the special Covington kids, there was a secret handshake. Her stomach growled. Time to put this away and go eat.

When she got downstairs, Jessi was pulling on her jacket. "Dinner plans?" Cat asked.

"Actually, no. Cora mentioned seeing a pair of earrings like the ones I lost last week in the pawn-shop down on Main. They went shopping after we left Bernie's, but I didn't feel like it, so I came back here to try to write." Jessi flipped her hair out of her jacket. "I'm so wired on all of this stuff, I'm not sure I'll be able to write again. So anyway, I'm heading there and then meeting the gang at Reno's. If Danielle pawned my earrings, I'm going to kill her."

The words hit her as soon as she said them, and Jessi sank into the bench by the door.

"It's okay, it's natural not to remember you've lost someone." Cat thought of the conversations she'd had with Linda Cook after Linda lost her husband. Sometimes, she'd get so caught up in a story, she'd forget that Tom wasn't coming home. Not this time. "It takes time."

"I was so mad at her right then." Jessi wiped away tears. "Mad because of some stupid earrings, but my grandmother gave me those hoops. I've lost a lot of items over the years, but I was kicking myself for losing those."

"I'll go with you." Cat patted Jessi's shoulder. She thought the odds were pretty high that they would probably find Jessi's missing earrings up for sale at the shop. And if that was true, she might need Uncle Pete's help to get them back. "I need the walk anyway."

As they walked the few blocks into town, Jessi seemed lost in her thoughts. She needed to grieve the loss of her friend, but finding out about Danielle's secret life kept getting in the way.

"Do you know if they're going to have a memorial service for Danielle?"

"I haven't heard. I haven't even called her folks. What kind of friend am I? I should have called her folks." Jessi took a deep breath. "My emotions are all over the place. Mom thinks I'm still grieving losing my father, but I don't really think it's that.

He wasn't around much, and when he was, well, things were difficult."

"I'll stay with you when you get back if you want company while you call Danielle's parents." They turned on to the sidewalk for Main Street. The town looked like typical small-town America, except the streets were almost empty. Most of the townsfolk had finished their shopping chores and returned home to cook dinner. Reno's Pizza was across the street from where they currently stood as they waited for a car to pass before crossing the street.

Jessi strolled into the crosswalk and then back on the sidewalk, not even pausing at the restaurant where her friends sat near the front waiting for her. Through the large window, Cat could see Connie reviewing the menu, and Cora was animatedly chatting about something to Lisa. Kelly stared out the window, but she didn't even see Jessi and Cat as they passed by. *Typical writer,* Cat thought, *lost in her head while the world is spinning around her.*

"No, I can do it myself. I'm just beating myself up for not thinking about it earlier. Danielle and I were tight, even if she made some bad decisions." Jessi paused in front of the door to Randy's Pawnshop. The neon sign read *Cash for Anything of Value.* "Hopefully, stealing from me wasn't one of her bad decisions."

Cat followed Jessi into the room and was overwhelmed by the selection of items for sale. Guns, rifles, drums, flutes, guitars, and, as she followed Jessi farther into the store, jewelry. The store smelled of old leather, and as she passed by a hand-tooled leather saddle, she reached up to stroke the fine surface. Maybe she could find Shauna a place that rented horses to ride. She'd need a saddle, and this one looked perfect. She was still lost in the planning of the gift when she heard Jessi's muffled cry.

Looking up, she'd expected to see Jessi being carried off in some big thug's arms, but instead, she found her staring at a glass counter. "What is it?"

"My earrings. And the necklace I thought I'd lost at the park. And that's my bracelet. I thought it was in my jewelry box." Joy filled the girl's face as she pointed out more items that belonged to her. "I thought these were gone forever."

"The question is, how did they get here?" She dialed her uncle's number. "Hey, I'm at Randy's Pawnshop. Can you come down? We have a problem."

The clerk on duty frowned as he overheard her conversation. When Cat put the phone away, he stepped closer to the counter. "May I help you with something?"

"Who sold you these pieces?" Cat pointed out several items that Jessi had already identified.

"I'm not at liberty to release that information. We take our clientele's privacy concerns very seriously here at Randy's." He narrowed his eyes and repeated, "Is there a problem?"

"Yes, there is. Basically, these are all stolen items." Cat held up her phone. "I've already called Chief Edmonds, and he'll be here in a few minutes to help sort this out."

"I assure you, if the items in question had been stolen, they would have been on our listing, or once they came into our possession, we would have re-

ported as soon as the stolen property report came
from the police department. We got no such reports on these items. I handle that process myself."
He opened the cabinet with a key. "Which items
are supposedly yours?"

Jessi pointed out a total of twelve pieces. Then she
grinned at Cat. "My mom's going to be so happy we
found these. I'm glad you came with me."

"There's a protocol for returning property to its
rightful owner." The man straightened one of the
ring boxes. "You have to prove the items are
yours."

"No probs. I'll have my lawyer fax over the insurance description sheets." Jessi ran a hand over
the blue and silver bracelet closest to her. "This
has totally made my day."

When Uncle Pete came into the store, he had
the clerk bag up the items and write out a receipt.
"Jessi, you go back to the dorm room and make
sure there's not anything else missing. If there is,
have the insurance company send me the pictures
of that as well. We might still be able to trace the
sales of anything that's not here."

"Who sold this to you?" Cat pinned the clerk
with a look. "Do you have records?"

"Of course we have records, but we will be re-
leasing that information to the proper authorities,
not some woman off the street." The guy tried to
pull off a proper butler sniff, but it didn't come
across as haughty as he'd expected.

"George, just go get the receipts. My niece may
not be law enforcement, but she's smart enough to
know you have some information we need to solve

this little situation." Uncle Pete stared down the guy and finally, George twitched.

"Fine, but Arnold's going to be upset about this whole thing. We're following all the rules. It's not our fault that she never reported the items stolen." He turned on his heel and stomped back through the opening that must hold the office.

"Who's Arnold?" Cat leaned against the counter and glanced at the selection of saddles. They might not want to sell to her after she caused this upheaval. But then again, a sale was a sale.

"He's the owner." Uncle Pete took all the smaller bags filled with jewelry and put them in a large plastic bag.

"Wait, I thought it was owned by some guy named Randy." She glanced up at the banner over the counter announcing Randy's twenty-fifth-year celebration and sale next month.

"It was. Years ago. Arnold bought it in the early nineties, I think. It was right after Randy died."

"From an illness?" Cat had never heard this story before. But then again, she'd never been in the pawnshop before today.

Uncle Pete shrugged. "I think it was cancer. I don't really know."

"It's nice that the new owner kept the name of the place." Cat glanced over at Jessi, who was sitting on a bench, talking to her mother on the phone. "She's hurting. And every time we learn something new about the girl she thought she was her friend, she gets another cut."

"It's a sad fact that secrets tend to come out when we're investigating a murder. This might have nothing to do with who killed Danielle, but I'm glad we could get at least some of the jewelry back to her. The girl seems sweet." Uncle Pete stopped talking when George came back into the room. "You got the records?"

"Mostly. I guess Arnold didn't ask for a driver's license for the seller. Which is normal if he knows the guy. Maybe I should call him." George glanced at the phone on the counter like it was a life preserver in the middle of the ocean.

"Let's just look and see what you do have. Then you can call Arnold and let him know I'll be over at his house in a few minutes."

George sighed. "You're not going to like this."

When he turned the card toward Uncle Pete, Cat read the name. Ernest Hemingway.

"Well, at least our thief is well read." Cat glanced at the signature. "But it looks like he almost signed his real name. Does this look like a 'K' to you?"

"It's definitely not an 'E.' " He slipped the cards into a different evidence bag. "Anything else I should know, George?"

The clerk blanched but was able to spit out a shaky "No sir."

Uncle Pete turned to Cat. "Would you go with Jessi to check out her jewelry? I hate to blame a dead girl, but it looks like she might have gotten the items out of the room and into this joker's hands." He turned back to the clerk. "I suppose it's too much to hope that you have video covering the last time he sold something to you."

George brightened. "Probably. Looks like the guy came in last week. We keep tapes two weeks before recycling. Do you want me to check?"

"Please." He leaned on the counter. "Go with Jessi and I'll wait for this. Keep your phone on you so if I get a decent still, I can send it to see if Jessi can identify the guy. I'll probably be able to get a match from the college database. It's usually about the college."

There was an air of tiredness in his voice, and Cat glanced over before she went to gather Jessi off her phone call. "Are you all right?"

"I'm fine. It's been a busy week since I got back from Alaska. I haven't even had time to unpack my suitcase yet." He made shooing signs with his hands. "Get on out of here. I think you scare George more than I do."

"He should be scared." Cat gave her uncle a quick peck on the cheek. "You make sure you come over for dinner soon. You need some downtime."

"As soon as I get this murder and the college peeper behind me, I'll be over." He chuckled. "Okay, that's a lie, I'll probably be over sooner than that. I don't have anything in the fridge since I haven't stopped at the grocery store yet either."

"Whenever. You know Shauna will be happy to see you." *And*, Cat thought, *maybe it might pull her out of her funk.* She filed away the idea of buying the saddle and headed to the bench.

Jessi looked up at Cat and nodded. "Hey, Mom, I've got to go. I'll call you on Sunday. Just make sure the insurance company sends pictures of the jewelry to the Aspen Hills police station." She rolled her eyes. "I know, Mom. I should be more careful. Look, I really have to jet now."

Cat watched as Jessi ended the call, cutting off a

barrage of parental advice midstream. "Your mother must be happy that the items were found."

"You would think so." Jessi rubbed a hand over her face. "I think she was more content when I looked like a total loser for misplacing them."

"I don't think that's true. You mother must love you." Cat held the door open for the young woman and they stepped back out into the bright sunshine.

"That's what she keeps saying." Jessi hunched her shoulders and walked next to Cat, not speaking for a while. Finally, as they got closer to the college, she turned toward Cat. "So did your mom hate you for a while? I mean once you came of age, did the relationship turn a little bad?"

Cat thought about her relationship with her mom when she went off to college. They'd started to become friends instead of just mother and daughter. If anything, having Cat out of the house had strengthened their bond. "No, we got along fine."

"Okay, so let's change the subject before I get all depressed about family." Jessi side-eyed Cat. "You're doing that Seth guy, right?"

"Seth and I are dating." Cat smiled at the inference.

"Come on, you can tell me. I need to know someone has a good relationship. It will help me get over this hump." When Cat just shook her head, Jessi opened the door to the dorm room. "Fine, be all secretive. But you know that I know. Let's get this done. It feels really creepy in here knowing that Danielle isn't ever coming back."

"Are you going to ask for a new roommate?"

Jessi shook her head. "I don't think so. I'm actually going to look for a place off campus. I can afford my own place, and that way, I can get a dog. My dog, Whiskey, died last year. Mom was taking care of him for me. The only reason I stayed in the dorm room was it was cheaper for Danielle."

While they'd been talking, Jessi had pulled out her two jewelry boxes and was going through each item. "I'm missing my diamond earrings too. I'm sure I'm missing a few more items, but it was costume and not worth anything."

Cat made a note to have Uncle Pete ask the pawnbroker if he'd ever turned down an item. As she watched, Jessi got down on the floor and slid under the bed. "Son of a . . ."

"What?" Cat bent down to see if Jessi was stuck or something.

She slid back out, a small safe in her hands. She flipped it open and looked inside. It was empty. "I can't believe she took my money. I mean, I never told anyone I had this stashed."

"You had what stashed?" Cat wasn't sure she really wanted to know the answer.

"My father taught me as a young girl to always have getaway money. He gave me five thousand dollars in cash when I left for college. He didn't trust banks." She closed the empty safe. "Why would Danielle steal from me?"

Cat wondered if the better question was who Danielle had told about the money and if that was why they killed her.

# CHAPTER 10

When they got back to the house, the group was waiting for them in the lobby. Cora took one look at Jessi and put her arm around her, sensing her pain. "I'm so glad you got back in time. We're going to eat bowls of pasta and drink wine."

Kelly held up a hand. "Even me. I just finished a first draft, so before I start a new book tomorrow, I'm celebrating."

"You're starting a new book tomorrow?" Cat winced. Even with her hectic schedule she tried to take at least a few weeks in between books.

"What can I say? I have deadlines." Kelly grinned. "But tonight, I'm not worrying about anything."

"She's a machine." Connie glanced around the group. "I wrote two thousand words today. I'm happy with that."

"You should be happy with that." Cora smiled. "We all should be celebrating for getting words on the page."

Jessi took a deep breath. "I got seven hundred fifty this morning. I would have gotten more . . ."

"The day's not over yet." Connie pointed to the clock. "We'll go eat and then I'll get into my writing pajamas and write until I fall asleep in bed. I do this at least a few times a week. I'm more creative at night."

As the group made their way out the door to the restaurant, Cat watched them leave the house. She loved this part of the retreat, when they celebrated each other's joys and accomplishments. Typically, it happened as they were reviewing the week, but this group had bonded quickly.

She went into the kitchen and found Shauna standing at the stove. Cat sank into a chair. "I'm beat."

"Hey, I was wondering where you were." Shauna turned off the oven and set the salad on the table.

"I took Jessi to the pawnshop, where we found most of her jewelry." Cat held up a hand when Shauna started to ask a question. "Let me grab a beer and I'll tell you everything. Can I help with dinner?"

"Nope, we're all ready. I decided to put the soup away for another day so it's chicken enchiladas and salad. That way, if Pete doesn't have time to eat with us, he can at least take food back to the station." She pointed to the table where her phone sat. "Oh, your uncle called about five minutes ago. He said he couldn't reach you."

Cat pulled out her phone to check for a missed call. It was dead. "I must not have charged it last night."

"My spare plug is in the top drawer." Shauna

pointed to her kitchen desk, where she did her meal planning and retreat work.

While Cat got her phone charging, Shauna grabbed two bottles of beer. She set them on the table and sank into a chair. "What a crazy day."

"You're telling me." Cat sat and took a long sip of her beer. Then she caught Shauna up. Halfway into the story, Uncle Pete and Seth came into the kitchen and she had to start over. Finally, she told them about the missing money.

Seth whistled. "Man, that's a lot of mad money."

"I tell the families time and time again not to send cash with their kids. But they never listen. I had one kid lose twenty thousand dollars last semester when his date from another school found the money and ran. We got most of it back, but she had some fun at the mall before we tracked her down." Uncle Pete passed plates around the table.

"Who is stupid enough to steal from these kids?" Seth shook his head. "I'd be worried about the consequences."

"Kids don't think of those things. They just think the kid was stupid to have so much cash." Uncle Pete took the baking pan from Shauna. "Let me rephrase that. Kids don't think."

"Hey now, I used to be one of those kids." The spicy, cheesy smell made Cat's mouth water. Even with all the sadness that had surrounded them this week, she loved having her family together to eat a meal. It felt comforting and real, and this was where she got her real energy.

"Are you putting yourself up as an example?" Her uncle grinned at her. "Because I have a few stories maybe even Seth hasn't heard . . ."

"Stop, I beg you." Cat held her hands in front of her. "So how was your day, Seth?"

Seth layered some of the enchiladas on his plate, then passed the food on to Cat. "I don't know, maybe I need to hear what Pete has to say. I thought I knew all your stories."

"I don't want to talk about it." Laughing, Cat filled her plate and took a bite before she continued. "Let's let the past stay in the past."

"Now I'm even curious." Shauna laughed when Cat threw her a look to kill. "But I'll let it go. For now."

"So what are you working on, Seth?" Uncle Pete didn't look up from his plate as he asked.

"Not going to happen. It's a surprise, and everyone can just wait until it's done. Besides, you'll all know on Saturday."

"Seriously? What's happening on Saturday?" Cat paused her fork midway to her mouth.

Seth shrugged. "You'll see. Can you have the group meet up in the lobby around ten? I'd like all of you to see it."

"I guess. We didn't have anything scheduled except the dinner. You are going to be able to be our designated driver, right?" Cat ladled another enchilada onto her plate.

"I know you love your margaritas. Yes, I'm set as your driver." He shoved the rest of the food into his mouth, wrapped up two brownies, and stood, taking his plate to the sink where he washed it off and set in in the dishwasher. "Sorry, I've got a game on tonight. I'll be in my room if you need me, but don't, okay?"

They watched him leave the room.

Uncle Pete cleared his throat. "So do you know what this surprise is yet? You typically knew all your Christmas presents before the first of December."

"Not a clue. Every time I even think about heading out there, he's there to stop me." Cat took a sip of her water, considering the last few days. "It's like he has a tracker on me. Of course, I've been unusually busy with this retreat group."

"You can say that again." Shauna put her plate in the sink and poured hot water for a cup of tea. "If I look out the window, he's either coming or going back to the project. I'm betting on a gym. He wasn't too happy with the way the basement was turning out."

"Well, whatever it is, he's kept the secret pretty close to his chest. And that's not easy in this small a town. Seth's always been an upstanding and loyal young man. If he says you'll love it, you will." Uncle Pete stood and took his empty plate to the sink and mimicked Seth's movements of a few minutes before. "Well, I've got work to do anyway. Crimes don't solve themselves, you know."

After her uncle left, Cat helped Shauna clean the kitchen. "I can't wait until Saturday. The suspense is killing me."

"I've been meaning to ask you a question. How serious were you and Seth when you broke up? Sounds like your uncle was betting on Seth."

Unsure of how to answer, Cat finished wiping down the table and then excused herself and went into Michael's study. She'd put all her memorabilia in this room. Her scrapbooks and the yearbooks from her high school years. From *their* high school years. Every candid picture of her had Seth nearby. They had been a couple since he brought her a rose on Valentine's Day from the booster club freshman year, but even before that, they'd been friends.

"I really messed this up, didn't I?" She ran her hand over the picture of the two of them at senior prom. She'd loved that dress. But when her mom tried to give it to her when they'd sold the house, she'd told her to donate it. Old memories were better left in the past.

She'd been wrong. Wrong about the dress. Wrong about the memories. Wrong to assume one fight would end their relationship.

Danielle had been in love too. With the wrong guy, obviously, but still in love. Maybe that was the reason she'd been stealing from Jessi. Take her man, her jewelry, her life. Danielle had wanted to be a carbon copy of Jessi Ball, no matter what the cost.

She took out a notebook and started playing with theories. At least when she was looking into who killed Danielle, she wasn't thinking about the way she'd messed up her first love. Having a second chance meant she couldn't make that same mistake again. And she wouldn't. Not this time. Now she just needed to convince Seth of that fact. Feeling like she was going nowhere except down memory lane, she set aside the notebook.

Instead, Cat opened her laptop and typed in *Outlaw, Colorado* and *unsolved murders.* She got a listing of several sites but as she scrolled through she found there had been four murders of young women before Danielle. Each ten years apart. Mrs. Rice had been a little off on her dates. Each strangled in one of the rooms above the saloon. Were they all unsolved? She reopened her notebook and started making notes.

By the time she was done she had a list of similarities and differences. Then she highlighted the ones that matched what she knew of Danielle's death.

There were at least fifteen points that matched. She needed to talk to her uncle. Even if it wasn't the same killer, someone was trying to make it look like it was. Danielle might have just been in the wrong place at the wrong time.

Curious, she dug more into the history of Outlaw. Jessi had said a corporation owned all of the town. Could she find out who the man behind the curtain was? It didn't take long to find that Joseph John Robertson was the man behind the big ideas. He had a lot of things going on in Colorado. Outlaw was only one of his many projects. He'd built high-end shopping malls on the outskirts of some of the largest ski resorts ever. Outlaw was only one of the "ghost towns" where he'd bought the entire town and turned it into a tourist draw. But Outlaw had been his first.

She did a web search on Joseph John and found he was teaching a summer class at Covington's business school. She opened another tab and found out that his class ended at nine. She had fifteen minutes to get to the school and see if she could corner the guy after class. She wasn't sure what he'd have to tell her, but maybe he had more information on the early murders.

Cat laced up her tennis shoes and headed downstairs. No one was in the kitchen, but Cora sat in the living room alone, reading. Cat leaned inside the doorway. "Hey, I've got to run an errand. You doing okay?"

Cora grinned. "Happy as a clam. I can't remember the last time I curled up with a book on a Wednesday night. Typically, I'm writing my daily words at this time since I still have the dreaded day job."

"Well, enjoy. I'll try not to bother you when I come back in." Cat didn't wait for a response as Cora had already returned her attention to the book.

The June night air held a touch of a chill, so Cat zipped the jacket she'd grabbed out of the coat closet. Summers were short here, and from what the weather guys said, the winter was going to be icy and cold. She hoped this time the weatherman had it wrong, but she wasn't counting on it. She power-walked past Mrs. Rice's house and only paused a second as she crossed over the street where Dante lived. The house was dark with only a few lights on in one corner of the house and security lights around the driveway. The owner apparently was still involved in meetings in Boston. She needed to talk to him about Jessi and the missing money, but she would wait until he got back into town.

As she opened the door to the business building, students poured out of the large first-floor lecture hall. Apparently, Joseph John couldn't be bothered with a normal-size classroom. Cat had been assigned a classroom on the third floor when she had started teaching, and that was a full-time professor position. She guessed money talked in more ways than one on campus.

She slipped inside and the man was talking to a pretty blonde. He sat on the side of the stage and swung his leg as she chatted about some issue she was having in class. Before he could gather his papers and leave, Cat hurried down the stairs and blocked his exit.

"Thanks for the direction, Professor. I'm sure I'll be able to finish the assignment now," the woman gushed as she turned to leave. Narrowing her eyes, she glared at Cat as she made her way down the aisle between the now empty seats.

Joseph John smiled, and Cat realized the guy could sell ice water to people in a snowstorm. Then he turned his gaze on Cat, and she felt the full force of his gaze. "What can I do for you? I know you're not in my class. I would have noticed you by now."

"Guilty as charged." Cat sat next to him on the stage. "Actually, I'm interested in the history of Outlaw. I'm a writer and the place just sounds so fascinating. What do you know about the murders?"

A look of shock covered his face and he raised a hand to his heart. "I don't know what you are talking about. I don't know anything about that poor girl who was murdered."

"I actually was talking about the past murders. Before you bought the town." Cat paused and watched his reaction go from shocked to what she might even call sly. "You must have done your research before you bought the place. You have a reputation of being a smart businessman."

"Of course I did my research. Those murders

were years ago. There is no way this current unfortunate business has anything to do with that mess."

"Why are you so convinced of that?" Cat opened her notebook. "Weren't they all killed in the same room?"

"You need to do your research. The girls weren't killed in the same room." He stood and went to retrieve his briefcase. "I think someone thought the legend might just hide their actions. Especially when yellow journalists like you look for the sensation instead of the truth."

He turned toward the stairs.

She waited for him to be on her same level. "One more question. Why did you purchase Outlaw?"

He glared at her when he paused by the bottom of the stairs to the stage. "Because it made good business sense. If you have additional questions, please reach out to my company public relations department. If you can actually do some research and find the number."

And with that he stomped out of the lecture hall, leaving Cat wondering what exactly he hadn't told her. Because even she could tell that the man was holding something back.

As she walked back to the house, she saw Seth walking toward her. He grinned his easy smile as he paused to wait for her to catch up to him. "So you had an errand?"

"I did. Who told you I was out? Cora?" She put her arm in his as they walked toward the house.

"I went looking for you after I got done with a few things. I wanted to know if you wanted to share

some ice cream. I think she was annoyed I interrupted her reading." He moved around her so he
was walking on the outside and retook her arm in
his. "Cora said you'd left about twenty minutes
ago. I was starting to worry."

"You have kind of a white knight addiction, you
know that, right?" Cat leaned into his shoulder.
Walking next to him felt good, like all of her concerns had been put on pause for a second. Then
reality struck again. "I wanted to talk to Joseph
John Robertson."

"The guy who runs Outlaw?"

Cat looked over at him. "I didn't realize you
knew anything about the corporate structure."

"I may not know a lot about business, but Outlaw started as a hobby for this guy. I tried to bid on
some of the work, but he went with an out-of-state
crew that undercut me on everything. But I heard
he's had to bring people in to fix the shoddy work-
manship ever since. You get what you pay for." He
paused at the gate. "I take it you were looking for
answers for Danielle? Did you get any?"

She shook her head. "No, just more questions.
Let's sit in the kitchen and have some iced tea while
you tell me what you know about Joseph John. I
know the guy is hiding something, but I don't know
what."

"We could still have ice cream." Seth held open
the kitchen door. "I've been working hard trying
to get this done before the end of the week. I de-
serve ice cream."

"Trying to get what done?" Cat hoped her question sounded casual when really, she was dying to
know.

"You're not that tricky." Seth grabbed two bowls out of the cabinet as she got the ice cream from the freezer. "You'll find out Saturday along with everyone else."

"Sometimes you're a tease." Cat grabbed toppings like crushed walnuts and chocolate sauce. "Chocolate syrup?"

"Of course." He reached around her to the fridge. "I'm pulling out the huckleberry jam too."

They'd fixed their sundaes and Cat was just starting to tell Seth about the meeting she'd had with the ghost town mogul when Shauna came into the room.

"Hey, I didn't mean to bother you two." She moved toward the desk. "I forgot my planner. I've been talking to Connie, and I think I'm going to call that grief group that meets over at the Baptist church."

"That's great." Cat patted the table next to her. "Come sit with us and celebrate with some ice cream."

Shauna picked up her planner and set it down on the table. Then she got a bowl and dished up ice cream, pouring on the chocolate syrup. Finishing it with a mountain of whipped cream, she finally took a bite. Then she looked up at Cat and Seth, who were watching her. "What? So I like a lot of toppings on my ice cream. Change the subject. What were you guys talking about?"

Cat caught her up on what she'd already told Seth.

Shauna stuck her spoon into the ice cream. "What is he lying about?"

"If I knew that, I'd know everything." Cat sighed,

eyeing the ice cream container. Her thoughts of more were shattered when Shauna screamed.

Seth stood and whirled around and followed Shauna's outstretched hand. Even Cat could see the man running toward the street.

"Did you see him? He was there, staring at me through the window." Shauna turned wide-eyed at Seth and Cat. "That wasn't just my imagination, was it?"

"Definitely not." Seth stood and strode to the door. "Lock this after me."

Cat followed his instructions, then thought of the front door. She glanced at the clock. Not quite nine. The front would be wide open. "Stay here and let Seth back in when he comes. I'm going to go lock the front."

Shauna nodded. Her words didn't match her calm demeanor. "I hope you're not too late."

# CHAPTER 11

Less than twenty minutes later, they were all back at the kitchen table, plus one. "Maybe I should just open a satellite office here in the house. At least on retreat weeks." Uncle Pete sat with his notebook out. His deputy, Brenden, was canvassing the neighborhood, but so far, no one had seen the man who'd been outside Shauna's kitchen window.

"Maybe it was just a fluke. A prank." Shauna stood and refilled her coffee. She'd thrown away her ice cream after it melted.

"Could be, but I don't like the fact that we've been having more of these issues on and off campus. Outlaw, the dorms, and now here. And these things only have one person in common." Uncle Pete looked at Cat. "Maybe we should contact her family and get her out of town for a while."

"You know that won't solve the problem. If

Jessi's in danger, she's probably safer here than in Boston." Cat held up her hands. "What? You know it's true as well as I do."

"Anyway, for once, my niece is right. I agree that keeping Jessi here is probably safer for her than sending her home. But there might come a time where my hands are tied. I need to figure out who killed Danielle and why, so we can keep Jessi from being the next victim."

"So, I talked to Joseph John about the murders at Outlaw. He wasn't very forthcoming. The only thing he did say was the murders weren't all in the same room. Then he took off and told me to call his public relations guy if I had more questions on the self-made millionaire."

"I already had that piece of information. One woman was killed in the blacksmith's shop, one outside the saloon, one downstairs in the saloon, and only one upstairs. I've looked at the cases, although there isn't much. One killer was arrested, but the other three cases went cold. I'd hate for Danielle's to be number four." Uncle Pete frowned. "The guy is a big shot in Aspen Hills. He should have known who you are, especially after the paper did that three-week write-up on you and the retreat. He didn't recognize you?"

"Not even a second glance. He was charming at the beginning when he thought I might be another groupie, but he hightailed it out of there as soon as the questions got hard. What did you know about the murders? I did a comparison, and they all have a lot in common with the way Danielle was killed."

"Interestingly enough, so did I. Well, I guess,

since it's my job, it's not that strange that I did the comparison."

"Do you want to fight or share information?" Cat met his gaze and didn't waver.

Sighing, he leaned back in his chair. "The first guy was put in jail right after the murder. He'd been stalking the girl for months, and when she dressed up as a saloon girl for Halloween, the temptation was too much."

"He didn't kill the other three?"

Uncle Pete shook his head. "Now the other three were never solved, but the theory I'm finding in the case files is they were a crime of passion by a copycat. The guy or guys who killed the other girls, wanted it to look like Gus's handiwork. Including Danielle's."

"Then it has to be Max. He's the only one with a clear motive for wanting her dead. He wanted to be with Jessi, and Danielle was just a passing fling." Seth looked hopeful.

"I've been trying to get Max in for an interview, but his lawyer is telling me he can't be bothered until tomorrow's Summer School final is over. I've got him scheduled to be in my office at five minutes after three. I might just send him a ride to make sure he gets there."

Brenden opened the back door and stepped inside. "No one saw nothing, Chief."

Uncle Pete stood. "You three go to bed. Let the professionals find your murderer and the peeper. Just make sure you lock up."

As Cat walked him to the door, she asked, "So what happened to the guy who fenced Jessi's jewelry?"

"Arnold is conveniently out of town. I have a guy trying to track him down. Tomorrow should be interesting if all goes well." He rubbed his face. "But then again, they could all be dead ends and I won't be any closer to solving that poor girl's murder than I am today. Go get some sleep. You look beat."

She said good night to her uncle and turned to find only Shauna left in the room.

"Seth went to check the basement door and then he was turning in. I'm heading up now. Are you okay?"

"I will be. I just don't like the thought of someone sneaking around here after Jessi. We're going to have to keep a close eye on her." Cat followed Shauna out of the kitchen toward the stairs.

"We can talk to her tomorrow morning. Let her know we're concerned and want to make sure she's safe." Shauna flipped off the lights.

Cat wondered if that would be enough. After the talk, either Jessi would realize the danger she was in or it would wind her up more to try to solve the murder of her friend's death. As she turned in to bed, Cat thought she knew which one it would be, because she would probably do the same thing.

Thursday morning came early after a night of tossing and turning. Cat grabbed a quick shower, then headed down for coffee. She thought she might work in Michael's study rather than heading back upstairs to her turret. She loved the spot she'd set as her office, mostly because of the remoteness, but today it seemed a little too far out of the way. Besides, she wanted to talk to Jessi sooner rather than later. This way, both she and Shauna could keep an eye out for her.

When she walked into the kitchen, her wishes were answered. Jessi sat at the table. A hot chocolate in front of her along with a few of Shauna's muffins seemed to have relaxed her into telling her story to Shauna.

"Good morning." Cat went to the coffeepot and poured a cup. "How are you this morning?"

"Feeling dumb. I think I know the guy who was hanging outside the house last night." Jessi pushed her hair up out of her eyes.

Cat's heart stumbled. She managed to get her coffee to the table and sat before she answered. "Really? Who and why?"

"Keith. He works at Outlaw. He's been trying to get me to go out with him, but really, he's been Danielle's boyfriend." Jessi blanched and picked up the cup, taking a big swig. "I was so mean to him. He must have found out about Danielle and Max, and that's why he pushed me so hard on Sunday."

"You saw him on Sunday?" Cat thought she might just get the real story about what had happened to Jessi at Outlaw before lunch.

Jessi blushed. "When I went back to the car, he followed me out to the parking lot. It got a little heated because he tried to get me to make out with him. Danielle had told me she was head over heels for this guy but when I told him that, he laughed at me. Said I didn't know my roommate as well as I thought."

"That's why you were late? You were fighting

with Keith?" Cat sipped her coffee, letting Jessi talk it out.

"I was so ticked. I can't believe how mad I was. I was going to tell Danielle to dump him. Not really tell her what he'd tried because I didn't want to hurt her feelings. What an idiot I was, right?" Now she picked at the muffin in front of her, not eating, just tearing it apart. "He even invited me to spend the weekend with him at his cabin. Like I was even interested."

"You were the one betrayed. That doesn't make you an idiot. That makes you a victim. And that's a role you can walk away from anytime." Shauna took her cup and refilled it with cocoa. "You hurt now, but it will be okay, I promise."

"Seems silly to be mad at her for this when she's dead. I should be remembering the things she did that were funny and uplifting. My mom said the same thing when my father died. I shouldn't remember the bad things about him. I should remember the little things that remind me that he loved me. Like taking me for ice cream and the time we rented a paddleboat in Central Park. Mom tried to talk him out of it, but he said, whatever his little girl wanted. That's a good memory, right?"

Instead of listing off her own version of how to deal with losing someone, Cat just smiled. "Your mom gave you great advice."

"She's solid, you know? Sometimes I think she's all caught up in decorating the house or something, then she'll step in and take care of something she thinks I shouldn't have to deal with. She was the one who wanted me out here to get one more degree. That way, when or if I went back, I'd have options. I could choose my own path." Jessi smiled as she lifted her hot cocoa. "And no matter what was going on, she was always there when I got home from school with cookies and hot cocoa. I liked talking to Mom."

"You should call her today. I know you want to get some words down, but you've had a crazy week. Maybe words will have to wait until you're more settled." Cat watched her and wondered what it might be like to live a pampered kind of life. "So where does Keith have his cabin? Do you know?"

After Jessi told her the area, Cat excused herself and went to look it up on the computer in the study. She glanced at the distance and thought about grabbing Seth to run up there with her to see if Keith was still hanging out there. Then she thought of Uncle Pete and the lecture she'd get even with taking Seth along for the ride. If she could even convince him to go with her. He'd probably be on the tell-her-uncle bandwagon if she told him why she wanted to take a short ride with her. Following the good angels, she called her uncle and left a voice message with the information. Then she took her coffee upstairs to her writing cave and sat down to get some words in.

Shauna opened the door at ten, and Cat swung around and grinned. "I can't believe how much I got done for a retreat week."

"When you didn't come down for breakfast, I figured you got caught up, so I brought you some food. It's a Greek egg scramble with feta, tomatoes, and onions. I added a couple of slices of toast to go with it." Shauna set down the tray on the coffee table. "And a pot of coffee with a glass of orange juice. I took a similar tray up to Kelly, as she's lost in her story as well. You writers are easy to predict. If you don't come down for meals, you're writing hard."

Cat sat down in front of the tray and drank half of the orange juice. "Thanks. I was planning on only writing for an hour. I guess I got a little lost."

"No worries. Seth ate early, then went into the back where I swear he's building a man cave for himself. I don't think we'll get rid of him any time soon. I saw a truck from the lumber yard dropping off more wood yesterday. I know why he doesn't have money for food—he's spending it all on two-by-fours." Shauna sat on the couch and poured herself a cup of coffee out of the pot. "Then the guests all gathered in the breakfast nook, well, except for Kelly, and they took off about twenty minutes ago."

"For the library?" Cat put huckleberry jelly on a slice of toast. She was starving.

Shauna took the other slice of toast and spread jelly as well. "I guess. They didn't say where they were going, but Cora hired a taxi. I heard her talking about it. They're used to using Uber in their area, so she was amazed she had to call someone to come and get them."

"I wonder if they are going into Denver. Connie was talking about visiting the train station. I guess she's writing a mail order bride story." A niggle of concern nagged at Cat as she ate. "I wish they would have told you where they were headed. I don't like the idea of Jessi just running around."

"Believe me, those women aren't going to let

anything happen to that girl. She's been adopted into their clan, even if she doesn't write historical romance." Shauna glanced at her watch. "Time to start cleaning the rooms. You might as well stay up here and work unless you have an appointment, since everyone else is occupied."

"Do you want help?" Can took a bite of her eggs and groaned. The flavor hit the right spot. "This is awesome. You're kind of magic in the kitchen."

"There's nothing a good cookbook and a little time can't produce." Shauna finished her coffee. "And no, this is my part of the deal. You bring in the writers and talk about that crazy magic of making stories, and I keep you all fed and in clean towels. It works for me. Besides, I feel better when I'm keeping busy. This week has been just what I needed."

After Shauna left, Cat finished eating and then stood and looked out over the backyard. The roof of the old building that Michael had called a barn peeked out from the edge of the trees. Maybe she should go out there and find out exactly what Seth was doing. He'd been less than pleased with the area in the basement that they'd started remodeling into a gym. Maybe he had taken it on himself to remodel the barn. Cat thought of the one time she'd gone out there to look through the building. There had been birds in the lofts and the place had been filled with old straw and still smelled of the animals who had lived there years before. Michael had talked about making it into a storage shed, but before they'd even finished remodeling the house, they'd had their issues. Cat had moved to California and the barn had been forgotten.

Now Seth was turning it into a workout place.

She guessed the barn could have worse uses. And at least he had a project to work on. His handyman business had slowed down a little this year as the college was reevaluating renovation plans that he'd counted on and had turned down other work to make sure he had time to devote to the larger project.

She left the window and went back to her computer. Finding writing time during retreat weeks was rare, and she was going to make the most of the gift she'd been given.

At noon she was reviewing the day's words. She was happy with the work she'd finished and excited to get back to the writing. If she got to work before everyone woke up each morning of the last few retreat days, she might even get to a place where she could finish up a week early. She made notes in her calendar of what she needed to write to make that happen. Her phone rang and Uncle Pete's name showed on the screen.

"Hey, what's going on?" She shut down the computer, making sure she saved her document one more time, just to be safe. She also emailed it to herself at the end of every writing session, just in case her hard drive gave out in the middle of writing a book.

"I need you to come get your guests." Uncle Pete's voice sounded taut, and Cat recognized the anger behind them.

"Uh-oh, what did they do now?" Cat had a sinking feeling she didn't want to know. The pause on the other end of the line had her scared, but finally, her uncle answered.

"I hate to say it, but they probably saved this guy's

life." He barked an order to one of his men. "Sorry, just come and get them."

"Where are you?" Cat figured she already knew the answer.

"At Keith Anderson's cabin. The guy had been beaten to an inch of his life. If they hadn't come when they did, he probably would have been dead in a few more hours."

Cat called Seth as she walked down the stairs. Shauna was in the kitchen folding laundry and took one look at her before setting the towel back down, unfolded. "What happened now?"

Cat held up one finger. "Hey, can you drive me somewhere? Like right now?"

When the answer came, she nodded. "I'll be out by the SUV with the keys. Hurry, okay?"

"What happened?" Shauna repeated again.

Cat grabbed the keys to the car off the rack and grabbed her purse. "They didn't go to Denver. They headed out to find Keith and his cabin."

"Oh, no. Was there a fight?"

"I guess there was before they got to the place. Uncle Pete says they saved his life." Cat paused at the door. "I'll call you when we get there if there's going to be a delay, but you should see us in ten to twenty minutes. I'd have coffee going."

"I might have the whiskey available too just in case." Shauna made shooing movements with her hands. "Go on. Go save the day. This group thinks they are in one of those television murder mysteries. I can't believe what they're doing. Don't they realize they could be putting themselves in danger?"

Cat hurried out to the car and unlocked it, then

slid into the passenger seat. She turned on the engine, and it was ready to go by the time Seth came out from behind the trees. He was covered in sawdust and tried to brush himself off before getting into the car. Cat waved him in. She didn't want Uncle Pete to be any madder than he already was.

As he slipped into the driver's seat, she took a sliver of straw out of his hair and threw it out the window onto the driveway. He back up and paused at the street. "Where are we going?"

Cat rattled off the address, and he turned right toward the road out of town. As he headed toward the cabin, he glanced over.

"Can I ask what we're doing?"

She turned off the radio that had been blaring when she got into the car, finally noticing the noise. Shauna liked her show tunes. "The guests are at another crime scene, and Uncle Pete would like us to come and get them as apparently Affordable Taxi got another call and left them at Keith's cabin before they found the guy all beat up in his kitchen."

Seth let out a low whistle. "Those women know just how to get in the middle of things, don't they?"

"I thought they were doing research for Connie's book. I didn't realize they were trying to confront a guy who was supposedly dating Danielle. I guess they thought they were helping Jessi heal from her broken heart, but seriously, what if this guy had murdered Danielle?" Cat shook her head. "They could have been killed and I would have been up in my office writing."

"Did you get a lot of words?" Seth didn't look at her as he turned the car onto the mountain road and decreased his speed.

Cat tried to hide the grin. He knew her too well. "About three thousand, and I'm close to finishing a chapter. What about you? How was your day before this emergency taxi run?"

"Good. I still should be finished by Saturday morning for the big reveal." He shook his head. "And before you ask, don't. I'm not talking about it."

They drove in silence until Seth turned onto an unmarked side road. "I did some work up here a few weeks ago for one of the neighbors. The road is a cul-de-sac and has three other houses. One of them must be Keith's."

As they turned a corner, they saw the entire road was blocked with emergency vehicles. He pulled over onto the side embankment, and an ambulance with its lights on took off out of the area. "I'm glad we didn't run into him on the main road. He needs to put on his siren too."

Then, as if the driver had heard Seth's muttered complaint, the sirens went on and echoed down the mountain. The sound made goose bumps pop up on Cat's arms.

# CHAPTER 12

Cat and Seth walked through the line of police cars, all with their lights flashing, and headed to the cabin where the historical writers stood outside in a circle with Jessi in the middle. When they approached, Jessi held up her hand.

"Really, Cat, we didn't hurt him. He was like this when we got here. Then we saw him on the floor and the taxi guy took off to call your uncle. And now you have to come and rescue us again. Seriously, I don't know how things got so bad, so quickly. All I wanted to do was to let Keith know he was such a jerk. He probably didn't even know about Danielle since he came up here after his shift on Sunday."

"Did you ever think that Keith might have been the one to kill your friend?" Cat glanced at the other three women. "I should have thought after the last field trip, one of you might have thought twice about this adventure."

Cora stepped toward Cat. "You're right. I should have nipped this in the bud as soon as Jessi brought up the idea, but I really didn't think we'd even find the cabin. It's crazy what you can find out about people on Google."

"Let's get you all back to the house where you can get back to the reason you signed up for the retreat: writing. I'm sure Kelly's probably finished four or five books by now." Cat nodded to Seth, and he took Jessi's arm and started to lead her to the car.

"Kelly's a machine. Besides, I've gotten more words this week than all last month," Connie groused on the way past Cat. "And it's been exciting. I may just have to write a contemporary mystery or suspense after this week. Historical seems so tame now."

Lisa followed her friend. "Leave it to Connie to see the bright side. I'm just glad I'm not going to town in the back of a police car."

"Don't even joke about that." Cora paused by Cat. "I really am sorry. I didn't even think that this Keith guy could have been more than just a bad boyfriend. Too much romance writing, I guess."

"No worries. You're all safe. I was just concerned when I got the call from Uncle Pete." She turned and saw her uncle by the side of the house. "Would you let Seth know I'll be right there? I want to check in with my uncle."

"Sure." Cora paused. "You don't think this was because of Danielle at all, do you? You think Jessi is somehow involved."

"I think *involved* is a strong word, but she may be part of the answer here." Cat glanced toward the car. "Let's just keep that between us for a while, okay? And try to keep her under control? We only have three more days of the retreat, and I'd like to not lose any of you before you leave on Sunday."

"I'll do my best. She has a way of talking people into things. I swear, she's a trouble whisperer." Cora turned and moved toward the car.

When Cat got near her uncle, he was on the phone. She waited for him to get off before asking, "Is Keith going to be okay?"

"They think so. That was the EMT. I told Jake to call when he got the guy stable. He just gave him a quick glance, but in his opinion the injuries are not life threatening." He glanced over at the car where Jessi sat. "Too much damage for that little thing to have done it, and besides, it looks like he was beaten sometime yesterday. The last call recorded on his cell was yesterday afternoon, and I've talked to the girlfriend who left the cabin around ten yesterday morning."

"Who would do this?" Cat looked around the small cabin, the room a mess from the struggle. Keith had tried to fight back.

"My guess? He was beaten right after Jessi talked to her mom about the missing jewelry." He held up pawn slips and Cat saw the name on the top—Ernest Hemingway. "I think someone got to George at the pawnshop before I did and traced Danielle's fence down to Keith."

"But why would he kill her?"

Uncle Pete slipped the bag with the pawn slips back into his pocket. "I don't believe Keith killed Danielle. She was his money tree. The good thing is I have the last piece of jewelry Jessi declared as missing in evidence now. I guess he didn't have time to pawn that yet."

Cat was quiet as the car made its way back to town. The women in the back talked about the way the trees shadowed the road. Seth told them that the road closed from the first heavy snowfall until spring thaw.

"So people just let those cabins sit in the winter?" Lisa glanced back up the road. "Seems like a waste of a house."

"Believe me, they get plenty of use during the summer. We have tourists up here all season wanting to be part of the wilderness adventure." He glanced over at Cat. "There are all kinds of people who show up for the experience. Hikers, kayakers, people who like to fish, and in the fall, a lot of hunters come in to bag an elk or a deer."

Back at the house, the guests headed into the dining room for some coffee and treats while they planned their lunch adventure. Cat thought about handing them delivery menus, but they were adults. If they wanted to go get in trouble again, all she could do was go and rescue them yet another time.

In the kitchen, Cat sank into a chair cradling a cup of coffee. "I swear, this retreat is going to be the death of me."

Shauna giggled. "My mom used to say that about me. I was her wild child. It's probably why I took off for California. I was always living down to expectations."

Seth set a cup of coffee in front of Shauna and then sat down with his own. "You wanted to be an actress? I didn't know that."

"Actually, no, I followed a guy who wanted to be an actor. Then he dumped me for some chick who worked at a studio and had connections. The loser tried to stop by and get some on the side at first, but I had the apartment in my name, so I just changed the locks." Shauna sipped her coffee. "Not all men are as upstanding and honest as our present company."

Seth blushed and Cat smiled. Shauna seemed happier the last two days. Had she already started attending the grief group? Or were her chats with Connie helping? She didn't really care, she was just glad to see her coming back to normal.

The door opened and Uncle Pete wandered inside. He took off his hat and set it on the bench by the door. "Mind if I steal some coffee?"

"Help yourself." Shauna popped up. "I can make you a sandwich or we have some clam chowder just about ready for lunch if you can stay."

He got his coffee and sat next to Cat. "I'm heading back to the station as soon as I take the women's statements. Are they all here?"

"In the dining room." Cat studied her uncle. He looked tired. "You should eat."

"If you could have some ready for me after the interviews are done, that would be great." He smiled up at Shauna. "I feel like I'm always mooching food."

"You're family. There's no mooching involved." Shauna set a piece of blueberry cobbler in front of him. "And we'll start with dessert. Life's too short."

"Isn't that the truth." He gave in and picked up his fork.

Cat waited for him to finish, then asked, "How's Keith?"

"Dehydrated. He lost a lot of blood. His kneecaps were smashed, so he's going to have to have surgery, but he's lucky to be alive. Arnold's been known to rough up customers who cause him problems. I've got an APB out on him for questioning, but I'm sure he'll have an airtight alibi." He pushed the plate away. "He doesn't get his own hands dirty."

"You think it's just that?" Seth had been quiet, but Cat had noticed him watching her uncle closely.

"I got an anonymous tip this morning before the taxi driver showed up." Uncle Pete sipped his coffee. "They told me that Keith should have learned his lesson by now and where to find him. The caller also said that finding him would solve the active case I had on my books."

"Maybe they were talking about another one?" Cat wasn't hopeful. Jessi and Dante's family had a way of taking care of their own problems.

"I only have three active cases. The murder, the loss of Jessi's jewelry, and the missing money. Since he didn't have the money at the cabin, just the earrings, I'm thinking someone else has the money."

Cat thought about that. "I'm not sure Jessi has called her mom since we found the empty safe. Have you called her mother?"

Uncle Pete sat back in his chair. "No. I haven't. I reached out to my contact at the college, but I didn't hear back from him. Jessi's an adult. I want to let her deal with her family. Besides, right now we're just guessing that she's in trouble."

The other three at the table didn't speak and finally, Uncle Pete stood. "I better get these interviews done. I'll stop back in for a small cup of that soup and maybe a sandwich if you don't mind?"

"When you're ready, let me know." Shauna took his plate as he tried to rinse it in the sink. "Go work. The sooner you figure all this out, the sooner life will go back to normal around here."

After Uncle Pete had finished with his interviews, he quickly ate the lunch Shauna had prepared for him, then excused himself from the table. Seth was the next one to finish and he left, saying he had work to complete. So then it was just Cat and Shauna.

"Did the guests go into town? Including Kelly?" Cat had been in the foyer with the others as Uncle Pete did his interviews in the study. No one stayed in longer than ten minutes, except for Jessi. She was in the study almost twice as long. As soon as she got out, Cora bundled Jessi and the others outside to go get lunch. When she went into the kitchen to eat with Shauna, she updated her on their status. "These are people after my own heart. Food solves everything."

"That's my motto." Shauna pushed away her soup bowl. "I'm sorry I've been horrible lately."

"Stop apologizing. I get it. You have had a bad couple of months." Cat ran her spoon through the creamy soup, making figure eights. "What's helping? You seem better."

"Talking to Connie has really been helpful. She was married for so long, and when he died, she hated him for changing her life. Then she hated herself for hating him. Just listening to her helped me realize my crazy emotions are normal and it's time to get past this. I called the attorney and told her I wasn't going to wait any longer for Jade's excuses. I'm pushing for the will reading to be on Monday. I want to be done with this whole thing next week." Shauna sighed. "Then I can start healing and get this behind me."

"That's great. I'm glad Connie had some good advice."

Shauna picked up her dishes and started cleaning up the lunch mess. She kept her back turned away as she spoke. "She just told me what had happened to her. Knowing I wasn't alone in this really helps. Thanks for being there for me."

"Any time." Cat paused, wondering if she should say more, but the outside door opened. Seth came back into the kitchen. "I thought you were working?"

"I was, but I got a call from Joseph John himself. He wants me to go check out the security system out at Outlaw. I guess the other company he hired is getting a little tired of the constant travel out here from Denver. I even doubled my hourly rate for this emergency trip, and the guy didn't blink." Seth ran a hand through his hair and studied her. "I'm going to regret this, but do you want to go up with me?"

"You'll let me into the crime scene? Won't Uncle Pete be mad?" Cat didn't want to talk him out of it, really. She just wanted him to think she was second-guessing herself when in fact, she'd been chomping at the bit for a chance to get back to the saloon in Outlaw.

"I just talked to him. He cleared me to go." Seth shrugged. "I didn't mention having a ride-along."

"You're devious. I like it." Cat grinned. "Let me get my tote."

As they drove up to the ghost town, Cat checked the camera on her phone. Sometimes just being able to see where something happened let her think about what shouldn't be there. And even though her uncle and his team were professionals, they didn't deal with murder a lot. Maybe Jessi could spot some inconsistencies that Cat could point out to her uncle. She was feeling kind of lost on this investigation. Every time she looked at one thing, a totally unrelated clue popped up and made her question the few ideas she'd had.

"So I knew Keith."

Seth's statement was out of the blue and made Cat look up from her phone. "You never said you two were friends."

"It wasn't like that. We played on the same baseball team for Aspen Hills rec last summer. This year I was too busy with the retreat to sign up for the league. He was a pretty good outfielder, but he couldn't hit worth crap. I think he was doing it more for fun, although he claimed he'd been a star player on his high school team. All I could think of was it must have been a small school."

"Was he on scholarship at Covington?" Cat turned in her seat so she could see Seth as he drove.

"He talked about coming from a little town north of Denver. I guess he was on scholarship, but I think he dropped out and just worked odd jobs. He had a friend who owned the cabin and let him stay there." Seth glanced over at her.

"Uncle Pete thinks he was beat up by someone

Arnold hired after finding out the jewelry was stolen. Do you think that's what happened to Danielle too? Could this all be just revenge for stealing jewelry?" Cat played with the theory in her mind. In some ways, it had merit. And the place was known for other murders that anyone could copy to make it seem like there was a different motive.

"Why kill Danielle but beat up Keith? And someone called the police so Keith wouldn't die from his attack. To me, that's teaching the kid a lesson. He won't ever steal from anyone again. Danielle's death feels different." He pulled the car into the parking lot, but instead of stopping, he drove around the edge to a dirt road with a sign at the edge marked *Service Trucks Only.* "You'll get to see the working side of the town."

They drove through a stand of trees and came up on a large flat building hidden from view from the town sites. On the backs of the old buildings were doors marked with the name of the shops. Photo gallery, souvenir shop, saloon, they all had doors that must have gone into the back of the building for deliveries and employee entrances. On the top of each door was a warning: *Do Not Enter Without Changing Into Costume First. Not Even for a Quick Peek.*

"I guess they are strict on the rules for their employees." Cat mused as they pulled up in one of the marked spots.

"Even the cooks and cleaners had to be in costume if the town was open for business. They do a lot of the work on Thursdays, before the weekend starts. Someone's supposed to be here by two to

get my report, so I think you have about thirty
minutes to check out the saloon building before
you'll have people wondering what you're doing."
Seth walked her over to the door and keyed in a
code. "I'll get my work done and be back here in
twenty minutes. Don't make me wait long. Do you
have a timer on that phone?"

"Actually, I have one on my new watch." She set
the alarm for twenty minutes. "I'll be at the door
just a few minutes after the alarm rings."

He kissed her, then held the door open. "Call
out if you run into a murderous ghost. I'd hate to
lose my girlfriend again."

"Especially since you're the one who let me into
the building. I bet Uncle Pete would have a hard
time explaining that so you wouldn't go to jail."

"The ghost won't take another life for at least
ten years, if you believe the stories." He squeezed
her arm. "Just be careful. I don't believe in ghost
stories, but I do believe that some people just like
to kill."

He handed Cat a flashlight and nodded to the
larger service building. "I'll be in there checking
out their system. I should be able to hear you if
you call out the window."

"I'll be fine. Don't worry." Cat put on a wide
grin she didn't feel and stepped into the darkness.
The small windows only let in so much light, and
as she walked through the hallway, she heard the
door close behind Seth. She was alone in the saloon. Or at least she hoped she was alone.

Moving forward, she saw a glow ahead of her.
This room must be the large room where they'd

eaten lunch on Sunday. Servers had been coming out of the back area throughout the meal and taking the dishes back that way as well. This must have been the hallway they'd used. She turned the corner, and there was the main room of the saloon. A wooden bar stood at her left. Bottles without labels with what looked like whiskey gleamed in the sunlight from the large windows in this room. She could see Main Street from where she stood, but the dirt road was empty of life.

Except the cat was sitting on the windowsill, looking in at her. She heard the meow through the glass. She walked over to the window and touched her hand to the pane. The cat touched her nose to the other side. "Hey, Angelica, why are you here and where is your owner?" As soon as they got back in town, she'd have Seth stop at the woman's house and ask if she knew her cat was at Outlaw. The cat looked down the street and took off.

Cat went to the back of the room and found the ornately carved wooden stairway that made its way up to the rooms above. During Sunday's lunch, the saloon girls had taken turns standing on the stairway, swishing their skirts and calling out suggestions to the men eating lunch below. Cat hadn't tried to identify Danielle since when the meal first started, Jessi had been among the missing, and then when she did come in, she'd been visibly upset.

Cat wished she'd pulled her aside that day. Maybe this wouldn't have happened if Uncle Pete had known what was happening, but Cat realized even Jessi didn't know what was going on with her life then. She'd just thought Keith was a bad boy-friend to Danielle.

She was stalling and still on the bottom step, looking up to the second floor. Cat forced herself to go up one step, and then another. With each movement, she wondered when she'd hear a scream.

# CHAPTER 13

Cat made her way up the stairs and stood in the hallway. Her heart was pounding so hard, she knew she could be heard a mile away. Here the light was dimmer but she could see exactly where they'd found Danielle's body. The crime scene tape hung loosely around the door. The room wasn't sealed anymore, so either Uncle Pete was done with the area, or someone else had been here before Cat.

She started snapping pictures as she made her way to the room. A small window at the end of the hallway kept some light in the dusty walkway. Three doors lined the rest of the hall and a table sat near the window with an old water pitcher and a large matching bowl. Lace curtains hung over the sides of the window, faded from years of sunshine.

Cat paused at the edge of the room, taking in the scene. She took several pictures of the room, not seeing much except the crime scene techs' dust and footprints. The team had come down from Denver to do the investigation, and her uncle was still waiting on the lab reports. She took a deep breath and stepped inside the room.

She expected to feel a chill come over her or some type of physical reaction to moving inside, but there was nothing. She laughed at herself and muttered, "I guess I *was* expecting a ghost."

Walking over to the window, she saw Seth outside the building looking up. She waved at him, letting him know she was fine, and he waved back. He turned and walked toward the service building. He'd been waiting to see if she'd made it upstairs. Turning back to face the room, she tried to imagine the murder scene.

From what Uncle Pete had said, Danielle had been found on the bed, still in her saloon girl outfit. Had she been up here waiting for Max to show up? Or Keith? Had she been stringing both men along? Cat couldn't tell from the diary entries, but Danielle had been head over heels with Max. Was that because he was unavailable and Jessi's? The girl seemed to have a need to have what her roommate possessed.

She glanced around the room, then made a circle, taking pictures of all the areas. After making sure she had everything, she glanced at her watch. Ten minutes had already passed. She needed to hurry. This would probably be the last time she was able to actually be in the room, so she needed to get as much seen as possible. There was a small dresser with a mirror and three drawers. All three were empty, and Cat leaned down and looked underneath as well. Nothing seemed out of place. She'd found a secret compartment in

Michael's desk, so she was always looking for another one. She looked under the bed; nothing.
Then in the wardrobe that served as a closet for
the room. Again, nothing, and nothing out of
place.

Frustrated, she glanced at her watch again. She
had five minutes or less before someone would be
here from the company, questioning her being in
the room. She slowly spun around. Was there anything that looked out of place?

The mirror on the dresser was slightly tilted.
And from the bed, Danielle would have been able
to see it. Cat ran her hand back between the mirror and the wall. Her fingers stopped at a pad of
paper taped to the wooden backing. Hoping it
wasn't the original sale invoice, she pulled off the
taped package and opened the envelope.

Three typed pages had been folded together. Cat
read a running list of Jessi's activities for the last
month, ending with a paragraph about the writing
retreat she'd been chosen to attend. The address
and Cat's name were highlighted.

Cat considered the pages. Was Danielle report-
ing everything Jessi had done, bought, drank, to
someone? Who would have paid for this information? Or was it just Danielle's way of keeping track
of her friend?

One thing she did know as she tucked the envelope and the pages into her jeans pocket: If Jessi
found out that Danielle had been spying on her,
she would be devastated. It was hard enough trusting someone, but Danielle had broken that trust
over and over again with the person she claimed to
be her friend.

When Cat got downstairs, she had just enough time to get into the car and grab her phone before she heard the car come up the road behind her. Her body froze when she realized she'd forgotten about the cat. She couldn't go looking for it now. She needed to stay in the car so it looked like Seth had brought a passenger to keep him company for the trip, rather than brought someone to snoop around in the buildings. The Range Rover pulled alongside Cat's door and Joseph John got out of the driver's side. He glanced her way but quickly dismissed her. She guessed he didn't recognize her, which was good. If he had, he might have wondered what a journalist was doing sitting in a car in the employees-only section of his ghost town.

Cat didn't know if she should feel offended or not. She'd just talked to him last night, but maybe he hadn't looked closely, thinking she was somebody's wife or girlfriend. Men were funny. She took out her phone and called Uncle Pete. She got voice mail, so she hung up. She'd call him when they were back in town. The crime scene guys were going to get a strong talking-to for not finding the envelope and pages, if she knew her uncle.

Of course, she might get the same lecture, but this one she could kind of blame on Seth. She started playing with her phone and was surprised to see she had internet access, probably due to the staff building they had parked in front of. She started researching Joseph John and after ten minutes found an old college paper from Covington where he'd examined the killings at Outlaw. She looked at the publication date. It had been more than twenty years ago. Joseph John had been part of the *Covington Chatter*, the college newspaper when he attended. And apparently a big Outlaw history buff.

Big enough to buy the place after he'd made his money as a local developer. Or maybe he had other connections to the town as well. She'd have to ask her uncle.

When Seth came back, she was just finishing the paper. "You get something?" he asked.

Looking up, she grinned. "I got a lot of something. Or at least it feels that way. Probably not enough to do anything with on Uncle Pete's side, but really, really interesting."

She started to pull out the envelope she'd found to show him. Seth shook his head. "Let's drive out of here to the overlook. I don't want Joseph John to overhear this."

"Definitely." She buckled her seat belt, then sat back, waiting to talk until Seth had driven the five miles to the top of the mountain.

When they parked, he turned off the engine and took the envelope. After he finished reading the pages, he whistled. "Man, someone had it in for this girl. Danielle was really digging the dirt on her."

"There's notes about who she saw, where she went, and how much money she spent." Cat shook her head. "Nothing about this makes any sense."

"It did to someone. Anyway, I think we can take Keith off the list of killers. At least all he wanted from Jessi was her jewelry. Your uncle may keep him on his list just for principle."

And that was the problem, Cat thought as they

made their way down the mountain. Everyone wanted something from the girl. All Jessi wanted was to be a good friend and daughter and to find her way in the adult world. Cat didn't think that was so much to ask.

As they started into town, she sat up, watching for the first house. "Do you know where Mary Davis lives?"

"I knew where she lived." Seth pointed to a small white cottage on the right side of the road. The lights were all off and the house looked deserted. "Why, did you know her?"

"The vet says Angelica is her cat. Did she move away? Maybe the cat walked home. You hear about those things all the time." She turned toward Seth. "Where did she move to?"

"Cat, she passed away a few months ago. From what I heard, she called 911 and said she was having a heart attack. By the time they got her to the hospital, it was too late." Seth slowed near the house. "She didn't have any relatives. The house is in probate. I've made a bid on doing the renovations to get it up to code. I guess no one thought about the cat."

"So the cat has been on her own for a couple of months?" She turned back to look at the mountains in the darkening light. "We have to go up and get her."

"We'll go back tomorrow. I'll call Joseph John in the morning and tell him we saw a lost cat on the streets." Seth patted her leg. "You know we wouldn't be able to find her in the dark. Angelica has been on her own for a while now. One more day isn't going to make a difference."

By the time they got back to the house, the guests had left for dinner. Kelly and Jessi had been included in the group. Cat wondered how much work Kelly was really getting done since she seemed to be around every time the group got themselves into a pickle. Seth went off into the extra lot to work, and Cat, finding the kitchen empty, went to Michael's study. She wanted to reread Joseph John's undergraduate article on Outlaw. It might give her a deeper understanding of the guy.

Settling down into her lounger with a tablet, she accessed the article. As she read, it occurred to her she'd done the same thing when Michael was alive. Come into his office and curl up with a book, or, sometimes, a stack of papers to grade. He'd be working on one project or another. She joked that he must be writing his biography, but he'd always laugh and say he was too boring. There were too many great biographies out there, no one wanted to hear about the day-to-day life of an economist.

Shauna opened the door a few hours later. Cat was making notes in a notebook about the things she'd found odd. Like why a teenager had been so fascinated with the grisly history of a ghost town. She wondered if Uncle Pete had questioned him yet. She'd love to be a bug on the wall for that discussion. She put a period on the last sentence and looked up at her friend. "What's going on?"

"I was wondering if you were hungry. Seth and I waited for a few minutes, but then I decided to come find you. I think he started eating already." Shauna looked tired. She had bags under her eyes that wouldn't classify as carry-ons, they were so large. She rubbed her arms, apparently chilled. "So are you coming?"

Cat eyed her. Maybe she was coming down with a cold. She seemed a bit out of breath, and the kitchen wasn't more than a few steps away. "Let me just bookmark this site and I'll be there."

When she got into the kitchen, Seth was telling Shauna about their trip to Outlaw. Cat's eyes widened. "Crap, did you call Uncle Pete?"

"Call Pete about what? Don't tell me you guys actually found something." Shauna sat a plate of spaghetti with two large meatballs in front of Cat.

"No, you said you would. I was outside working until just a few minutes ago." He took a bite of the spaghetti. "Don't blame this on me."

"I wasn't blaming you." Cat eyed the food, then sighed and picked up her phone. "Maybe he hasn't eaten yet."

After inviting her uncle to dinner, Cat ended the call.

Seth pointed a fork at her. "I didn't hear you tell him about the pages we found at Outlaw."

"I thought that conversation might go over better once he has food in his stomach. He gets a little grumpy when he's hungry. Tell Shauna what we found out about Angelica." Cat dug into the spaghetti in front of her and didn't even look up a few minutes later when her uncle came into the house.

"Pete, sit down and eat. What can I get you to drink?" Shauna dished up a bowl of spaghetti and stood, watching him as he walked to the table.

"Iced tea will be fine." He glanced at Cat as he sat down. "I take it I'm not here just for supper?"

"Of course you're here for supper." Shauna sat the bowl and a glass in front of him.

Cat squirmed uncomfortably in her chair. Her uncle could always read her. It really wasn't fair. "Well, there is this thing I found—"

"We found," Seth interrupted.

Cat shook her head. "No, I found it. You were outside doing what you were supposed to be doing. I was the one snooping."

"But you wouldn't have been there if I hadn't invited you. So partially, this is my fault too." Seth turned toward Pete. "Don't be too hard on her. Like I said . . ."

"Believe me, I know, it was your fault too. There's plenty of blame to go around here." Uncle Pete set his fork down. "How bad is this? Do I want to try to eat before you tell me? Will I have to take off for some remote spot as soon as you spill whatever you're holding back?"

Cat glanced at Seth who shook his head. "I don't think so. But let me tell you while you eat."

He picked up his fork gingerly and took a small bite. Waving at Cat to continue, Uncle Pete ducked his head down and focused on the plate of food rather than her words.

"I went to Outlaw with Seth this afternoon."

Now Uncle Pete's head came up and he stared at her. Finally, he broke eye contact and went back to eating. Cat had gotten the message. The act had been foolhardy and dangerous. Something she wouldn't have even let her fictional character perform because of the fear of being labeled Too Stupid to Live. Not seeing any other choice, she continued.

"I went upstairs in the saloon, found the room where Danielle had been killed, and since the crime scene tape was off, I entered the room. I looked around for anything that you or your sweepers hadn't seen."

"Or your band of Nancy Drews who brought me that nice present of all the litter they'd found in the room." He waved a fork filled with pasta at her. "Sorry, go on. I promise not to interrupt again."

"Anyway, I didn't find anything, and I was about to leave when I noticed the mirror was cockeyed. And when I reached behind the glass, I found an envelope."

Shauna leaned forward in her chair. "What was in the envelope?"

"A report of what Jessi had been doing for the last month." Cat set her fork down and pulled the pages out of her back pocket. She tossed them on the table in front of him. "Uncle Pete, someone was stalking that poor girl and using her best friend to do it. That's just so not fair."

"You're right. Jessi has had a heck of a week. And if I were her, I'd never trust another human again in my life. But the girl seems resilient." He took a bite and chewed it thoughtfully. "Well, Keith is out of the picture for this bit of stalking. All he wanted was the jewelry, and once that was done, he had moved on to other marks."

"You talked to Keith?" Cat sat her fork down on her plate.

"A few hours ago at the hospital. He was so scared, he told me everything. He thought those guys were going to kill him." Uncle Pete met Cat's eyes. "Arnold has a lot to answer for when I find him."

"But I don't understand why Keith couldn't have killed Danielle."

"Because he was with his new girlfriend at the cabin from Sunday night until Tuesday night when she had to go back to work." Her uncle took a slice of garlic bread from the basket in the center. "Being out of that house probably saved that girl from being hurt. But all she can think of is that maybe he wouldn't have been attacked if she'd been there."

# CHAPTER 14

After Uncle Pete left, Cat went into the living room to wait for the retreat guests to return from dinner. She couldn't go to bed knowing that they were out there, maybe in danger. This must be what having children felt like. She was frustrated and wanted to wrap them in bubble wrap and keep them safe in their rooms. She didn't know if she even wanted kids now.

She heard the women talking as they came into the lobby and stepped out into the foyer.

"I am so embarrassed." Jessi was talking to Cora. "I promise I'm going to the bank first thing in the morning to figure out what's going on."

"It's no problem. I can buy you one dinner. My last royalty check covers at least that." Cora patted Jessi on the arm. "I'm sure it was a mistake."

"What happened?" Cat wasn't sure Cora was right. Someone was targeting Jessi, but she didn't know why or for what end. The girl wasn't having a good week.

"My debit card was rejected. I know I have money in the bank. I get an allowance every month and I barely used anything this month. And what, it's the tenth? I should have more than enough money for a pizza." Jessi shook her head. "I can't call Mom because she'll think I've been overspending again."

"Now, Jessi, I'm sure she'll understand. Bank errors happen." Cora glanced at Cat, and Cat could see she doubted the truth of what she was saying. Cat knew Jessi had shared some of the complex relationship she had with her mother with the other women in the group. That was the magic of the group—it led to strong bonds and the ability to understand each other's pain. Writers got each other.

Cat tried to deescalate Jessi's emotions. "Well, there's nothing we can do about this issue tonight. Let's go into the dining room, grab a dessert and coffee or hot chocolate. I feel like we haven't talked a lot during the retreat. I'd like to touch base on how your writing is going."

Cora sent her a grateful look and put an arm around the clearly upset Jessi. "That sounds wonderful. I've got a couple of questions I'd like to throw out, if you don't mind. I've been thinking a lot about senses this week. And I've been dying for a brownie all day."

As they moved into the dining room, Jessi paused and turned back toward Cat. "I'm really thankful that I'm here with you all this week. I don't know what I would have done by myself after Danielle . . ."

Cat saw the girl was fighting back tears and she shook her head. "We're here for you. Good or bad, this is your week too."

As they gathered with their treats and drinks, Cat hoped that the feeling of home would help shelter Jessi from the pain she was going through that week. Her house was supposed to be a place of comfort and creativity. Cat relaxed into the discussion of writing and words. That was a place where she felt at home and comforted. She hoped the discussion would ease others' minds as well, if just for the evening.

Seth met her in the lobby when the group broke up after ten. "Hey, the back door and the cellar are locked up tight. Your uncle called earlier to make sure I double-checked this evening."

"He's worried about Jessi." Cat glanced up the stairwell where the women had disappeared a few minutes ago.

"He's worried about all of us," Seth said flatly. "If someone is set on taking her out, locked doors aren't going to stop them."

"You think I haven't thought of that?" Cat rubbed her face, trying to get the tiredness to stay at bay for at least a few minutes. "Although why someone would be targeting that poor girl is beyond me."

"All I know is I'll be glad when Pete catches this guy." He walked over and double-checked the locks. "I'm heading upstairs to read, but if you need me, just knock."

"I'll come with you." She turned off the main lights. "I'm beat." She wanted to tell him she appreciated him. She wanted to tell him she loved him. But now didn't seem like the right time.

They walked upstairs together but with a canyon of feelings separating them. When she lay down on her bed, the exhaustion took over and she fell asleep, but dreams kept her restless. When Seth shook her awake, she thought it was part of the nightmare.

"Wake up, Cat. Someone is in the house." He shoved his phone into her hand. "Call your uncle."

She sat up and stared at the phone in her hand and Seth's back as he started to leave the room. "Where are you going?"

"Downstairs. I want to check the guest rooms." He turned and repeated, "Call your uncle. Then go wake up Shauna. If you don't hear anything, come down to the second floor and meet me. I'll be in the hallway."

She followed Seth's instructions, first calling Uncle Pete, who told her to stay in her room. Ignoring his orders, she went to Shauna's room and knocked before moving into the room and flipping on the lights.

"What's going on?" Shauna was wide-awake. Cat wondered if she had even been asleep. Cat crossed the room and sat next to her.

"Seth says someone's in the house." She glanced at his phone, fear running through her. One a.m. Was this the witching hour, or was it supposed to be midnight?

"Cat? Are you calling the police?" Shauna's voice cut through her thoughts.

Cat watched as she pulled on a robe to cover the long, silky nightgown. "Already did. Uncle Pete's on his way. We're supposed to wait and see if Seth finds someone on the second floor."

"How will we know?" Shauna pulled Cat to her feet. "Let's go downstairs now. I'm sure the guests are frightened."

Cat followed her, listening for trouble. The last time she'd dealt with a problem in the house, the creep had actually been one of the guests. This time, at least she knew the threat had come from outside the house. Cat wasn't sure which was better. She felt scared and longed for this whole thing to go away. "Buck up," she whispered. "Stop being a whiner."

Shauna looked back at her. "Are you okay?"

Cat took a deep breath and pushed the fear away. This was her house. No one was going to make her afraid in her own house. She grabbed a heavy iron statue from the table in the hallway. "I'm fine. Let's go downstairs."

Softly and slowly, they descended one flight to the floor that held the guest rooms. Cora and Connie stood in the hallway, and Kelly was with Seth farther down the hall. Lisa appeared in the doorway, and Kelly motioned her toward the other women, a finger on her lips indicating that Lisa should be quiet. The last room was Jessi's. Kelly knocked quietly, then opened the door. Cat could see Seth's reaction when he saw the empty room. He rushed inside, then came back out and headed directly to Cat.

Flashing lights from the police cruisers filled the street-side windows. Seth glanced at Cat before making his way downstairs to let Uncle Pete in. "Jessi's not in her room. She's gone."

"Stay with the guests," Cat glanced at Shauna. "I'm going downstairs to check the other rooms."

Uncle Pete stood in the lobby, directing officers to check the rooms. When Cat moved toward the study, he called out, "Where do you think you're going?"

Cat froze at the edge of the steps. "Jessi's not in her room. I wanted to check the study."

He shook his head and waved her toward him. "Come stand by me. Brenden will go check the study."

"But I'm right here."

"Cat." In one word, her uncle stopped her in her tracks. She'd heard that tone before.

Sighing, she turned away from the hallway and walked toward her uncle. "I'm sure she's just working. Maybe she's in the attic writing."

As if she'd called her, Jessi came out of the hallway that led to the study. She held a cup in her hand and her eyes widened as she noticed Brenden walking toward her, dressed in his police uniform.

"Oh my God. What happened? Did someone get hurt?" Jessi hurried toward Cat.

Cat took a deep breath. At least Jessi was okay. She motioned to the bench. "Sit down there for a minute. I need to talk to my uncle."

Cat and Seth gathered around Uncle Pete. He lowered his voice and asked Seth, "Tell me what happened."

Seth pointed to the front door. "The sensor went off about twelve forty-five. I woke Cat and told her to call you. We gathered the guests together on the second floor, but Jessi wasn't there."

"It is a writer's retreat." Cat turned toward Jessi. "Hey, did you go outside a few minutes ago?"

Jessi gripped her coffee cup and shook her head. "No. I've been writing since about ten thirty. I couldn't sleep, so I came down and was working in the study. It's a great desk. The chair is really comfortable. I started to get sleepy, so I thought I'd fill my cup with the last of the coffee. Is this all because I wasn't in bed?"

"No. You didn't do anything wrong." Cat turned back to her uncle. "So someone at least tried to break into the house. Maybe they didn't actually get inside?"

"Take Jessi back upstairs and send the guests back to their rooms. I'll send Irene up with you to clear each room before they go back in. Then you three wait for me in the kitchen."

Cat followed her uncle's instructions, following Sara upstairs. When Shauna approached her, she waved her off. "Let's get everyone settled first. Jessi? You're in the last room, right?"

Cat worked with Irene as the officer cleared each area and then Cat invited each guest back to their room. Jessi sank onto the bed and Cat gave her an encouraging smile. "Go to sleep. We'll talk in the morning."

"I'm exhausted." The girl curled up on the bed. Cat wanted to cross over and cover her with a blanket. Instead, she turned off the lights and closed the door. Connie's room was next, and Irene had already cleared it.

"This is so exciting. You really know how to throw a writers' retreat." Connie patted Cat's arm as she walked toward her room. "I may just have to write a contemporary story after this. Maybe even a romantic suspense."

Cat couldn't believe how comfortable the women were with the middle-of-the-night disruption. Writers. You could never tell what was going on in their heads.

Cora was the last one waiting for Irene to clear her room. She pulled Cat aside. "Now, you don't worry about this. It's not your fault and you can't control what goes on."

"I don't need mothering but thank you." Cat smiled at Cora. "I just hope your retreat has been worthwhile. I apologize for the distractions."

"You are kidding, right? Distractions make the writer's life." Before she stepped into her own room, Cora glanced down at Jessi's door. "That poor girl, someone really wants to mess with her life."

By the time Cat got back downstairs, Uncle Pete had cleared the house and was standing talking to Seth. "I think someone tried to get in but didn't make it past the security on the door. We're doing a canvass of the neighborhood, but most people were probably asleep when this happened."

"Do you think it was just random?" Seth put an arm around Cat as she joined the group.

"Normally, I'd say yes. A lot of the kids walk this way back from Bernie's to the dorms. I've had reports of them just going into houses and passing out on the first available couch." He shrugged. "But with what's going on? Being random seems unlikely. Keep an eye out on that girl, and I'm going to suggest to her family that she go home after the retreat is over. The security at the dorms isn't going to keep her safe."

"She's not going to like that," Cat stated, fear gripping her stomach. She had come to care for the kid. "And I'm not sure she's any safer there."

"Maybe I'll figure out what's going on before your retreat ends. What, I have all of two days to find out who killed Danielle and why someone is trying to at least mess with Jessi." He straightened his jacket. "I have to go back to my lists of possible suspects now. I was really betting on Keith for this whole thing. I need some sleep. Let's button this up and all go to bed."

Cat nodded and watched as the police officers who had gone over her entire house in less than thirty minutes started returning to their cars. Her uncle was the last to leave. He paused as he closed the door and then pointed to the lock. Cat smiled. Uncle Pete used to do that when he came over for dinner on nights Michael was out of town. Now instead of just a lock on the door, she had a security system that sent alarms to their phones when something was happening.

She didn't feel much safer.

Friday morning, Cat was still lying in bed trying to push the sleep from her eyes when a knock sounded at her door. She sat up and grabbed her robe. Pulling it on, she moved toward the door. "Just a minute."

Standing outside her room was a visibly upset Jessi. "I'm sorry to bother you, but I really need to talk to someone. Cora's nice, but she tries to fix everything. I just need a sounding board, do you mind?"

Cat opened the door. "Come on in. Or we could go downstairs and grab coffee if you'd rather."

Jessi plopped down on the bench on the edge of Cat's bed. "That's okay. I couldn't sleep last night, so I'm a little wired this morning. I'll probably try to take a nap after the bookseller talks."

Cat smoothed the comforter over the bed and sat in the middle watching Jessi. "It's your retreat."

"You always say that. Like we can just come into your life for a week and uproot it with no consequences." Jessi pulled back her blond hair. "I'm so sorry my life has inconvenienced you this week."

Cat glanced at the clock. It wasn't quite six a.m. Jessi was on a roll already this morning. "Don't worry about me or Shauna or Seth. We're here to make your week the best it can be. I'm sorry that life issues have made it hard for you to truly get into the retreat spirit. From money issues, boyfriend problems, and, of course, Danielle's death, you've been a rock through this entire week. I'll tell you that I wouldn't have been able to be as calm and levelheaded as you've been."

Jessi laughed. "I don't think Max would call our fight me being levelheaded."

Cat curled her legs up underneath her. "Relationships are hard. Especially when you're betrayed. You didn't grab a hand weight and try to hit him. I'd call that restrained."

"The last thing I needed was to attack someone. Then Chief Edmond would be inviting me to his jail retreat and really looking at me for Danielle's death. I know he thinks I'm a spoiled rich kid, but honestly, the money doesn't mean that much to me. I just want to be comfortable, you know?"

Nodding, Cat knew exactly what Jessi was saying. Not that she'd ever had the chance to be one of the ultra-rich, but sometimes, that much money made more problems than it solved.

Jessi continued. "Anyway, after that mess with someone trying to break in last night, I got to thinking that maybe someone was actually trying to kill me instead of Danielle. I haven't asked your uncle—in fact, I'm kind of scared too—but what do you think? Am I in danger?"

Cat thought about how to play this. The girl needed to know to protect herself, but she didn't want to scare her on a maybe scenario. "Honestly? I don't know. But I would be very careful about going off on your own until Uncle Pete gets this solved. You're just going to call the bank today, right? Or maybe have the others come with you before lunch to visit the branch?"

Jessi's eyes widened. "I'd forgotten about that. Yeah, I guess I better handle that too. So much for a short nap for me."

"But you won't go alone." Cat watched the girl's face.

She held up a hand in some kind of salute. "I promise, on my honor, I will drag someone along with me to find out why the bank messed up my accounts."

"If the other women are busy, let me know. I'll walk with you." Cat couldn't hide the yawn, but she covered most of it with her hand.

"And that's my clue to get out of here." Jessi popped up off the bench.

Cat stood too. "No, don't go on my behalf. I'm just trying to wake up."

"I'm heading to the shower, then down for coffee. I've bugged you enough for the morning." She gave Cat a quick hug. "Thank you for helping me calm down. I feel so much better after talking to you."

Cat closed the door and headed into the bathroom to get ready for the day. She wasn't convinced that Jessi wasn't in danger, but apparently her words had calmed Jessi. She needed to think about everything and maybe pop into the gym again and talk to Max. If he was just the no-good boyfriend, then he could go off the list, at least as far as Jessi's safety was concerned.

She closed her eyes as the warm water tried to wash away her tension, but for some reason, something was nagging at her and making her even more anxious. Jessi had passed on the worry with one quick chat.

When Cat came into the kitchen, Shauna took one look at her and poured her a cup of coffee. "I was just about ready to bring coffee up to your office since I assumed you were working this morning."

"No such luck." She took the cup and sank down into a chair at the table. "Jessi came to talk to me this morning, and now she feels better and I feel worse."

"You have a habit of taking on others' problems." Shauna arranged two slices of French toast on a plate and slathered them with butter and syrup. She then set the plate in front of Cat. "Eat. You'll feel better."

The maple smell reminded her of Sunday mornings with her mom and dad. She would have said she wasn't hungry before entering the kitchen, but now her stomach gurgled in delight at the upcoming meal. "Thanks."

"Before you ask, Seth already ate. We had a perfectly polite and civilized discussion about the craziness last night. Even with the Peeping Tom the other night, Seth's convinced it was a student messing with us." Shauna took a sip of her coffee. "Sometimes he's just so practical, it's frustrating."

"But you're not as sure," Cat deduced from the look on her friend's face.

"The guy was staring into the kitchen right at me." She set the cup down and played with her spoon. "Honestly, I don't know what to think. But there's been too much happening in the last month to that girl. She loses her jewelry and finds out her best friend has been stealing it and another friend has been pawning the stuff. Then she loses that friend to what may be random violence or may have been a failed attempt on her own life. And that's not even bringing in the cheating boyfriend. I swear, Jessi needs a whole crop of new friends and business associates."

"I agree. And I should have told her that this morning during our talk. But she kept apologizing for the mistakes she'd made during the retreat. Like all this was her fault, just for being Jessi. I swear, she had some unhelpful messages drummed into her as a child."

"She looks so confident, but really, she's always trying to make everyone else happy. I guess I can understand her a little, at least. I'm probably a pot calling the kettle black." Shauna got up and made a second plate of French toast for herself.

"You're strong. Yes, you like taking care of people, but you also take care of yourself." Cat paused, wondering if she should say more. A knock came to the kitchen door.

Glancing through the window, Cat's heart sank. Martin Mathews stood outside the door. The guy was the last person she wanted to talk to or even let in her house. She turned toward Shauna. "Make sure Jessi's not going to pop in the kitchen, would you?"

"Do you want me to stay?" Shauna set her plate down on the counter. "Or call Pete? Or at least Seth?"

"I can deal with one wannabe gangster." Cat put on a smile, then went to open the door, hoping her words were true.

# CHAPTER 15

Martin Matthews stood in the doorway, his hands up in surrender. "Look, I know I told you I wouldn't come by again, but I need to talk to Jessi. Uncle Dante asked me to check in with her."

"I'm not sure I should let you." Cat leaned on the doorway, watching the young man in front of her. "I really don't want you in my house."

He ran a hand through his too-long blond hair. "I'm sorry. I know I was a jerk. I just heard about the break-in last night, and I want to make sure she's all right."

Cat's gaze narrowed. She lifted her hand to look at her watch. "It's just past seven and you've already heard about something that happened six hours ago?"

He shuffled his feet. "I kind of have people watching out for her. Especially after I heard about Danielle. I never trusted that chick. When I'd visit her at the dorms and Jessi wasn't looking, she got the strangest gleam in her eyes." He turned to Cat and smiled. "I know I've been a jerk, but can I just talk to her?"

Cat moved to unblock the doorway, then swept her arm out in a welcoming manner. "Wait here. I'll go and ask her if she wants to talk to you. Don't touch anything."

He plopped down in a chair, so much like Jessi had earlier that morning, Cat had to bite her lip to keep from smiling. He held up his hands. "I'll be right here. Touching nothing. Man, you know how to hold a grudge."

"You're lucky I didn't press charges on you."

He flushed. "Point taken."

In the hallway, Shauna was standing outside the kitchen door and rushed to her side. "You okay?"

"Fine. Where's Jessi? I told him I would let her know he wanted to talk to her." Cat rolled her eyes. "Although I don't know why. The kid is so full of himself."

"She's in the study. I can go get her."

Cat put a hand on her friend's arm. "Let me. Maybe I can soften the request a little."

"Then I'll just stay outside this door and make sure he stays in there." Shauna folded her arms and leaned against the wall, staring at the kitchen door.

"I'll be right back." Cat made her way to the study. Shauna was tough. She'd been as effective in moving out troublemakers as the bouncers in the bar where she used to work. If Martin tried anything, Cat was certain that he wouldn't get past the fiery redhead. Especially not in the mood she'd been in for the last few months.

She found the study door open. She paused at the doorway and glanced inside. Jessi was sitting with her feet curled under her in Michael's chair. A laptop rested on her lap, and a notebook and pen were on the desk in front of her. If Cat wanted to snap a picture of a day in the life of an author, she couldn't have staged it any better.

"Jessi? I hate to bother you, but do you have a minute?" Cat saw the flint of irritation of being interrupted on the girl's face, then she glanced at her watch and sighed.

Jessi hit some keys on her laptop, then closed it and put it on top of the notebook. "I need to get up and stretch anyway. I try not to sit more than an hour at a time. But I can get lost in the story. I have a watch that alerts me, but I'm not sure where it is."

Cat moved into the room and shut the door behind her, just in case any of the other guests decided to use the study this morning. She crossed over to the desk. "I'm just going to ask this, but you don't have to say yes. Remember that."

"You're making me a little nervous. What's going on?" Jessi's hand went to her hair and pushed it back away from her face. Cat had noticed the tell before. It's what the girl did when she was concerned about something or unsure of what was happening.

"It's not a bad thing. I just want you to understand you are under no obligation to see him."

"Who? Max? Is he here?" Jessi's eyes widened. "I can't believe he got the balls to try to fix this with me. The guy's such a loser."

"No, it's not Max." Cat held up a hand before

Jessi could guess again. "Martin Mathews is here, and he would like to talk to you."

Relief came over the girl in an instant, and Cat watched as Jessi's shoulders dropped into her more relaxed stance. "He's cool. Kind of full of himself, but he's part of Dante's family. You know, my mom's friend? He comes by once in a while just to chat. I wonder what he's doing here?"

"He heard about the break-in, and I think he just wants to make sure you're okay." Cat glanced toward the door. "Do you mind talking to him? He's in the kitchen. I can stay with you if you want me to."

"I don't care." Jessi glanced at her laptop and notes. "You mind if I keep those here? I'd like to finish up this chapter before I go figure out why my bank hates me."

"Saving your space?" Cat crossed over and opened the door for her.

Jessi caught up. "You better believe it. These women have rules, and if you don't mark your territory, it's up for grabs. I learned that the hard way on Monday. Connie commandeered the study and I had to beg to get my notebook out so I could keep working. Where's Martin?"

"In the kitchen." Cat followed her out of the study and into the hallway. When they got to the kitchen door, Shauna held it open for her. If Martin thought he was going to bully Jessi into doing something, he was going to have to go around both Cat and Shauna to get to her.

Martin sat in the same place Cat had left him, but this time, he had a plate of French toast in front of him and he was halfway through eating.

He looked up and grinned. "Whoever made this is a goddess. A food goddess. I swear, I'm moving in."

"Not in my lifetime." Cat pointed Jessi to a chair. "I thought I told you not to touch anything?"

"I didn't touch anything. Well, except the food. I was just hungry." He molded his face into a look of pity and innocence. "You wouldn't turn away a hungry child, would you?"

"Martin, you're such a user. You're not starving. Besides, I bet your debit card still works. You seem to always have money to burn." Jessi tried to grab the plate, but Martin held it up out of her reach.

"Sorry, kid, you're not getting this until I'm done. Seriously, who's the chef? This is better than the Diner's French toast, and I thought they were top notch." He took the last bite of the stolen breakfast, then stood and took the plate to the sink to wash. "I'd pay just to eat meals here. You're the lucky one, Jessi. I can't believe you get to spend all day with this kind of food."

"Can we get past the love fest? I don't have time to play your games, Martin. I have to go clear up a banking issue."

He turned and watched her. "Buying too many purses again?"

"No, I've been good." Jessi frowned and rubbed a spot on the table. "I must have messed up my accounting, but the last time I looked, I had tons in checking. There's no way I spent that in the last month. It's got to be a bank error."

"No weekend jaunts to the Caribbean?" Martin sat down next to her.

She slapped his arm. "I think I'd remember something like that. And before you ask, no, I don't do drugs. I don't know where that rumor came from, but according to both Max and Danielle, it's all over the school. I had more than one dealer come up and try to sell me stuff."

"Wait, you've never done drugs?" Cat thought about her talk with Jessi's money manager, what was his name? Darryl? Hadn't he insinuated something similar?

Martin laughed. "Jessi tried pot at a frat party her first year here. She choked, then went on to tell everyone how stupid they were for even trying it. She's a bit of a straight arrow in that area."

Jessi held her hand up in a salute. "They all called me Girl Scout after that party. And since then, I haven't been invited to the really wacked-out ones. Anyway, as fun as chatting has been, why are you here, Martin?"

As they talked, Shauna and Cat stood in the corner. Shauna leaned close, then asked, "So now the rumor of using drugs has been taken off the table. What do you think that Darryl guy was talking about?"

Cat looked over at the two, who seemed to be actually talking and not just rubbing each other the wrong way. "I don't know, but I think we should try to find out. If he'll actually tell me anything. He's supposed to be confidential with her dealings."

Jessi walked over and stood in front of the women.

"Cat, Martin's going to go with me to the bank. He's sure it's just a glitch. But sometimes, it's easier with a guy around. Stupid, I know, but true. I'd call my money guy, but I don't want to drag him down here from Boston if it's something I can take care of. I guess we all have to learn to adult sometime." She glanced at the clock. "If I don't get back before lunch, tell the group I'll meet them at Reno's at eleven thirty. I owe Cora a meal."

"Be careful, and if something weird is happening, call me." Cat watched as Martin pulled out his phone and appeared to check his messages.

"I think you need to be more specific. This week, a lot of weird crap has been happening." Jessi grinned. "I'll text you when I'm at Reno's. That way you don't have to worry."

"Thanks."

Cat and Shauna watched as the two left the house.

"Do you think she's safe with him?" Shauna asked as the door closed.

Cat considered the question. "If he fears his uncle, then yes, she's safe."

Shauna went back to her plate she'd left on the counter and put the cold food in the microwave. "Well, at least the kid knows good food. I was afraid he was serious about moving in with us. I'm not sure we could afford to keep food in the house if he was here."

"You *are* a food goddess." Cat grabbed a cup of coffee and a couple of cookies. "I'm heading up to my office to check email and maybe grab some words. The idea of a long-lost brother showing up for Tori is plugging away at my subconscious. Maybe I just found a new plot line for this book."

"You mean the book that's almost done?" Shauna leaned on the counter and watched her.

As Cat pushed the kitchen door open, she paused.

"It's not done until deadline. I thought you knew that about me?"

Laughter followed her into the hallway. Cat knew Shauna didn't think she was serious, but she was. Deadly serious. She quickly made it up the two flights of stairs and went into her office, closing the door behind her. Grabbing a notebook, she brainstormed all the ideas running around in her head about the story she was working on. Then, drained, she turned her focus to her email. She'd let the ideas percolate a little before inserting them into the current plot, but she thought she had a great addition to the series.

When that was done, she still had an hour to kill before Tammy from the bookstore came to talk to the group. She hoped Jessi would be back in time for that, but she guessed money issues took time to unknot. She put on her tennis shoes and made her way downstairs.

Popping her head into the kitchen, she saw Shauna on her laptop. "Hey, I'm running into town for an errand. If Tammy shows up before I get back, can you help get her set up? I should be back in plenty of time, but I don't want you caught off guard."

"Of course I can." Shauna considered Cat over the edge of the laptop. "You're not doing something that Pete is going to make you regret, right?"

"No. I'm just running in to check on something." Cat hurried out of the room so she wouldn't have to lie again. Besides, she *was* just running into town to check on something. Shauna didn't need to know what exactly she was checking on. Or should she say who?

The June morning was beautiful. Birds sang in the large oak trees that lined Warm Springs. Some of the houses still had the original hot springs heating system from when the houses were built. Cat's house had been renovated to a gas furnace before she'd bought the house. That was her one regret, that the house had been modernized. Although Shauna seemed to love the kitchen, so she guessed it wasn't all bad.

When she walked into the gym, Cindy shook her head. "Please tell me there's not going to be another fight? My boss told me I should have called the police the other day."

"There's not going to be a fight." Cat smiled, holding up her phone. "And if there is, I'll call Uncle Pete myself. I don't want to get you in trouble. I take it Max is here?"

"In the weight room like normal. I swear the trainers have told him to follow an actual schedule, but he thinks he knows everything. No wonder Jessi dumped him. The guy's a tool." She glanced around the open area of the gym. "You know the way, right? I'm working on the monthly billing, and if I stop, I have to log in and get all set up again. Their billing system is an antique."

"I know the way. Good luck with your project." Cat made her way through the empty cardio room. Every time she came into the gym, more machines were empty than actually being used. Didn't matter what time of day, or what day of the week. She wondered if the ratio changed during the first two weeks of January where everyone was on a weight loss challenge. She had to admit it, she was looking forward to Seth getting their private gym completed. If she was going to sweat, she might as well do it at home.

She walked through the small hallway that went past the locker rooms and then paused at the door to the gym. Max was alone, sitting on a bench, his elbows on his knees and his head in his hands. He must have heard her footsteps because he jumped up and spun around to face her. Disappointment filled his face.

"What are you doing here?" He picked up a towel and wiped his face.

Cat didn't think he had any sweat to wipe away, but she had seen tears in his eyes. "I wanted to ask you about Jessi."

"What about her?" He sank back onto the bench. "She and I are done. You heard what she said."

"You were sleeping with her best friend." Cat leaned on the doorway, watching for a reaction. Instead of the defiance she thought she'd hear, Max let out a sigh.

Running his hand through his hair, he nodded. "I really screwed that up. I mean, I never thought Jessi would even care. It's not an excuse, but Danielle threw herself at me. And then when Jessi asked for a break at the beginning of summer, I thought maybe she wanted to sow some wild oats too. I'd already started seeing Danielle on the side by then. I should have known better. That girl is as loyal as you can get. And I blew it."

"I've heard that Danielle thought you were going to ask her to marry her."

"You've got to be kidding. Like I could take her back to introduce her to my family? No way. Jessi has the right creds for my mother. Danielle wouldn't have made it a week." He shook his head. "I know she kept pushing me about staying together. Like she could drive up to Harvard and see me. But I told her after September, this was over. That I had to get back to my real life."

"That must have made her feel special." Cat hated this guy. She had hoped he had killed Danielle because he deserved to be in jail just because he was a jerk. But she was losing that hope. All she saw was a spoiled little rich boy who didn't want to be alone when his girlfriend wanted some time.

"I know. I'm a jerk. I've always been a jerk." He rubbed his neck. "Frankly, I was shocked when Jessi said yes to our first date. I should have changed my ways then, but hindsight, you know."

Cat decided to be direct. "Did you kill Danielle? Or should I say, arrange for her death?"

Shock and grief filled his face. "No. You can't believe that. Tell me Jessi doesn't think that. I know Danielle was a horrible friend to her, but Jessi, she loved her like a sister."

"Do you know who would want Danielle dead?"

Max shrugged and a touch of pink covered his cheeks. "Honestly? I didn't really listen when she talked, and, man, the girl loved to talk. When I finally realized she was planning us a future, I decided to break it off early. I hadn't seen her in two weeks."

Cat decided to turn the tables a bit. "Do you know who would want Jessi dead?"

Fear filled his eyes and he jumped up. "Jessi's in danger? Where is she? I'll get her a room at my parents' house. No one will find her there."

Cat was shocked at the quick protection reflex she'd just witnessed. She stood staring at him. "You really care about her."

"I do. Is she safe?" He stood, ready to take off to save his ex-girlfriend.

"For now." Cat knew she wasn't going to get any more from the guy. He loved Jessi. He'd screwed up their relationship, but that hadn't kept him from wanting to save her. "I don't know if she can ever forgive you for what you did, but you might want to try to be friends. She doesn't have a lot of real friends who care about her."

Max stared at her. "You seem to know her well."

"Take care, Max." Cat left the room and made her way out of the gym, waving at Cindy as she passed by her desk.

She didn't know who had killed Danielle, or who was after Jessi and why, but she knew one thing. Even if she didn't like him one bit. Max Trandor, wasn't the one who was trying to kill Jessi. And Cat didn't believe he had it in him to kill Danielle just to protect his relationship with Jessi. One more possible suspect off her list.

Her detective skills were totally off base with this murder. Maybe she should stick to writing books where she could control the characters and what they did and said.

Like that ever happened.

# CHAPTER 16

When she got back to the house, Tammy Jones, owner of the Written Word, Aspen Hills's only bookstore, was setting up a table in the living room. Cat picked up one of the books she had unpacked. "I appreciate you bringing in craft books to sell. I always tell them to go visit your store, but the week goes by fast."

"I always bring books to these things. Mostly they are from local authors or focused on local history. Of course, for your groups I'm always looking for the next big craft books. I sell enough to make it worthwhile." Tammy set down the box and moved closer, her arms outstretched. "How have you been? I haven't seen you since last month. I hope that means you've been writing."

Cat laughed and gave her a quick hug. "I have been writing. I'm close to deadline, so the next week or so, I'll be locked in my office, but it's nice to have the retreat to force me to take a break now and then."

"I'd bet that you've gotten words down, even this week." Tammy eyed her carefully. Then she lowered her voice. "I have a message from Dante for you."

"You what?"

She passed a white note folded in two to Cat. "He emailed me and asked me to print this and give it to you. I didn't read it. He asked me not to and, well, he's a really good customer."

"I'm sorry he imposed on you this way." Cat wanted to kill Dante. What was he thinking with all the cat-and-mouse games?

"Oh, it's not an imposition. I guess he knew I was coming here today anyway." Tammy went back to setting up her display. She emptied out the last of the boxes and tucked them under the table. Then she sat her prepared notes on the lectern and glanced around. "I think that does it. Do you mind if I help myself to some coffee and a cookie?"

"Go ahead. In fact, some of the group is probably in there getting refueled before your talk." Cat hesitated. "Do you know Jessi Ball? She's our Covington student this session."

"Of course. That girl is a reader. She comes in probably once a week to get one or two books. I don't know how she has time to read so much. She works and takes classes. I would think someone that pretty would be going out and finding the one."

"You're a romantic." Cat smiled as Tammy made her way out of the living room.

Tammy paused at the door. "Some of us have to be romantics and dreamers. The real world is too hard and negative sometimes. Having dreamers keeps it sane."

She waited for Tammy to leave the room before she opened the note and started reading.

> DEAR CATHERINE,
> FORGIVE ME FOR THE SUBTERFUGE. I DIDN'T WANT THIS INFORMATION TO FALL INTO THE WRONG HANDS, AND I KNOW I CAN TRUST MISS JONES. IF YOU EVER NEED TO REACH ME, JUST LET HER KNOW, SHE CAN REACH ME AT ANY TIME. BUT THAT'S NOT WHAT I NEEDED TO TELL YOU. IT DOESN'T SEEM THAT JESSI IS BEING TARGETED BY THE FAMILY, OR ANY OTHER FAMILY, AT LEAST THAT'S WHAT I'M HEARING. I'M STILL NOT SURE SHE'S SAFE, BUT I SHOULD KNOW MORE BY THE END OF THE WEEK. I'LL COME AND GET HER MY-SELF ON SUNDAY. I DON'T KNOW IF I'LL BRING HER HERE TO BOSTON OR JUST INVITE HER TO STAY AT MY HOUSE ON WARM SPRINGS. I'M NOT SURE I'M READY TO SHARE MY HOME WITH SUCH A VIBRANT YOUNG WOMAN, BUT THE SACRIFICES WE TAKE FOR THOSE WE CONSIDER FAMILY. OF COURSE, YOU KNOW ALL ABOUT SACRIFICE. ANYWAY, JUST KEEP AN EYE OUT FOR JESSI, AND I'LL BE THERE ON SUNDAY TO TAKE HER OFF YOUR HANDS. THANK YOU FOR THIS, CATHERINE. I AM IN YOUR DEBT.
> ALWAYS, DANTE

Cat folded the note and tucked it in the back pocket of her jeans. She wasn't sure what to do with the information. At least Jessi wasn't being targeted by the family. It had been a long shot, but in Aspen Hills, it was something you needed to scratch off the list. Glancing around the living room, she decided to go join Tammy in grabbing some coffee.

As Cat crossed through the lobby, Jessi burst through the front door. "You won't believe what happened."

"We're just getting ready for Tammy's program. I'm glad you're back." She crossed over to where Jessi stood and lowered her voice so she wouldn't be heard in the dining room. "Is this about the visit to the bank?"

Jessi looked around, then led Cat to the bench in the foyer by the window. "Someone transferred all my money out of my accounts. It's been happening slowly over the last year. The manager says he doesn't know how it even happened. Apparently, it's not from the debit card I have, so they know it's not me."

"Did someone get another card for your account?" All Cat could think of was this was probably one more betrayal from Danielle. "Do they know where?"

"The bank is doing a full audit. They had me set up a new account, and I called Mom to give me enough to get me by until they figure this out." Jessi wiped at her eyes.

"It's only money." Cat put a hand on the girl's shoulder to comfort her. But when Jessi looked at her, she was smiling.

"You don't understand. She believed me. For months it's been like I'm this debutante girl who only wants to spend money. I told her I wasn't being reckless, but she didn't believe me. Now she does." She wiped away her tears. "She believes me."

Cat wondered if Dante's unexpected visit home had something to do with Jessi's mother's change of heart around her daughter's actions, but she didn't want to ruin the girl's good mood. "I'm happy for you. Well, it's too bad it had to go to this extreme, but I'm glad she is supporting you now."

"I know. Isn't it great?" She glanced up and saw the other guests moving to the living room. Jumping up, she spun around in a circle. "I better go join them. I'm so glad I can talk to you."

As Jessi joined the group heading toward the living room, Cat leaned her head against the window and closed her eyes. Poor little rich girl, she mused. Jessi was a lovely young woman who deserved to be treated with respect and dignity. Her boyfriend and her best friend had betrayed her. But at least now her family was stepping up and being there for her. She thought about Danielle's death. If it wasn't Max, maybe someone was playing with the ghosts of the past. Only one person was that vested in the killings at Outlaw.

The new owner of the town. She needed to do more research. And there was one woman who had her pulse on the gossip trail in Aspen Hills. Lucky, or unlucky, for Cat, she lived next door. She poked her head into the kitchen and saw Shauna stirring what appeared to be another soup creation for lunch. From the smell in the kitchen, it had something to do with chicken. "Hey, do you have some cookies I can snag?"

"Sure. Why are we out in the dining room?"

Shauna set down the spoon and headed to the cabinet to grab a plate.

"No plate. I need a Tupperware container." She crossed the room and grabbed one out of the cabinet and handed it to Shauna. "Maybe six? Or a dozen if they're small?"

"When have you ever known me to make a small cookie? Except of course during the holidays. I do so many gift baskets, if I didn't make them small we'd be broke." She layered twelve pecan shortbread cookies in the container. "Who are you trying to bribe?"

"Mrs. Rice. I need some gossip." Cat shrugged off Shauna's laughter. "What? You know if anything happened in this town, she'd know about it."

Shauna handed her the container. "Just don't trade off my job for your information. I kind of like working here."

Cat went out the back door and headed to the sidewalk. Mrs. Rice would probably be inside, cleaning the house that no one but her got dirty. Cat wondered what she would do all day without Seth, Shauna, and Uncle Pete to talk to, not to mention the retreat. She might be as starving for conversation as her neighbor seemed to be every time she caught Cat walking by. Her mother would have told her to be generous with her older neighbor. Cat tried, really. She put on a smile and was about to knock on the door when it swung open.

"I thought that was you walking up my path. I told Mr. Peeps that our neighbor Catherine was coming for tea, and he took off and hid upstairs. I don't think Mr. Peeps cares for you, my dear." Mrs.

Rice stood in a cotton shirt dress and fuzzy slippers. "I've got bridge tonight with the girls, so come in quick and let's get this over with."

"Get what over with?" Cat didn't know who Mr. Peeps was and really didn't want to ask. She followed Mrs. Rice into the dark hallway. All of the blinds were closed. How she'd known she was coming, Cat couldn't guess. Unless she had cameras set up. Paul Quinn had been selling camera security systems up until a few months ago. Mrs. Rice could have been one of his victims. Or customers. It all depended on how you looked at it.

Mrs. Rice turned into an open doorway where light filtered out into the hallway. "Your monthly visit. I'm sure your mother must have talked you into coming and visiting. She was always so friendly."

"My mother speaks highly of you, but no, she's not why I'm here." Although—Cat kicked herself—now that Mrs. Rice had it in her head that Cat should be visiting, she would probably get a guilt call in the next week or so.

Mrs. Rice sat on a sofa covered with plastic. It squeaked when she sat. "Oh, well, then, tell me what's going on. Do you need help?"

Cat opened the container of cookies and held it out to Mrs. Rice. "Shauna sent these over. She thought you might enjoy them. It's a new recipe she's trying out."

She lifted her eyebrows and sniffed at the container. Then she lifted a cookie out and held it under her nose. "They look attractive and smell good."

"I've had one, they taste even better." Cat smiled

and perched on the edge of the sofa. It crackled under her weight. She held back a grin as Mrs. Rice bit into the cookie and the joy filled her eyes. It was time to ask. "So I was wondering what you knew about Joseph John Robertson? He grew up here, didn't he?"

Now those eyes gleamed. "Yes, he did. The boy was a joy to his parents, but honestly, I thought he was a little shit."

"You knew the family?" Cat kept her questions short, to give Mrs. Rice room to reminisce.

"Of course. They lived just down the street. In the house your friend owns." Mrs. Rice smiled deviously when she saw Cat's confusion. "You know, Dante Cornelio? He's always over at your house, visiting. I was sure you were all friends."

"Oh, yes, I didn't realize." Cat let the sentence fall. Obviously, Mrs. Rice had been keeping a closer eye on the house and their comings and goings than she'd known. "They owned Dante's house? Why did they sell?"

Mrs. Rice picked up a second cookie and frowned. "I believe Joseph John sold it as soon as his mother went into a facility. His dad had passed the year before, and poor Penelope just wilted. She didn't last much longer, especially not in that place."

He sold the family home but bought a ghost town? The guy had a weird way of holding on to history. Cat decided to be polite. "Maybe the memories were too close in the house."

"He wanted the money. The man has always been about the money. Even when he was a kid."

Mrs. Rice shook her head. "It was disgraceful. Of course, he didn't have time to change his mind. As soon as it went up for sale, the Cornelio family bought it to use when they came into town for their college visits. Then Dante took it over when he graduated."

Cat took one of the cookies and took a bite. She almost choked when she saw the glare she got from her neighbor. "I guess I didn't realize he was from Aspen Hills."

"If you read his official bio, he's not. He claims to be from Denver. And yes, the boy was born there, but he spent his first eighteen years here in Aspen Hills. Sometimes children don't realize what they have until it's gone. He bought that old town right after he sold the house. Everyone thought he was crazy, but he's turned even that money pit into a profitable business. I hear he has three more in different states in various stages of development. I guess he realized the value of history, finally. But he still only sees it in terms of money, not emotion."

Cat wasn't sure how to ask, so she just blurted it out. "You don't think he had anything to do with the other murders there, do you?"

"Of course not. He would have been maybe twenty and off to college when the last girl was killed. Well, the last girl before this one last week. You can't tell me your uncle is really looking at Joseph John for this murder? He's probably the most non-physical man I've ever met. In fact, I'm not sure I've ever seen him with a woman. He tends to enjoy one-night stands, from what I hear.

Killing someone would be such a commitment for him. Besides, it would interfere with business. Nothing interferes with his business."

Cat said her goodbyes and then walked back to the house. Shauna was still on her laptop when she came into the kitchen. "You find out what you needed to know?"

"Not really. More questions than I had, I guess. Did you know that Joseph John's family lived down the street in what's now Dante's house?" Cat grabbed a water from the fridge and sat at the table.

"Really? I thought he was from Denver. Kevin took me to a party he gave last Christmas. It was a huge house in the old part of Denver. I'm sure he said his family had owned it for generations." Shauna hit some keys on her laptop. Then she turned the computer toward Cat. "Here, he did an article for *Denver Homes and Gardens*. He opens with a statement that the house has been held in his family for years."

"Mrs. Rice said he was born there. Maybe they had two houses?" Cat scanned the article. The picture showed Joseph John in front of what looked like an old plantation-style house, his arms crossed. The title of the article was "Family History Is Big Business." She passed the laptop back to Shauna. "Why didn't the journalist research where he grew up? The article reads like it was all from the real estate mogul's interview."

"Good question." Shauna started looking for something on her computer, then frowned. "The writer resigned and moved a month after the piece was published. It doesn't say why."

Cat picked up the notebook in the middle of the table and ripped off a sheet of paper. "What's the reporter's name? Does it say where she was going?"

"Nothing. Just a thank you for her years of service." Shauna closed the laptop. "Maybe she retired?"

"Maybe. I wonder if Miss Applebome knows her. She seems to know a lot of writers in the area." Cat folded the paper and put it in her back pocket. She felt the note from Dante and thought about sharing it with Shauna.

"I have to tell you something." She squirmed under Shauna's gaze. "Tammy brought me a note from Dante."

"What? Doesn't he know how to use a phone?" Shauna shook her head. "First the guy just appears in Michael's study waiting for you, then he's sending secret missives to the bookseller? You know with all this undercover stuff, he's making it look like there's more going on with the two of you than just friendship."

"Tell me about it. Now Tammy thinks we're in collusion together on this whole thing. The only thing holding her back from telling everyone in town is how good a customer Dante is to her store." Cat put the paper on the table. "According to this, Jessi wasn't being targeted by the Mob. So that's one suspect off the list. Well, maybe not for Danielle's murder."

Shauna read the letter, twice. Then she pushed it back to Cat. "I'd put that away. Seth's uncomfortable enough with your relationship with Dante.

Now he's sending you secret messages? It would be hard to swallow."

"I know, but I'm going to tell Uncle Pete what he said and then burn this in the fireplace. I hate keeping secrets."

"Trust me, all this one would do is cause hard feelings. And if you're not interested in Dante . . ." Shauna paused until Cat nodded. "Then it's better being water under the bridge."

"I'll think about it. The last time I tried to keep something about Dante a secret from Seth, he was across the street, watching us talk." Cat glanced at the clock. Ten thirty. She could still pop into Tammy's session and be the perfect host instead of pretending to be an investigator. "I'm heading into the living room. Let me know when you want to have lunch."

When she got to the hallway, she paused and pulled out both sheets of paper, rereading Dante's message. She was going to share the information with Uncle Pete. So why did she feel that withholding it was lying to Seth?

Because she was?

Shoving the papers back into her pocket, she took a deep breath and headed to the living room. She had two more days to play hostess, and she owed it to her guests to focus on their retreat, not who killed Danielle. Other people, like Uncle Pete, were looking into that. And Dante, she added as she walked into a discussion she'd heard many times.

As she walked in and took a seat near the back, Tammy gave her a knowing look. A look that said,

We share a secret. Cat pretended not to understand the significance and turned away, looking out the back window. She hated that she held this secret with Tammy and wished she could just stand up and tell everyone. But sometimes, secrets were best held close to your heart.

She felt the papers stuffed in her back pocket and grinned. Or close to your butt. Either way.

# CHAPTER 17

Cat and Lisa were chatting about the state of the book business as the group started gathering in the lobby for their next-to-last lunch together at Reno's. The house phone rang, echoing in the almost empty foyer.

"Better get that, it's probably someone making a reservation at next month's retreat," Lisa said to Cat. "Or do you want Shauna to handle it?"

"Shauna just ran up to her room. Sorry, I guess I'll have to answer. But hold that thought, I think it's an interesting take." She crossed over to the desk and picked up the phone. "Warm Springs Writers' Resort, how may I help you?"

"Hi, Catherine. This is Bob Nagel from the bank. I just needed to chat with Jessi a moment, is she there? I hate to bother you, but I tried calling her cell and it went right to voice mail. There's been an incident and I wanted to make sure she hadn't made a mistake and was using the wrong card and withdrawing the money before I finalize the trace." The bank manager's voice seemed strained and tired. Kind of like her uncle had the other night.

"Sure, you just caught her. They just had a session with Tammy Jones from the Written Word. I'm sure that's why she turned off her phone. Hold on a second." She glanced around the lobby and was about to ask Lisa to run upstairs to get Jessi, when she saw her bouncing down the stairs. "Jessi, you have a call."

The girl froze at the bottom of the steps. "Me? Who would be calling me here at the retreat?"

"It's the bank manager." Cat waved her over. "Come talk to him."

The room quieted and Cat noticed Lisa and the other women moved into the dining room to give Jessi her privacy for the call. They all acted more like sisters to her than acquaintances who had just met on Sunday. Cat waved the still-frozen Jessi to the phone. "He just wants to ask you something."

"Okay," Jessi moved toward her, but her voice hadn't sounded as strong as it had during the lecture when she asked Tammy all kinds of insightful questions. This subject had her rattled. Cat wondered if she still thought there was a chance her brother or someone else in the family was behind the disappearance of her money.

Cat handed her the phone and stepped away. She saw the fear in Jessi's eyes. "I'll be in the dining room with the others, waiting."

Jessi swallowed, then focused on the call. "This is Jessi Ball." Cat heard the pause, then a short laugh. "Hi, Mr. Nagel. Of course I remember you . . ."

Relaxing quite a bit, Cat entered the dining room and went to pour a cup of coffee. When she turned with the cup up to her lips, she saw all the eyes on her. "What?"

"Is Jessi okay?" Cora took her role as mother hen seriously.

Cat sat at the table where the others gathered, worried hands clasped together on the table in front of each woman. "She's talking to the bank. I'm sure she'll update you as soon as she gets off. Don't worry. You all look like something bad is going to happen."

"With that girl's track record? She'll be lucky if her dorm room doesn't spontaneously combust. She's had a bad week." Connie shrugged when everyone stared at her. "What? You all are thinking the same thing."

Cat nodded. "Jessi has had more than her share of blows this week, but she's strong, and it's better she knows this now than when she thought everything was fine before."

"Exactly. At least she can have a plan for the future when she knows the whole story." Connie stood and grabbed a cookie. "It's when they don't tell you anything that you get sideswiped."

Cat assumed Connie was talking about her husband's illness that had taken him away from her. The woman had a strong constitution. No wonder Shauna was enjoying talking to her and getting back on track after losing Kevin.

No one said anything, but Cat saw the gentle pat on the arm that Cora gave Connie when she returned to the table with the chocolate chip cookie. Connie sent her a smile, then glanced around the table. "I know it will go right to my hips, but I don't care. I've gained ten pounds this week just from my cookie addiction. I'm going cold turkey as soon as I get home, so you all might want to tread carefully around the critique table next Thursday. I might not take kindly to your valid suggestions."

"You're always grumpy when we tell you the work needs something." Kelly laughed as she eased back into her chair, the tension from the earlier moment gone as quickly as it had come over the group. "You should see her, Cat. She grumbles about how stupid we all are all night after her turn to workshop a piece. Then the next week, she comes back and tells us we were all brilliant."

"I don't think I've ever said brilliant." Connie leaned over to fake whisper the next to Cat. "Sometimes I just let them think I changed something due to their comments. Sometimes I just let it be."

Laughter lit up the room at that comment, and Cat smiled. Writers were the best people in the world to hang out with. They wanted to talk about everything and nothing. The chatter dropped as Jessi walked into the room.

She held up her hands. "Someone tried to access the old account just a few minutes ago. Five thousand dollars. I guess they didn't realize they'd drained the account with the last withdrawal. The bank manager just wanted to confirm that I hadn't initiated it myself."

Kelly let out a whistle. "Five K? What did they think you were buying? A cruise for all your new friends?"

Cora laughed. "It's been a while since you've

been on a cruise, I can tell. Five thousand would take probably two of us, maybe three, but not the whole group."

"Who said you were invited?" Kelly shot back as she stood. "I'm starving, let's get going."

"Sounds like a plan." Cora stood, and as she walked by Jessi, she paused. "You still want to go?"

"Definitely. I'm starving too." Jessi glanced at Cat. "I just want to talk to Cat a second. I'll catch up."

"As slow as Connie walks, I don't think we'll get far." Cora winked at Cat and Jessi. "Come on, you old women. Let's go get some lunch."

Jessi waited for the room to clear, then turned back to Cat. "He thinks it's a good thing. Like they can really catch this guy now. I tried calling Darryl to let him know what's happening, but he's not answering. So if he calls here, could you let him know what's going on?"

"Are you sure? I mean, I can ask him to call your cell."

A smile curved Jessi's lips. "Actually, it's upstairs on the charger. I forgot to plug it in last night. I'm sure he's in some sort of meeting. He probably won't call me until Monday. He likes to take off early on Fridays. I guess he has a cabin in Tahoe."

Cat walked Jessi out to the door and waved to her as she jogged toward town and to meet up with the group. When she hit the street, a black car zoomed by and swerved up on the sidewalk. Jessi had just paused at Mrs. Rice's gate, and when the old woman pointed to the street in horror, she jumped the little fence and landed in the middle of the yard.

The car hadn't expected her to stop walking

and skimmed the fence line, tearing up the petunias Mrs. Rice had planted that spring. It swerved back on the street and sped away. Cat ran over to Jessi, dialing 911 on her phone as she did. When the dispatcher answered, Cat spurted out the description and what she'd seen on the license plate.

"Calm down, what happened?" On the other end of the phone, Katie tried to take charge of the situation.

"A car tried to run down Jessi Ball. I'm checking her out now to see if she needs medical attention, but you need to get a cruiser on Warm Springs and see if you can track that jerk down." Cat paused as she saw Jessi stand up next to Mrs. Rice. "Are you okay?"

"Fine." Jessi ran her hands down her jeans-clad legs. "I don't think I even have grass burns thanks to Mrs. Rice. She saved me."

Cat turned to Mrs. Rice. "Did you see what happened?"

"A car was sitting down the street for the last ten minutes, waiting, its engine on. I called it in, but no one came." Mrs. Rice smoothed Jessi's hair. "Relax now, it's all over. Breathe."

Cat turned away and spoke quietly into the phone. "Mrs. Rice called in the car a few minutes ago. She gave you a full plate."

"Hold on, I'll send that information to the car I just dispatched. Are you sure you don't need medical?"

"We're good. Hey, is my uncle in the station?"

A pause came over the phone. "Yes, he is."

"Have him call me." Cat hung up the phone and dialed another number. When she reached

Dante's voice mail, she left a quick message. "She's not safe here. Someone just tried to run her over with a car."

She turned back to Jessi and Mrs. Rice, but before she could move closer, her phone rang. She didn't recognize the number. "Hello?"

"Tell Jessi we got put in the back room. I guess they think we're too loud or something." Cora giggled over the phone. "I guess they know us too well, right?"

Cat made eye contact with Jessi. "I'm not sure she's coming."

"Darn, I already did an order for her. Does she want me to make it to go?"

"Is that Cora?" When Cat nodded, Jessi ran her hands over her face. "Tell her I'll be right there."

"Are you sure? You may be in shock." Cat didn't see any visible injuries, but Jessi had hit the ground hard after she'd jumped the fence. Had she landed on the rock path to the house, there would had been some cuts, maybe even a broken bone. Instead, she'd landed on the soft grass.

"What's going on?" Cora's concerned voice came over the phone.

"I'm going to eat lunch. No one is going to stop me." Jessi brushed off the grass from her jeans. "I'm a Ball. I'm strong and determined. And I don't scare easily."

Cat saw a layer of steel in the young woman she hadn't seen yet this week. She guessed that this was one too many attacks on her well-being. Now Jessi was mad. Cat nodded and answered Cora. "She'll be right there. I'm walking with her."

Cat hung up before Cora could ask any questions. She turned to Mrs. Rice. "If my uncle shows up, let him know that Jessi's at Reno's Pizza eating lunch. I'll be home in a few minutes after I make sure she gets there this time."

As they walked down the sidewalk, Jessi didn't look at Cat but spoke anyway. "You don't have to do this. I don't want you hurt."

"They tried, they missed. They're on the way out of town. You know they can't try again. They're thinking you're at either the police station or the hospital by now. No one would suspect you were one of the ladies who lunch at Reno's." Cat took a deep breath as they passed a flowering apple tree. The fragrance of the blooms was slight, because the tree did actually produce fruit, but she could still smell the sweetness.

"So you're hiding me in plain sight." Jessi grinned but she sobered immediately. "I like your reasoning. Seriously, can they just give me a break? First Danielle, then Max, then the jewelry, and don't forget the money. Someone has it out for me, or a whole bunch of someones, and this is just the next battle."

"You have had a horrible week." They stood at the one light and crosswalk, waiting for the light to change. Reno's Pizza was on the other side, and all Cat wanted to do was go inside with Jessi and have a beer. Instead, when they crossed the street, she paused at the doorway. "Don't be alone, and watch out for cars, flying bullets, and any other weird thing you don't expect. I think you're safe right now, but I've called in reinforcements."

"Don't tell me you called Dante. Seriously, I

hate it when he gets involved." Jessi shook her head. "You know he'll call my mother."

"Jessi, this is serious. You need to be protected until Uncle Pete can figure this out." Cat studied Jessi's face. "I could call Uncle Pete and you could get a ride in a police car home. Would that make you feel better?"

"No." Jessi sounded like a petulant child. "I'll be careful. And thanks, Cat. I know you don't typically have this kind of disruption at your retreats."

"I wouldn't say that." Apparently, Jessi hadn't heard the gossip about Warm Springs Writers' Retreat being a murder haven. Or maybe she thought murder wasn't such a big deal. "You haven't been a bother. Just keep yourself safe. I've got to get home and make some calls."

When she came into the house, Shauna met her at the kitchen door. "Your uncle stopped by and wondered where you and Jessi were."

Cat sank into a chair. "I hope he doesn't go and pull her out of lunch. She needs some normal right now. Besides, I know what she saw, because I saw the same thing. What I want to know is why they didn't send a unit to check out the parked car when Mrs. Rice called."

Shauna set a bowl of soup in front of her. "He explained that. Apparently, Mrs. Rice calls a lot. They don't ignore her reports, but the school was having an issue and there wasn't a free car to send."

"Well, I guess they'll be taking her more seriously from now on." Cat took a few sips of the soup, then pushed it away. "I've got some explaining to do."

"You're really not responsible." Shauna stopped when Cat shot her a look. Holding her hands in the air, she stepped back. "Fine. I get it, you feel responsible."

"Let me get this call done and I'll come back and finish my lunch." Cat stood and walked out of the kitchen to the hallway. She dialed Dante's number again. This time he picked up on the first ring.

"What happened?"

Cat took him through the entire incident. After she finished, there was quiet on the other end of the line. She thought he'd hung up or they'd been disconnected during her spiel. "Dante?"

"I'm here. It just doesn't make sense. I'll admit, it feels like a hit, but no one here is claiming responsibility. In fact, I've got a few who want in on the hunt. Jessi is well liked among the families. She did a lot of babysitting when she was in high school."

Cat smiled, thinking of Jessi in the big houses, watching over one or two little kids. "I can see that. Anyway, I just wanted you to be aware of the problem. I hope we won't have another incident before Sunday, but you never know."

"Where is she now?"

"Having lunch with the other writers," Cat continued, knowing he'd be yelling at her that she wasn't keeping Jessi safe. "Before you go off, she has to have a life. She has to feel normal at least part of the time. Besides, the guy in the car is long gone. He knows someone got at least a partial plate and he's on the run for a while."

"Until he gets a new car." Dante didn't say anything else.

Finally, Cat broke. "Well, she'll be home from lunch by then and he'll have to start over. I'm running a retreat, not a safe house."

"You're right. I'm sorry to have put so much on you." He paused and Cat could feel him picking his words carefully. "I appreciate everything you've done for Jessi. I know I've put you in a bad situation."

She thought about how to respond, but before she could say anything, he ended the conversation. "I'll be there on Sunday to retrieve Jessi. Please let her know I'm coming."

She heard the click in her ear before she could respond. He wasn't happy with her. Which suited her just fine. Maybe now he'd stop asking her for favors and sending her secret messages through the bookstore owner. Part of her just wanted him to leave her alone. The other part enjoyed talking to him as a friend. Just a friend. But she wondered if that was like trying to pet the tiger at the zoo. Sooner or later, the tiger was going to bite your hand. She went back into the kitchen, pocketing her phone. Glancing around as she started eating, Cat paused. "Where's Seth?"

"He hasn't come in yet. I'm worried that he's working too hard on this secret project. He keeps telling me I'll be happy, but that's all I can get out of him." Shauna stared out the window toward the tree line that covered the pasture from view. "Maybe I should just go tell him to get his butt in gear and come eat lunch."

"You sit." Cat stood from the table and crossed over to the door. "I'll go get him. I don't want you to ruin his surprise."

"He's really a great guy. You know that, right?" Shauna sat and picked up her spoon.

"He's the best." Cat paused at the door. It had been a surprise seeing Seth when she came back to Aspen Hills, but now it felt like they'd never broken up. "I'm really glad the two of you are friends."

There was an old stone path in the backyard that the original owners had put in, and she followed it to the tree line. Her thoughts were on Jessi. With this last attack, it was becoming clearer that maybe Danielle was just in the wrong place and Jessi was supposed to be the first victim. As she thought of all the secrets surrounding the girl, Cat pushed her way through the hanging branches and ran right into Seth.

Her hands flew up to his chest to help stop her forward movement and she looked up into his face in surprise. "Hey, I was coming to get you for lunch."

He took a leaf out of her hair. "I told you to stay out of the area until Saturday. You don't listen very well, do you?"

Cat leaned over and tried to see around him. "I'm here now. What are you working on?"

"Oh, no, you don't get to worm your way into seeing." He spun her around and gently pushed her back onto the tree-lined path. "Let's go eat lunch."

As they walked toward the house, Cat thought about the peak she'd seen around Seth. The barn looked like he'd been working on it. Now she was sure he was going to unveil an uptown workout space. Maybe they would have to add a small hot tub or an indoor pool once the original renovation loan was paid off. Oh, well, she'd find out tomorrow morning. And besides, she had to keep Jessi safe until Sunday. One secret project at a time was all she could deal with. She linked her hand with Seth's and headed to the house.

# CHAPTER 18

The retreat guests arrived back at the house precisely at two. Apparently, Jessi had filled them in on the incident with the car because they all looked relieved to have made it the few blocks from Reno's.

"A life of intrigue isn't what it's cracked up to be in the books we write." Lisa sank into the bench in the foyer. "I swear, my heart started pounding every time we saw a car."

"I thought you were going to dive to safety when that elderly woman inched her baby blue BMW up Warm Springs." Cora giggled.

"It looked like she was scoping us out," Lisa explained to Cat, who'd been reading in the living room. Or trying to read. She'd been actually waiting for them to get back, so she understood Lisa's anxiety.

"She was hunched over the wheel and trying to see the road." Cora sat next to Lisa and patted her arm. "The woman must have been ninety and probably shouldn't have been driving."

"That's Mrs. Linklater. She bought that BMW new when she lost her husband twenty years ago. She says she's going to drive it until they take the keys away from her and put her in the Aspen Hills Nursing Home." Shauna had joined them in the lobby. "I think her kids are scared that if they do, she'll just give up. Most people around here stay off the roads on Friday between one and three because that's when she does her weekly shopping."

"I didn't know that." Cat glanced at her, amazed at the level of knowledge Shauna had about a town she hadn't even grown up in.

"You don't do the grocery shopping. I swear, if you need to know anything, you should head to the market. The things I learn would fill two of those books you all write."

"Maybe I'll go with you if you go shopping before Sunday," Connie mused. "Of course, it's the same in our town. I always get the best gossip from Milly at the deli. She's got her finger on the pulse of New Haven."

Cora shook her head. "The places we find our muse. Anyway, I've got words calling my name. Who's going to join me in the living room for a few sprint rounds?"

"I hate those." Kelly shook her head. "I'm going to the attic to write. If I stay on top of things, I should have this book in good shape before I leave."

"Which probably means she wrote two while she was here." Connie sighed and headed to the stairs. "I'm in for sprints. I need to increase my word count. Heaven knows I won't get anything on the plane. Cora likes to chat too much."

"Everything has a time. And I don't see you putting in your headphones like Kelly does and writing anyway." Lisa stood from the bench. "I'm in. I've got to get my laptop and my notebook and I'll be down."

Cora consulted the clock. "We'll start round one at two thirty. Don't be late."

"You've got a bit of a drill sergeant in you, did you know that?" Cat walked with Cora toward the stairs.

"Writing is less about inspiration and more about perspiration. You have to work to get the words down, they just don't magically appear on the page." She paused at the bottom of the stairs. "You're more than welcome to join us. I think the girls would get a kick out of it."

"I might just do that." Cat looked back and realized Jessi was still standing in the lobby. She hadn't joined in with the banter, which was totally unusual. Shauna said something to the girl that Cat couldn't hear and they disappeared into the dining room. "I'm going to check on Jessi."

"She's being quiet right now, which means she's processing what happened." Cora's gaze was focused on the open door to the dining room. "I can't believe what a rotten week she's had. I would have been hiding under my covers by now, not wanting to even get out of bed. She's a strong one. See if she wants to join us in sprints, will you? I think writing would be good for her right now."

"I think you're right." Cat moved toward the dining room. Writing had gotten her through a lot of bad times. She'd been devastated after the divorce, and writing Tori's fantasy witch world had given her a place to escape to. A place where husbands didn't cheat and women didn't move away from the only place they'd ever called home. When she entered the dining room, she realized Shauna was applying chocolate therapy to heal Jessi's emotional wounds. They sat at the table, a cup of coffee and a double chunk brownie in front of both of them.

"Hey, you got any more of those?" Cat moved to the sideboard where Shauna set up the dessert bar she kept stocked during the entire retreat. Unless they were having breakfast.

"To your left," Shauna called out. "Come sit with us. We're sharing our tragic life stories."

"Well, I have a few of those." Cat smiled as she crossed the room and sat with the other two women.

"You all seem so normal. I can't believe you've had problems." Jessi shook her head. "Not at the scale of my life."

"But think of all the writing fodder you have. I swear, you could write a best seller just from what happened this week." Shauna took a bite of her brownie.

Jessi sipped her coffee. "No, I don't think I'll do a memoir. But a romance or a mystery? My life experience might just get me some readers."

"A true writer takes all the crappy lemons given to her in life and makes lemonade. It's what we do." Cat broke off a piece of the brownie. When she popped it into her mouth, she almost groaned. As she'd expected, it was chocolate heaven.

Jessi nodded. "I hadn't thought of it that way, but you're right. Even the big guys had trouble in their lives. Look at Professor Turner's precious Hemingway. He took his own life."

"I think Professor Turner likes to imagine it was an accidental shooting." Cat smiled. She'd heard the Covington English professor bandy around his theories. "Or a conspiracy."

Jessi laughed, and for a second, Cat heard the relaxed young woman who'd started the retreat on Sunday. "He does love his Hemingway theories."

"The group's getting together to do writing sprints in the living room soon. Do you want to join them?" Cat finished her brownie, washing down the chocolate overload with a hit of dark coffee. No, her life didn't suck at all. "I think I'm grabbing my laptop and playing for a while."

"That sounds like just what I need." Jessi grabbed her brownie and stood. "I'll go get my stuff."

When they were alone in the room, Cat sipped her coffee. "You were good with her."

"I used to be a bartender. Helping people see the bright side of life was my specialty." Shauna picked up the empty plates. "But you, you gave her hope for the future. If I haven't told you this before, I'm proud to be part of this retreat. I love seeing writers grow and develop, even if it's just for a week."

"It's a pretty neat thing." Cat grabbed the cups and followed her into the kitchen. "I just wish people would stop dying during retreat week. It would make this whole process a lot easier to handle."

"I don't know, it's kind of a great marketing tool. *Come and visit the murder capital of Colorado.*

*And if you're lucky, you'll get to help solve the murder."* Shauna rinsed off the dishes and put them into the dishwasher.

"If you're not the victim." Cat shook her head. "No, I don't think that would sell a lot of spots in upcoming sessions. I'd rather stay with *We help bring out the story in you.*"

"I think you're missing a big market." Shauna waved her out the door. "Go get ready for your writer race thing."

"Sprints. It's sprints, not races. We start a timed writing session, and then at the end, we report our word count to the group. Then we start again." Cat explained the process.

"And they say writers don't know how to party." Shauna went to her laptop. "I've got to research some new breakfast items for next month. I'm getting tired of stratas."

Cat left her friend in the kitchen doing what she loved, thinking about food and recipes, and ran upstairs to get her laptop. She could access her Word document from the cloud storage where she kept the draft. A window was open in her office and the wind was blowing through the room. She crossed over and shut the window and watched as Seth walked out of the backyard and through the wooded path to the pasture. They all had the things they loved. And even though they were all different, they made a good team. Or maybe they made a good team because they were different.

Cat grabbed her notebook, her laptop, a charger, and a wireless mouse. And then she tucked a couple of pens into the bag where she'd put the rest of the items. The good thing about having an office on the third floor was it was away from everyone else. The bad thing? There were a lot of steps when she forgot something after deciding to write in a different part of the house.

They were near the end of the third sprint and Cat was feeling pretty good about her word count when Martin burst into the living room.

"Jessi, oh God, Jessi, are you all right?" He ran to her side and lifted her head to look at him.

"Stop it, Martin. Can't you see I'm writing?" She slapped his hand away and glanced at the timer. "Go sit quietly on the couch or something for five minutes. Then I'll talk to you."

Cat bit back a smile. The girl was growing a backbone, that was certain. Martin, apparently shocked at her response, glanced around the room and then followed her instructions. He pulled out his cell phone and started scrolling. At least he knew to be quiet. Cat wasn't sure who would have yelled at him if he hadn't, but she would put her money on Connie. The woman was so focused on her laptop, she barely wanted to stop when the timer went off.

Refocusing on her work, Cat finished a chapter and had the first line of the next one written when she heard the *bing* from the timer and Cora called time.

"Call out your word count, ladies." Lisa stood at the flip chart, ready to write down everyone's totals.

As the numbers were called out, Cat realized the session was really getting some words written. She'd have to make this a standard Friday afternoon session for the retreat, if not every afternoon. She might just be able to knock out some serious word count during a retreat if she did a few of these sprint sessions.

Everyone stood and high-fived one another as the totals were called out. "One last round will start in fifteen minutes. Go get drinks or snacks, go to the bathroom, or whatever," Cora looked pointedly at Martin, "but be back here ready to kill this thing in fifteen minutes."

The women left the room for Martin and Jessi, but Cat hung around. She glanced at Jessi. "Do you want me to leave you two alone?"

"No, stay." Jessi turned her attention to him. "Why are you here again?"

"You almost got killed by a hit-and-run, and you are wondering why I'm here?" Martin closed his eyes and took a deep breath. "Sorry, not the way I wanted this to go. How are you? Are you okay?"

Jessi smiled, and it appeared her demeanor lightened a bit, at least from Cat's point of view. "I'm good. I was a little shaken up, but no bumps, no bruises."

"I can't believe someone is trying to kill you. Uncle Dante says you've been the target all along, is that true?"

Jessi shrugged. "I don't know. All I know is the life I thought I had last Saturday has totally blown up on me. I have no best friend, my boyfriend is a cheating jerk, and my money keeps disappearing. I might as well tell you, the getaway fund my father gave me is gone. Someone took it out of my room."

"I can't help you with the loss of your friend. And I never liked Max anyway." Martin grinned, but then his lips tightened. "But you can blame me for the getaway fund. I took it and put it away with mine."

"Why would you do that?"

He shrugged, visibly shaken at her angry tone. "Uncle Dante told me to watch out for you. When he told me about the cash your dad had given you, well, I wanted to keep it safe. That Danielle chick, she just worried me. I was going to tell you, then I kind of forgot."

Cat smiled and moved toward the door. Martin was finally stepping up and taking his responsibilities seriously, even if he was doing it in all the wrong ways. He'd have to realize that Jessi was pretty strong herself. Or at least she was now.

She closed the door and met Cora's eyes. The other women had scattered after the writing session. "She's okay."

"I know." Cora flushed a little. "I just worry about her. She's had a hard week."

"Isn't that the truth? Hey, I wanted to thank you for setting up the writing sprint session. I think I'm going to add that to next month's retreat schedule. I know it won't work for everyone, but it's a new way for some to think about writing." Cat glanced at her watch. It was almost five. "Are you all going out tonight for dinner?"

"That was the plan. I don't know why, but it feels like we're on vacation or something but with people who understand you." Cora took one last look at the closed door. "I guess I'll go grab one last cup of coffee before we start again."

"Don't worry, I'll keep an ear out for any trouble." Cat patted the woman's shoulder. "You're a good friend."

"I'm a mother hen and I know it. But I care." Cora started up the stairs. "My youngest is just about Jessi's age. I can't even imagine Bethany going through what Jessi has this week. She'd be a wreck."

"If she's anything like her mom, I kind of doubt that." Cat followed Cora into the dining room to pick up and to check on supplies for Shauna as she was waiting for Martin to leave. She stacked the dirty dishes on a tray and threw away the leftovers. With ten minutes still to go, she went back into the study and grabbed a novel she'd been reading a few days ago. She sat in the dining room and started to read.

She was lost in the story when Jessi came and put a hand on her shoulder. "Martin's gone. You didn't have to wait for me. I know you have things to do."

"I'm just waiting for the last sprint." Cat put a bookmark to mark her place and rose, stretching. "Did you and Martin have a good talk?"

"We did. He's going to help me move into Dante's house until I find somewhere of my own after this thing is settled. I read him the riot act about the money, though. Why is it that men are always trying to take care of things that aren't their business?" Jessi's eyes looked haunted. "Don't get me wrong, I appreciate Dante's offer of somewhere to stay. It's a cool house, and at least I don't have to move back to Boston and live with Mom. I think I'd stay at the saloon and take my chances with the Outlaw ghost killer before I did that."

"Not funny, Jessi."

The girl smiled as she picked up the tray and

moved toward the kitchen. "Not even a little? Man, you're hard to crack."

"Okay, maybe a little." Cat picked up the empty trays for the treats and followed Jessi into the kitchen. Shauna wasn't in the kitchen, so they loaded the dishes into the dishwasher, then cleaned up the trays.

"Time for the next sprint. We're going to the Diner this evening for dinner." Jessi glanced outside at the darkening road. "You think I'll be okay walking, don't you?"

"Seth can drive you all there and pick you up if you want." Cat pulled out her phone. "I said that wrong. Seth will drive you there. What time are you leaving?"

"Everyone's meeting down here thirty minutes after the last sprint. Really, I'll be fine walking." Jessi shook her head. "You don't have to take care of me."

*Actually, I do because I promised Dante.* Cat caught herself before she actually said the words. "No problem at all. Seth probably has some errands in town anyway." Cat dialed the number but paused and waved Jessi away. "He'll be grumpy if you aren't ready at the time we set. Go tell them to start the sprint without me."

Jessi grinned and took off in a jog.

Cat hit the send button and the phone rang. And rang. Finally, an out-of-breath Seth picked up.

"What?"

Uh-oh, maybe he couldn't drive the gang. Cat would probably have to do it herself. "Hey, are you busy?"

"A little, why?"

Cat thought she heard voices in the background. "Who's with you? I thought you were in the back working on your project."

"I'm a little busy to chat. What do you need?"

He dodged that question, Cat thought. "Any way you can drive the gang to the Diner for dinner in about an hour?"

"The dinner's tomorrow. And I thought we were going to the Mexican place?" A large clang sounded and Seth swore under his breath.

"I just don't want Jessi walking around town after what happened this afternoon." Cat glanced out the window, trying to see through the trees. "You sound busy. I'll drive them."

"I'd appreciate that. Look, I've got to go. I may miss dinner. Please don't come looking for me. I'll eat when I'm done with this."

And he hung up. Cat tucked her cell into her pants and stood staring at the tree line in the backyard for a long time. Then she headed back into the living room to join the sprints.

# CHAPTER 19

Cat made Cora promise to call her as soon as they got their check for the dinner. "Jessi might make noises about walking, but I'd rather be safe than sorry, you know?"

The good thing was she didn't have to press very hard, Cat could see that Cora was still worried about the girl too. Coming into the kitchen, she saw Shauna at the stove, grilling burgers.

Hearing the door open, she grabbed a towel and wiped her hands. "I saw your note. Driving them from now on is probably a smart idea. Who knows when that crazy will show up again. Isn't Seth here?"

"He's out at the barn. Apparently, he was busy." Cat didn't expand on what he'd been busy with, because honestly, she didn't know. "He said he might not make dinner, so just set a plate in the refrigerator for him."

Shauna frowned. "That's not like him. He never

misses a meal. I wonder if he's going to be able to do the reveal tomorrow?"

"Who can understand the mind of a man?"

"Isn't that the truth." Shauna poured a glass of iced tea. With her back to Cat, she spoke again. "I had my first grief support group meeting this afternoon. I should have told you I was going, but I wasn't sure I was actually going until it was time to go."

Cat sat at the table and waited. Shauna didn't say anything else, just set her tea on the table in front of Cat. "How did it go? Or do you want to talk?"

"I'm about all talked out for today." Shauna's smile was sad, but it was a smile. "I'm going back next week. I think it helps."

"Whatever you need." Cat sipped her tea, not sure what else to say, but she didn't have to worry because Shauna kept talking.

"The leader is a counselor who teaches part-time at Covington. Sally O'Bryan? Maybe you met her when you were teaching?"

Cat tried to remember, but the faces of professors and students swam in her mind. "Sorry, I don't remember. Of course, if she wasn't in the English or Economics departments, I probably didn't know her."

Shauna stood and went over to turn the burgers. "She's good. Intelligent, sharp, and she doesn't let people get away with deflecting. I hadn't realized how mad I was at Kevin for dying and leaving me until today."

"Anger is part of the process." Cat thought about her first few weeks in California. If she had seen Michael, she would have physically attacked him. It was a good thing she'd put miles between them after the divorce.

"My head knew that, but my heart wouldn't let me feel it. Like I was being disloyal or something." Shauna laughed, and the sound made Cat's heart lift just a little. Her laugh was almost back to where it had been before Kevin's murder. She was starting to heal.

Cat stood and went to the sink to wash her hands. "What can I do to help for dinner?"

An hour later, they'd eaten, the dishes were cleaned up, and Seth's plate was wrapped up and waiting for him. Cora still hadn't called.

Cat picked up her phone again, glancing at the display to make sure she hadn't missed a call. "Maybe I should just go down there."

Shauna refilled Cat's tea glass. "Just relax. They're probably having a great time. It's the next-to-last night for them. I love watching their friendships grow and the bonds tighten over the retreat week."

Cat felt the smile creep on her face. "Me too. It's like they finally found their tribe. Of course, this group was different, as they already had a tribe when they came here."

"But they enveloped Jessi into their group almost seamlessly. It meant a lot to her to be included, especially with the week she's had."

Something about Shauna's words made Cat's alarms go off. "It's about Jessi. It has to be about Jessi, right?"

"I don't understand." Shauna was looking at Cat like she didn't understand the words.

"I don't think Danielle's death was random or some crazy ghost town serial killer. Jessi's the clue.

Danielle was working Jessi's shift. She drove Jessi's car to Outlaw. She was wearing Jessi's costume. What if someone thought Danielle was Jessi?" Cat leaned toward Shauna. "And when he found out he had the wrong girl, he came back to kill her again. Only this time, she was on her guard."

"So you don't think this hit-and-run was an accident or even the first attempt. Maybe it was a last-ditch effort to finish the job, which made him sloppy." Shauna added on to Cat's theory.

"I need to talk to Uncle Pete." Cat reached for her phone, but it buzzed as soon as her hand got close. "After I pick up the group, apparently."

Shauna waited for Cat to get off the phone with Cora and walked her to the door. "I'll call Pete. Maybe he can swing by here before he goes home."

Cat thought about all that had happened that week as she drove to the restaurant to pick up the gang. The problem was there were too many suspects. Except Max wouldn't have wanted to kill Jessi; he was still in love with her. Dante said there wasn't anything with the family, and Keith had an alibi. Besides, Danielle and Jessi had been his golden goose. He'd be stupid to cut off his money supply. Which left Joseph John Robertson. But was being rich and weird enough of a motive to try to kill two women? Somehow Cat didn't think so.

Anyway, she'd tell Uncle Pete everything, including Dante's information, and let a real professional take over the worrying. All she had to do was get through tomorrow and hand Jessi over to Dante on Sunday. Then she was out of the picture. The logic sounded good to her head, but her heart was arguing that she did have a responsibility to help keep Jessi safe, even after Sunday. The problem was she didn't have a clue how to even begin.

Uncle Pete sat at the table, a piece of strawberry shortcake in front of him with a cup of coffee. Shauna smiled as Cat came into the kitchen. "Taxi duty over?"

"The group has been returned to the house and I've locked the front door early." Cat grabbed a soda out of the fridge. "I was thinking on the way to pick them up that I really didn't need to bother you. I have nothing to help you with the investigation, well, except for what Dante told me."

The raise in Uncle Pete's eyebrow was slight, but Cat noticed it. "Well, I'm here and enjoying some of Shauna's delights. You might as well tell me what you're thinking."

So Cat walked him through her reasoning on why the intended victim had always been Jessi. She went through each of her contacts with Dante and handed over the message that Tammy had delivered. She didn't want to hold anything back from her uncle. Not if it was the piece that broke the case for him. "And that's why I think it had to be about Jessi. The only thing that doesn't fit is who's stealing her money."

"She lost a lot of cash." Uncle Pete had taken his notebook out and made several notes during Cat's monologue.

"Oh, no. The cash isn't lost." Cat explained Martin's unhelpful logic. She frowned when she remembered his explanation. "Someone has been spreading a rumor that Jessi is hooked on drugs and making bad decisions. Her mother heard it and told Dante, who told Martin. Her money manager told me, but that might have come from her mother. But Jessi swears she doesn't do drugs. She doesn't really even like to drink."

"When you look at someone stealing her money, spreading rumors isn't that big a deal." Shauna sipped her hot chocolate.

"If you take each thing separately, you're right. But this seems like a massive attack on the girl. Of course, there were a lot of players in this drama." Uncle Pete set down his pen. "There is one explanation we haven't looked at yet."

"The ghost killer of Outlaw?" Cat yawned. It had been a long day.

Uncle Pete smiled, "No, but I'll add him to my list of suspects. I was thinking about Jessi. Could she have been orchestrating all of this herself?"

"You have got to be kidding." The tiredness fell off Cat, and she was angry that her uncle would even think that Jessi might be doing this all to herself.

"Cat, I have to question her about everything. She was at Outlaw when Danielle was killed. Maybe she knew about Max."

Cat shook her head. "There's no way. I saw her confront him. She was shocked and hurt."

"I'm not saying she did any of this, and believe me, there's a lot of people out there who have been taking advantage of the girl. Maybe she just got tired of being the victim?"

Cat stared at her uncle. "Then who tried to run her over with a car? She didn't do that by herself."

"She could know someone to hire." Uncle Pete sent her a sympathetic look. "Don't look at me that way, it's just a theory I have to disprove."

Shauna went to get Jessi, and Cat waited for her at the door to the kitchen. When the girl bounded down the stairs, she smiled at Cat. "What's going on? Are we doing a movie night?"

Cat put a hand on her arm. "No, but maybe tomorrow. Look, my uncle is here and wants to talk to you about a few things. You don't have to do this. You can call your lawyer and have Uncle Pete schedule an interview through him. Or you can have me or Shauna sit in with you. Or call your mother."

"Why would I want to do any of those things?" Jessi shook off Cat's arm. "You think I don't know he's looking at me for some of this? But see, that's the thing. I know I didn't do anything wrong, so there's nothing he can do to make me say something that could hurt me later in a court setting. I'm the victim here."

"If you need anything—" Cat started, but Jessi cut her off.

"Stop pretending like you care. You're just hired for the week to provide an environment for my writing development. You're not my mother or my family. You're staff." With that, Jessi flipped her hair back and squared her shoulders. Then she marched into the kitchen, fully prepared for war.

"Cat, she didn't mean—" Shauna started, but this time, Cat was the one who cut someone off.

"She meant it all right. She's hurt and striking

out. But see, she doesn't know everything about me." Cat smiled as she headed to the living room to wait for Jessi and Uncle Pete to finish. "She doesn't know I don't give up on people I care about. And for some reason, that kid falls into that category."

It was over an hour before Cat heard the door to the kitchen open. She stood in the doorway watching as a clearly upset Jessi dragged her way to her room, one stair at a time. She waited for the sound of Jessi's bedroom door closing before she moved toward the kitchen. Seth was standing by the microwave, heating up his burger. And he was the only one in the kitchen.

"Where's Uncle Pete?"

Seth yawned and stretched. "No clue. Was he here?"

"Yeah, he was interviewing Jessi." Cat grabbed a soda. It was her second of the night, but she didn't feel like sleeping, not yet.

"When I came in, Jessi was sitting at the table crying. I asked if there was something I could help with and the poor thing looked at me with such pain." Seth put the hamburger on a bun he'd slathered a ton of mayo on as well as a slice of cheese and a slice of onion. "So I stepped toward her and she held up her hands. Then she told me she was radioactive and ran out of the room."

"Poor thing." Cat sank down to watch Seth eat. She laid her head on the table. "She doesn't have anyone she can truly count on. That's got to be the hardest part of this whole thing."

Seth sat next to her and rubbed her neck. "See, that's where you're wrong. She has you."

Cat laughed bitterly, thinking of the last exchange she just had with Jessi. "I don't think she sees it that way."

"It doesn't matter what she sees. I know you're standing up for her. You love fighting for the underdog." He kissed her head. "Now, can I eat? I'm starving."

"Go ahead. I think I'm going to join you for some dessert." Cat went to the cabinet and got out a plate. She set up a brownie and put it in the microwave for thirty seconds. Then she got out the vanilla ice cream and a scoop from the drawer. When the bell went off, she took the plate out, scooped up the ice cream, and put everything away. Then she took a bottle of chocolate syrup out of the fridge and added a final touch. When she took it back to the table, Seth was staring at her. "What?"

"Stress eat much?" He looked down at his burger and coleslaw. "You're making my plate look like diet food."

"Then hurry up and you can make your own brownie delight." She ran her spoon down the ice cream into the brownie, making sure she also got some of the syrup. Taking the bite, she closed her eyes and enjoyed the flavor. Besides the words she got in the sprinting session, this was the best thing that had happened to her today.

"Your relationship with food is a tad unhealthy. I don't think I make you smile like that." Seth chuckled as she opened her eyes and blinked at him.

"Sorry, I couldn't hear you, I was in bliss."

He took a bite of his burger and watched her. "We really need a date night. I think I can massage some of those kinks out of your shoulders."

"Can't be next week, I'm on deadline then." Cat considered her calendar. "But the week after I'm free. Maybe we could do a couple of nights away?"

"I'm off with the boys next week anyway. The week after would work. We could go into Denver and hit some of the clubs. I hear they have some new bands that are killing it." He polished off his coleslaw and took his plate to the sink. Then he got out a new one and repeated her movements with the brownie dessert, except he added a sprinkling of walnuts over the top. "Remember the Ice Cream Palace that was downtown when we were kids?"

"I loved the Court Jester. It was amazing." Cat took a bite of the ice cream and then went to the cabinet. "I wonder if Shauna has some salted peanuts. It would almost be the same."

As they reminisced about the past and the hangouts of their youth, Cat put Jessi's problems away for the night. Maybe not thinking about them would bring her some clarity in the morning.

Otherwise when Jessi left the writers' retreat, she'd be stuck at Dante's while Uncle Pete solved Danielle's murder. Being taken care of might be stifling for a young woman, but it beat the alternative. And it definitely was better than being in the Aspen Hills jail.

# CHAPTER 20

Cat lay in bed Saturday morning, thinking about the retreat and the last day. They had dinner plans at the upscale Mexican place just outside town. She loved the last night, where everyone knew each other and made plans for future contact. And it gave her time to hear what the writers had accomplished during the week. This group's word count, with Kelly in the mix, would probably be through the roof, even with the distractions that came with Danielle's murder and Jessi's issues.

Frustrated, she threw the covers off and got out of bed. She didn't know where Uncle Pete was looking, except at Jessi herself, and Cat didn't have any other suspect to point him toward. But she knew the girl. There was no way Jessi could have orchestrated Danielle's murder or the failed attack on herself. The girl had a positive streak a mile long.

When she came downstairs for coffee, Shauna and Seth were already eating. Cat poured coffee and grabbed a slice of toast and smeared on huckleberry jam. "So what's on the schedule today? Any changes I need to know about?"

"Cora and the girls want me to drive them over to the library right after breakfast at nine thirty." Shauna glanced at her calendar that was open on the table next to her. "Then Seth has his thing at ten. I'm picking the group up at Reno's at two. And dinner tonight. Are you doing a farewell session like you normally have last day?"

"Yeah, I will. Just let them know to meet me in the living room at three. Do we still have some treats we can serve with lemonade and iced tea?" If they debriefed the work part, dinner would just be about fun and friendship. Cat nodded, pleased with the change from her morning thoughts.

"It's not just a Seth thing at ten. You two have to be there too." Seth stared at Shauna. "You are going to be back from dropping them off by then, right?"

"Of course. I'm dying to see what you've been working on all week. It better be worth the hype. I'm thinking a nice spa area." Shauna picked up her plate and went to the sink. "Maybe with a hot tub and a personal masseur to ease the kinks out of my shoulders in the mornings."

"Ha, I thought it was a new gathering spot, with more bookshelves. We could call it the Annex." Cat poked Seth's arm. "Want to tell us who's right?"

"At ten, all will be revealed." Seth finished his breakfast, then went to the coffeepot to fill up a travel mug. "And no peeking before. Man, you two must have been bad to live with as kids around Christmas. Neither one of you can wait for a surprise."

"He's really good at keeping secrets. It's kind of scary," Shauna said as Seth left the kitchen.

Cat stood and walked to the back window, where she watched as Seth made his way out to the backyard. "I wonder what he's up to?"

"I have no idea, but he didn't flinch when either of us made guesses. Your man has a tell. When he's lying or he's trying to hide something and you guess, he flinches. It's not much, just around the eyes, but it's definitely there. I've tested him several times when he's bought you a surprise gift or is planning on some romantic getaway. When I hit the nail on the head, he reacts. So no personal masseur for me."

"I'm sorry for your loss." Cat thought about Seth's tell. She'd known him longer than Shauna, and she'd already picked up on one of his habits.

Shauna grabbed a bowl of freshly cut fruit for the dining room out of the fridge. "I know. And I was going to call him Ricardo and teach him to speak Italian."

"You might want to get a dog." Cat paused at the doorway. "They're cheaper than keeping a personal masseur on staff twenty-four seven."

"You're not going to laugh when I come home with a huge dog who has a habit of chewing on antique wooden furniture legs." Shauna leaned against the counter. "But if you're serious, maybe a cat. We'd have to announce it on our website, since some people are allergic and it might affect sign-ups."

"If you want a cat, we'll deal with the loss of income, if there is any. I think a pet would increase the feeling of home around here. Don't they have hairless cats?"

"They do, but not in my house." Shauna smiled. "Hey, what did you find out about that cat at Outlaw?"

Cat told her the story. "Seth and I were going to head up to Outlaw and try to catch it, but I think that was the night of the break-in. It's been such a crazy week, I'm not sure what day it is. Maybe he can run up there tomorrow with me after he does the airport run to Denver. Since they're all on the same plane, he should be back sooner than usual."

"So we're adopting Angelica? That sounds right." Shauna smiled and made a note on her pad of paper. "Are you going upstairs to write?"

"Yeah. With the words I got yesterday, I might just be able to meet my deadline next week easy." Cat glanced at her watch. "Will you come and get me when you're done playing chauffeur? I'd hate to disappoint him. Talk about being excited for the reveal—it does feel kind of like Christmas morning around here. Except for the lack of snow."

Cat didn't see anyone as she climbed the stairs to her third-floor office. The guests must have been sleeping in. Most of the group had a day job, well, except Kelly, and this week had been a vacation as well as a writer retreat. She felt thankful that so many people had chosen to take their limited vacation time to attend her retreat. The next three sessions were already full, and they had another one in which everyone was from the same town, so she assumed their members already knew each other. She hoped they would take the Covington student attendee under their wing as quickly as this group had adopted Jessi.

She sat in front of her computer, turned on the power, and went straight to her manuscript. No internet surfing today. No checking email. The words were first today. She even pushed the worry she felt about Jessi out of her head. She was working. And all that mattered for the next couple of hours was what happened on the page. She checked her notes and dove into the project.

The next thing she knew, someone was knocking at her door. Checking the clock on her computer screen, she was surprised to see it was already 9:50. "Come on in, I'm just saving and shutting down."

Shauna set a muffin and a travel mug of coffee on Cat's desk as she saved her document in two different spots. She was so close to being done, there was no way she'd be able to start all over if her computer died. Well, she guessed she could, but she wouldn't meet deadline. She'd heard too many horror stories about lost files to take a chance now.

Finished, she unwrapped the muffin and took a big bite of the spice cake and walnut treat. "How'd the morning go? Any problems?"

"Nope. Even Kelly decided to head out with them. She took her laptop, so I think she'll find a quiet hole somewhere in the library and write, but she did go with them." Shauna sipped on her own coffee. "They're a nice group of friends. Sometimes I really love what we do."

"I know, right? I was thinking that too this

morning. I guess we've survived another retreat. We should celebrate." Cat finished off the muffin.

"Knock on some wood, missy. We still have most of a day and the airport runs to get through. Survival doesn't count until the fat lady sings." She nodded to the door. "Ready to go see Seth's folly?"

"Isn't there a mining camp named that somewhere?" Cat stood and, after wiping her mouth, threw away the napkin. "Let's go see what the man has built for us. Make sure you ooh and ahh loud enough so he can bask in the glory."

"You're pretty snarky sometimes, you know that?" Shauna laughed as they made their way downstairs.

"And that's why we're friends."

When they got to the walkway that went through the tree line, the bushes had been cut back since when Cat had tried to go find Seth the previous day. Now the path was free of any barriers. Looking around once they passed the hedge, all Cat saw was the barn. The pastured fence around it had been refurbished with new boards in places. The door to the barn was standing open and Cat thought she saw at least one vehicle parked behind the barn. She couldn't tell who owned the newer-model pickup, but she knew it wasn't Seth's.

Shauna pointed to the doorway. "I guess we're supposed to go in there?"

"Let's go." Cat smiled, but she was uneasy. What exactly had Seth been up to for the last week? And why had it been such a secret? Maybe he'd decided the house needed a dog and had made a place for it to sleep out in the barn. But then why fix the fence? Too many questions. Cat followed Shauna into the barn's open door and almost ran into her when her friend froze.

Seth and Paul Addison stood in the middle of the barn. And to the left, a black horse stood in a stall. The nameplate on the stall was carved with the word *Snow.*

The horse saw the newcomers, nickered, and threw her head in a greeting. Shauna raced toward the stall and put her arms around the large neck, burrowing her head into the curve.

Cat made her way to Seth and kissed him. "Well played, Seth, well played."

Seth pulled her into a hug. "I had to do something to make up for being stupid. Shauna can hold a grudge for a long time. I went to Paul and negotiated the release of the hostage."

Paul grunted. "No one but Shauna wanted the horse anyway. She should have had it moved here weeks ago. I came by, and Seth was here. So we talked."

"Yeah, but I hadn't upgraded the barn yet." Seth pointed to the roof and supports. "The place had good bones, so it just took some TLC to get it going again."

Shauna turned, and with a watery smile, she beamed at the men. "Thank you. I don't care how you pulled it off, but I'm so thankful you did."

Cat walked over and stroked the soft leather on the saddle. Shauna's name was hand-tooled into the stirrups. A second, less decorated saddle sat on a second saddle horse. Bridles and lead ropes lined the wall next to the stall. And on the other side of the barn, a stack of hay and a second stack of straw lined the main wall. In the corner, there must have been ten bags of feed tucked nearby.

"If the food isn't right, Harrold at the feed store said you could exchange it, but he said that's what you used to order when you were taking care of Snow." Seth stared at Shauna, waiting. "So, it's okay?"

"Oh my, Seth, it's more than okay. This is the best thing you could have ever done for me. If I'm ever a witch to you, just say *Snow* and I'll back off. Thank you." And with that, Shauna launched herself into Seth's arms and hugged him. And she burst into tears.

Seth's eyes widened and he looked for guidance from Cat. She mimed patting Shauna's back and so, robotically, he did. "I'm really glad you like it. I'm sorry for causing you pain before."

Paul shuffled and stepped toward the door. "Well, I'll get in touch with you for the reading of the will, but this part at least is done. Take care, Shauna. It was good to see you again."

Cat knew Paul hadn't liked Shauna when his boss was alive, but maybe now that they weren't in competition for Kevin's attention, he didn't have to be quite the same jerk.

Shauna sensed Paul's movements and left Seth's arms to grab Paul before he could sneak away. "Thank you so much. I know you never liked me, but Snow needed me and I couldn't bear thinking that she was going to be sold, or worse."

Again, Cat mimed the patting on the back to the frightened Paul, and after a short hesitation, he too followed her nonverbal instructions. "You are most welcome Shauna. I'm glad you are so happy."

Now Shauna turned her attention to Cat. But instead of hugging her, she bounced. "This is the best day of my life, well, since, never mind, no sad thoughts. Snow and I will get through this. My grief counselor told me I needed to be more active. Now I can ride whenever I want to."

A meow came from the straw, and a white cat with black patches strolled out into the sunshine. Angelica found a sunbeam coming from the open door and lay in the dirt, rolling around on her back.

"Oh, my God. Seth, you brought the cat down from Outlaw." Cat knelt close to the feline and gently rubbed her belly. "Hey, pretty girl. Do you like your new home?"

"I wasn't sure if you wanted her to become an indoor cat, but since she's been hanging out at Outlaw for the last few months, I thought she might be a good companion for Snow." He leaned over and rubbed the cat on the top of her head. "I kept having to round her up as she kept trying to follow me to the house."

Paul had disappeared shortly after Shauna had released him from her hug. Cat went and grabbed Seth's arm. She nodded toward Shauna, who was talking to Snow like she was her best friend. "Let's give them some space."

A girl and her horse, Cat mused. And their cat. She looked back and saw Angelica sitting by Snow's pen watching the horse and Shauna reunite. "I don't think she wants to be a house cat."

Seth looked down at her as they walked back to the house. "I think one Cat is enough for a house."

"Funny." She leaned into him. "Thank you for doing this. She's happier than I've seen her in a long while."

"Since Kevin, I know." Seth glanced back at the barn. "She deserved a bit of happy in her life. She works hard. I hope she finds someone soon. And someone who really deserves her."

Cat knew that Seth hadn't though much of Kevin, but like her, he had kept his opinions to himself. As they came around the tree line, Paul stepped out onto the path to stop their progress.

"Good, you're alone. I'm not sure how much more positive attention I could have stood from Shauna. I know the woman hates me." Paul crooked his head around the corner just to make sure Shauna wasn't coming down the path.

"What do you want, Paul?" Cat knew Shauna had good reasons to hate her ex-fiancé's business manager, but she'd be polite for a while. Especially after what he'd done for her friend.

He turned back. "I realized I didn't finish answering Seth's question. The two of you interrupted us before we could finish the conversation."

Seth put an arm around Cat. "Paul and Joseph John went to school together. I thought he might know more about him."

"Well, that and he was a pretty strong rival in the construction business with Shield Holdings. When we found out Kevin had been murdered, Joseph John's name was one of the first ones I gave Chief

Edmond. But then, well, you know the rest of that story." Paul peeked around the corner again.

Cat bit back a smile. Shauna had the guy nervous. "So why the fascination with ghost towns?"

Paul shook his head. "It's not ghost towns, it's serial killers. The guy has a crazy collection of memorabilia of all the local murders that occurred. The kids at school used to tease him about reading all those freaky books. But he's harmless enough. I mean, he didn't kill pets or weird stuff like that."

Cat wondered if the guy's fascination hadn't led him down the wrong path, at least with Danielle.

Paul continued. "He's big into that fantasy cosplay stuff too. We had to postpone a meeting on a project we're providing backup support for last weekend because he was going out of town Friday to this crazy conference in Denver. Seriously, he was just in Denver. You would have thought he could spare an hour for at least a video chat, but no. We had to wait until Tuesday morning when he was back in town."

Cat thought about the timing. He could have been in Outlaw on Monday when Danielle was killed, especially if the conference was his cover. She'd have to text this information to Uncle Pete and see if he could verify it. But why would he try to run over Jessi? Nothing in this investigation added up. Nothing.

Paul left through the front of the house and then walked back behind the barn to get his truck. Apparently being hugged by Shauna had unnerved him more than he wanted to admit. Seth and Cat grabbed sodas and sat in the kitchen.

"I'm thinking we're on our own for lunch. Want me to order a couple of pizzas?" Seth's grin was a mile wide. "She liked the surprise."

"No, she loved the surprise. Get a veggie and whatever you want, I'll pay." Cat leaned her head against the back of the chair. "I really thought when Paul told us the story about Joseph John that it would prove he killed Danielle, but honestly, it just made more questions in my head."

"I seem to remember it's someone else's job to find out who killed Danielle, not yours." He picked up his phone. "I can pay for my own pizza, you know."

"We're paying for your meals this week. It's part of the deal. If Shauna's too busy to cook, I'll buy pizza." Cat didn't look up. "Besides, maybe it will force me out of my doldrums. I have to be a good hostess for half a day more."

"You're always a good hostess." Seth stood up and dialed his phone. He left the room to order, and Cat picked up her own to call her uncle. Maybe he could use the bits and pieces of information she was feeding him. Because to her, all it looked like was a bag of fabric scraps, with no pattern at all.

# CHAPTER 21

"Here's to the Warm Springs Writers Retreat. Thank you for hosting our little crew this week. It's been fabulous." A tipsy Kelly stood and held out her glass to the group. "I'll have you know I wrote more than twenty thousand words and finished one book a month before deadline. I love having some breathing room."

"You are horrible." Connie pulled on Kelly's arm. "Sit down and stop bragging. I thought I was doing great with having twelve thousand words. And I got a whole notebook of research stuff for my next book."

"You're both amazing." Cora wiped a bit of margarita off her dress where Kelly had spilled as she sat down. "If there's one thing to be said for our little group, Cat, it's that we're competitive."

"From the numbers you all reported this afternoon while we were talking, I think this is the most productive session we've ever had." Cat held a glass up. "To writers who find the words to make every story sing."

"Hear, hear," the group joined in, clinking glasses. Seth and Shauna sat together at the far end of the table, whispering.

"Something you want to share with the group?" Cora winked at Cat as she poked Shauna.

Shauna blushed, the margaritas giving her a happy glow. "We're just talking about Snow. She might be a little lonely in the barn. I think maybe we need another horse. You all did go visit her this afternoon, right?"

"Yes, we visited your horse." Jessi laughed as the others ducked the question. She glanced around the table. "Or at least I did. Snow's an unusual name for an all-black horse."

"One of Kevin's jokes. He bought the horse as an investment, then when I came into the picture, I just fell in love with her." She set the glass aside. "If I'm taking her riding tomorrow, I better slow down on the celebratory drinks. I can't believe Paul left her trailer as well as all her tack. I'm afraid I'm going to have to send him a thank-you note."

"Hold off until the will is read. Snow and her stuff might have been yours all along." Cat was happy for her friend. After all the sadness in the last few months, she'd finally found something to be happy about.

"Well, it looks like I'll be staying at Dante's for the time being, so if you need any help, I'll be glad to come over." Jessi pushed the food on her plate around with a fork. "He wants me to stop working at Outlaw until this guy's caught."

"It's not a bad idea." Seth took a bite of his last taco. Everyone at the table was staring at him. "What? I do have an opinion on this, and Jessi needs to stay out of places where there are a lot of nooks and crannies and fake guns, unless she wants a bodyguard following her around all the time."

"I don't think I'll get away from that." Jessi sighed. "I had a long talk with Dante this afternoon and he set out the ground rules. I want to argue, but in the end, he's only looking out for my best interest. Cat, I realize I was a total jerk to you yesterday. Thank you for not giving up on me."

"That's a very adult way of looking at these restrictions." Cora patted the girl's arm. "Don't worry. Cat's uncle will find whoever did this to Danielle soon. I can feel it."

Cat's phone rang, and as if he had heard his name, she saw from the display it was Uncle Pete. She handed the bill and its leather carrier to Seth. "Would you give this to our waiter when he comes by? I'll be right back."

"Sure." He looked like he wanted to ask, but then didn't.

She picked up the call before leaving the table. "Hey, Uncle Pete. Hold on a second and I'll go outside. We're at the restaurant."

"We'll meet you outside." Shauna waved her off. "Go handle this."

Cat weaved through the crowded restaurant, and when she reached the outdoors, sat on one of the benches on the walkway to the parking lot. The smell of flowers from the overgrown beds lining the parking lot and surrounding the restaurant was a sharp contrast from the food smells she'd just left inside. "Hey, sorry about that. What's going on?"

"I wanted to get back to you on your suspicions on Joseph John. It took some quick talking for him not to get his lawyer involved, but I've got enough I can take him off the suspect list. Not only was he at this costume thing in Denver, he ran a large segment of the activities right in the middle of the time Danielle was murdered. And they have him on tape. He was obviously amused when he realized he'd been considered a suspect. And yes, he admitted to having a serial killer memorabilia collection."

"So he's creepy, but not a killer." A couple passing by the bench looked down on her and quickly stepped away, deciding to wait on their car valet a little closer to the parking lot. Cat chose her next words carefully, making sure there wasn't anyone else close enough to overhear. "That's disappointing."

"You know I'm probably going to have to bring her in for questioning. She had good reason to kill her friend, and she was on the property when Danielle was murdered." Uncle Pete's words were hard, but his voice kind. "I know you like the kid."

"It's not just that. She's had a really rough week and she just seems to bounce back. I don't believe there is a snowball's chance in Arizona that she killed Danielle. I talked to her as soon as she got back to the house that afternoon. She wasn't stressed or anxious. She just wanted to assure me that she'd handled the problem and there wouldn't be any more interruptions."

Uncle Pete cleared his throat. "That sounds like—"

Cat didn't let him continue. "She handled it by talking to her supervisor. She didn't kill anyone."

"Look, I've got reports to get filed before I leave. Can we talk about this tomorrow?" He paused. "I am still invited to Sunday dinner, right?"

"Of course." Cat saw the group coming out of the lobby. "Look, find out who took her money. I think that's the key."

"The cash or the bank funds?"

"I told you that Martin took the cash." She turned her head so as not to be heard by the others.

"Exactly. Maybe he was helping himself to her bank accounts as well. I've got an interview with the kid first thing Monday morning. Get some sleep."

"You too." She stood and tucked the phone in her pocket. "We all ready?"

Cora came up to her. "Kind of. We have a favor to ask."

"Okay, what?" Cat hoped it wasn't ice cream. She didn't think she could turn down the soft serve that the local drive-in had in stock.

Cora looked around at the group as they walked to the SUV. Seth remotely unlocked the car, but no one got inside. "We'd like to go to Outlaw one more time. Jessi has her key and code, so we shouldn't trip any alarms. We just want to make sure there isn't anything we missed the first time."

"I want to clean out my locker. Dante's pretty firm on me not going back to work for a while. I've already cleared it with my boss. She said I could come anytime they aren't open to the public." Jessi stood next to Cora. "Do you mind taking us? That way, we'll be safe and I won't have to try to sneak onto campus to get my car. Besides, not all of us will fit in the convertible and there's strength in numbers."

"You have a convertible?" Kelly's words were still a little garbled from the alcohol. "Youth, they don't understand the value of delayed gratification."

"Take a nap, Kelly. We'll wake you up when we get to Outlaw." Connie gently helped her into the back seat.

"That sounds nice." Kelly curled up with her head resting on the window.

"I didn't say we were going to Outlaw." Cat glanced around the group, now watching her. "Look, it's not safe."

"We're not alone. We have you. You can call your uncle and tell him we're going up to get Jessi's locker cleaned out. The management knows. What could go wrong?" Connie got into the back seat with Kelly. "One last road trip."

Cat glanced at Seth and Shauna. "What do you think?"

"They make a good argument. Besides, I've always wanted to see the town in the dark." Shauna shivered. "I've heard all kinds of ghost stories."

"Okay, but we're only going into the staff building where the lockers are." Cat looked at the writers staring at her, waiting for permission for an adventure.

"And walking around the back? I'd love to see how they pull off the show." Lisa dove into the car.

"So glad I charged my phone. These are going to be amazing pictures."

Seth hung back as the rest of them climbed into the car. "Are you texting your uncle?"

"I don't know. He's already up to his eyeballs with work. You know he'd say to stay away, especially at night." Cat bit her bottom lip. "I'll text him once we're there and tell him I'll send a second one when we leave. That way he can't say no."

Seth moved closer. "This feels like that weekend we snuck into Denver for that music festival. You realize we both got grounded for that."

She kissed him. "And it was totally worth it. Besides, who's going to ground us now? We're adults."

"Then why does it feel like we're teenagers again?" Seth leaned closer and whispered, "Maybe we could find a dark corner for a few minutes when we get there."

She laughed and gently pushed him away. "Maybe we can carve out some time tomorrow before you leave for your trip. Otherwise, we're still on the clock until the guests leave. And that means no sneaking off."

"You're such a stickler for rules." His eyes twinkled in the dark. "But sadly, I'm leaving as soon as I get back from the airport run. I only have to do one, so the guys will be waiting for me at my apartment."

"Delayed gratification." Cat rubbed her hands on his chest. "It makes the time so much sweeter."

"Hey, you two. Are we going or not?" Lisa called out the open door. "We have adventures to complete."

Cat met Seth's gaze. "I'm going to regret this, I know I am."

"Yeah, probably, but at least we're all together. No one left behind. It's kind of like my army days, if the guys were all historical romance authors." Seth opened the front passenger door for her. "Besides, I'm in a great mood now that Snow is all tucked into her new home."

"That was the best gift you could have given her." She kissed him lightly and climbed into the car. Turning toward the back, she smiled at the group. "Let's go see if we can spot some ghosts."

# CHAPTER 22

The ride to Outlaw was like the summer Cat had gone to camp in eighth grade. Everyone was chatting and laughing and telling stories. Then the singing started. Fun rounds to keep the passengers awake—well, except for Kelly, whose snores sometimes added to the harmony.

Cat pointed to the turnoff for Outlaw. "There it is."

"Thank God. I don't think I could deal with another round of 'Ninety-nine Bottles.' I haven't heard most of these songs since I left school." Seth turned the car up the dirt road to the ghost town.

"Don't tell me they didn't have sing-alongs in the army. What about boot camp?" Cat reached for his hand in the dark. Seth hadn't talked much about what had happened while he was away. His conversations when he got back were all about their future and where he'd be stationed. Cat realized he'd been focusing on them, when all she wanted to talk about was what college would hire her and the writing projects she was planning. They'd been on two different paths that could have run the same way, but she hadn't seen it that way back then.

She felt his look before he spoke. "No, Cat, it wasn't like summer camp."

"Do you want to talk about it?" She hadn't ever asked him about his time in the service. Now she felt like a heel of a girlfriend.

He pulled the vehicle into the main parking lot, then made his way to the employees-only driveway that curved around the back of the town. She'd almost assumed he hadn't heard her when he answered. "Not here. Not now. But maybe someday soon."

And with that, he parked and shut off the car. "Okay, Cat, text your uncle. We have twenty minutes, folks. Make sure you get what you need done and are back here by that time, or we'll leave you for the ghosts."

Everyone giggled as they piled out of the car. Well, everyone except Kelly, who was still asleep, and Cat, who was still reacting to Seth's comment. "Jessi? Do you want to open up the staff building?"

"For sure." Jessi waved her friends toward the modern shed-type building. "Over here, guys. I can give you the grand tour of the employee holding pen."

Seth held up three flashlights he'd grabbed from the glove box. "If you want to look around town, take one of these. And don't go alone."

"Silly, no one is up here but us." Shauna grabbed one of the flashlights. "Come on, Cat, let's go walk down Main Street. I want to see the village."

"Seth? You coming?" Cat looked back at him as he leaned against the car.

He shook his head. "No, I'll stay here. That way I can watch both of the groups. Just don't run into a bear or something."

"You're kidding, right?" Shauna froze.

Cat pulled her forward. "Yeah, he's kidding. Kind of. There are bears in the woods here, but they won't come into the town. There's nothing here for them to eat."

"Besides you," Seth called after them. "Just be careful."

"Sometimes his sense of humor escapes me." Shauna stepped around the first building and they stepped back into time. Outlaw looked like it had in 1880 when the town was founded. Whatever type of man Joseph John was, there was no doubt he was a history buff. The hitching posts for the horses were worn and some even chewed down from a bored horse left too long on the street.

Shauna shined the flashlight on the buildings and then back down the long expanse of street. "I could have lived back here. I would have had an eatery for men who came off the trails and had nowhere to dine except at the saloon. My food would have been better. Or maybe a rooming house."

"Kind of like we do now, except we have writers, not dusty cowhands." Cat grinned. "Maybe that's who you were in another life?"

"You know I don't believe in reincarnation. We've had this talk." Shauna smiled as she stepped up onto the wood sidewalk that ran the length of the four buildings on the left. "Although, right now, I might just let myself be convinced."

They wandered down the sidewalk, glancing into the windows and talking. When they reached the end, Shauna grabbed Cat's arm. "Stop."

"What? I wasn't going to walk off, I knew the step was there." She started to move forward, but Shauna's grip tightened.

"No, it's not that. Don't you see it?" Shauna pointed toward the blacksmith's shop at the end of town.

"A bear?" Cat's breath stopped as she scanned the darkened area.

Shauna stepped backward and pulled Cat with her, out of the light from the overhead lamppost hidden in the back of the building. "No. Not a bear. A car. Someone else is here, Cat. We need to get out of here."

Cat barely saw the dark sedan parked next to the blacksmith's shop. "Who could that belong to? Maybe it's just a car one of the employees left behind this afternoon."

Shauna pulled her out of the light and back into the shadows. "I'm not willing to take that chance. One girl already died here. I don't want us to add to the body count. And I thought a bear would be the worst thing we'd run into."

"Don't get all worked up yet. We'll just go back, get everyone in the car, and head out of here. Uncle Pete said they'd had trouble with break-ins. Maybe some couple is just parking and getting busy." Cat hurried to keep up with her friend.

"You've been hanging around with Seth too

much. Sometimes bad things happen. Even in perfect little towns like Aspen Hills."

That stung. Cat almost stopped in her tracks but then she wondered, what if Shauna was right? Better be safe than sorry. They found themselves back by the vehicle.

Seth was looking at his phone. He put it in his pocket when he saw them walk up. "That was fast."

"Tell him what you saw. I'll go get the others." Cat moved toward the staff building, but then the door opened and Jessi came out with a box in her hands. The other women followed her.

"Hey, do we have room for this? I didn't realize how much crap I had in my locker." Jessi grinned, then looking up, dropped the box. "Son of a . . ."

Cat watched as she ran to the saloon's back door. She looked up at the building and saw what Jessi had seen, a figure in the window of the room where Danielle had been killed. "Call Uncle Pete. Get him here and get the rest of these people out of here."

"You've got to be kidding." Seth tossed the keys to the vehicle to Shauna. "You're not going in there without me."

"Guys." Shauna paused, then sighed. "Be careful. We won't go far." She turned to Cora, grabbing Jessi's box and shoving it on the floorboard. "Get everyone in the car. And call 911."

Cat didn't hear Cora's response because she was already inside and making her way through the dark hallway. "I should have grabbed Shauna's flashlight."

Light streamed from behind her. "I grabbed one."

"Thanks." They made their way to the stairway, and Cat caught a glimpse of Jessi at the top of the stairs, then she disappeared. "Crap, let's go."

They ran up the stairs, with Seth taking the lead. When they paused on the landing, he handed her the flashlight. "Stay here."

"Not on your life." She took the flashlight and gripped it like her life depended on it. Then they made their way to the room where she knew Jessi had disappeared.

When they got there, Jessi stood in the doorway, blocking their view.

"Move over, let me deal with this." Seth put a hand on the girl's shoulder.

Jessi moved and Cat gasped. The man sitting on the bed sobbing was Darryl, Jessi's money manager. "What are you doing here?"

"It wasn't supposed to be like this," Darryl sobbed. "I tried to make everything right, but then I just got in deeper. I'm sorry I took the money. I thought I could win it back and no one would notice."

"The police are on their way." Seth glanced over at Cat. "Do you know this guy?"

"He's Jessi's money guy, and apparently the one who has been siphoning off money from her account. I thought he was nice." Cat shook her head. "I called that one wrong."

Jessi spoke, her voice quiet. "You stole from me? And worse, you made my mom think I was the loser."

"It wasn't like that." Darryl didn't look at any of them. "I got in over my head. I borrowed a little here and there, then your father died and your mom asked for an accounting. Your father never asked for an accounting. We were friends, he trusted me. Your mother, on the other hand, she didn't. So I stalled."

"By telling her I was doing drugs." Jessi's tone was flat, emotionless. Now that the truth was out, she'd put together all the pieces. "Then you used my friend to gather information on me, but when I wasn't being the bad girl you'd hoped, I had to go."

"No. It wasn't like that. Danielle started pressuring me for more money. I could barely keep my head above water with the casino bosses, and this nobody threatens me? I lost my temper. I never meant to kill her. Why would I? She was keeping my secret."

"She was keeping everyone's secrets." Cat put a hand on Jessi's back. "At least it's over now. Uncle Pete will come and arrest this guy, and you can go back to your life."

Darryl started sobbing harder. "I just can't go on this way anymore. I came up here to end it. But I can't even do that. I'm so sorry, Jessi." He reached for the gun on the side table.

"Get away from him." Seth's voice was cold and he dove toward Darryl, knocking the gun out of his hands. He pinned him to the bed. "Grab that for me, would you?"

Cat picked up the weapon with two fingers, then moved out of reach. She felt a hand on her shoulder, then the gun was taken from her.

Uncle Pete let out a breath. "I swear, Cat, you're going to be the death of me. Brenden, get that idiot restrained."

Cat leaned into her uncle and watched as Darryl was put into cuffs and led out of the room. As he passed by her, he paused. "I really am sorry."

As they were walking down the stairs, Cat paused. "Wait, how did you get here so fast? Cora just called you."

"Seriously?" He shook his head. "Trouble follows you like a puppy dog. So when you texted me, Brenden and I took off after you. What were you thinking coming up here at night?"

Jessi paused as she moved in between them on the stairs. "I needed to clean out my locker. But now I think I can talk Dante into letting me keep the job. Isn't that great?"

They watched as she joined the other writers, who did a group hug around her.

Uncle Pete turned toward Cat. "Thank goodness you only do these retreats once a month. The death toll around Aspen Hills is getting a little high for my reputation."

"Ha, ha." Cat gave her uncle a hug. "You know it has nothing to do with my retreat."

"I'm not so sure of that." He squeezed her and then let her go. "I need to get this mess cleaned up. Go take your crew home. I have their information if I need to interview them sometime down the road."

Seth went over to the group. "Load up. We're heading back. And don't think you get to sleep in. We have to leave for Denver no later than eight to catch your flight. So if you want breakfast, you need to be packed and downstairs by seven."

Groans came from the women as they climbed

into the car and got settled. Cora spoke first. "You know it's almost midnight. Maybe we should take a later flight?"

"My guys' trip starts as soon as I get back from dropping you all off. If you want a ride, I leave Aspen Hills at eight. No exceptions."

"Cat, your boyfriend is kind of snippy. How do you put up with that?" Lisa called out from the back.

"He's had a busy week. He deserves a vacation." Cat turned in her seat and took in the group. "You all have been the most interesting retreat guests we've ever had."

"I'm not sure that's a compliment." Cora smiled. "Okay, ladies, you heard the man. Set your alarms for six. I want you all to be showered, dressed, and packed before breakfast."

A sleepy voice answered her from the back. Kelly had finally woken up. "When are we going to be at Outlaw? I want to get some pictures at night. Maybe I'd catch a ghost."

"Too late. We didn't catch any ghosts, but we caught a killer." Lisa waved the others around. "Don't worry about it, I'll catch Sleeping Beauty up on what went down."

"Hey, Seth? Can you turn the music up a little?" Connie leaned against the window. "This was my husband's favorite song."

The group was quiet on the ride back. The ride mirrored the trips home from camp. You went up loud and excited, and back home tired and thoughtful. This was the time everyone was tired and cranky and ready to be home. Cat turned to look at Seth. "You did amazing back there."

"I was stupid. I could have gotten you or Jessi killed."

"No. You couldn't have. You care for people." Cat put her hand on his arm. "And that's one of the reasons I love you."

"I thought it was for my charming wit and dashing good looks." Seth patted her hand.

"That too."

At least it was over. And Jessi was safe. Cat watched out the side window as they made their way from the wilderness into town. A town with a lot of secrets, but one thing she dtd know about Aspen Hills was that it was her home.

# CHAPTER 23

Seth was as good as his word, and at 8:05 he pulled out of the driveway on Sunday morning with Connie, Cora, Lisa, and Kelly tucked into the vehicle. He'd given them the extra five minutes to say their goodbyes to Jessi and Cat. And the group had made plans with Shauna to book a return visit to the retreat in six months. Kelly had offered to pay the entire cost if Jessi could come back as the Covington student.

"We'll figure out something," Cat promised as she shut the door. She, Jessi, and Shauna stood in the driveway and waved as the car left. "When is Dante coming to get you?"

Jessi grabbed her duffel and her laptop bag. "He's not. I told him I'd walk down to his house. He's expecting me for breakfast, so I better get going. My mom flew in last night and will be there too."

Cat gave the girl a hug. "Don't let them bully you. You are amazing. You can do anything."

"I'll second that." Shauna stepped in for her hug when Cat stepped back. "And you know where we are. You're welcome anytime you want to stop in."

"Thanks. I'll take you up on that." Jessi started humming as she made her way to the sidewalk. She turned back and waved when she cleared the gate. Then she was gone.

"It's like sending the baby birds out into the wild, isn't it?" Shauna stared after Jessi until they couldn't see her anymore.

"We got attached to this group." Cat turned toward the kitchen. "Do you need help cleaning up?"

"Nope, I'm good. But I will be out riding this afternoon, so don't come looking for me. Pete will be here at seven for dinner, and I'm making a roast chicken."

"Sounds wonderful." Cat walked back with her into the house. "I'm going upstairs to spend some time with my book. See you at dinner."

When seven came, the three of them sat down in the kitchen for Sunday dinner. Uncle Pete passed Cat the chicken. "Well, Darryl is out of my jail and off to Denver. They're going to do some psych tests on him. All he did was cry the entire time he was in my cell."

"It's been a crazy week. I almost feel sorry for him." Shauna dished up a tower of mashed potatoes and then poured gravy in the middle.

Uncle Pete took the potatoes and filled his own plate. "I'm really glad it's over. I can't believe I almost charged Jessi with her friend's murder. Your faith in her kept me from making that mistake."

"She's a good kid." Cat smiled at the memories from the last week. It had been an interesting retreat.

"Oh, and I've caught our Peeping Tom." Uncle Pete ran a hand over the back of his neck. "Apparently, the college got a copy of one of the frat's entrance dare lists. And peeking into your house and being seen was worth five points. Getting the cops called was worth ten. And if you got away with it, fifteen. We're going to be revoking their charter and sitting all the pledges down for a long talk about right and wrong."

"It's always something with the college." Cat tore off a piece of the breast meat and nibbled on it. "Do you have any more clues on the string of murders at Outlaw? Did Darryl just try to make her murder look like the others?"

"Now that we've eliminated Joseph John from the murders, yeah, it looks like they're not connected, although Shirley thinks the cases would be great training tools for new officers to learn how to investigate." He blushed at mentioning her name. "I guess we could be solving those someday."

"I got a call from Paul today." Shauna changed the subject quickly, sensing the unease Pete was feeling after mentioning Shirley. "The will reading is scheduled for next Wednesday. I'm so glad this nightmare will finally be over."

"So you'll be taking off for the islands when you inherit all that wealth?" Cat took a bite of the potatoes. "I better enjoy your cooking now."

"Even if he left me something, you're stuck with

me. And by the way, remember when you said I could get a pet?"

"You want something besides a horse and a cat?" Cat asked, not sure where this subject was going. The place was going to turn into a zoo if they didn't watch out. Maybe they should talk about Jessi instead.

"Well, Angelica solved that problem. I think we have enough pets for a while." Shauna smiled at the confusion on their faces. "She made a nest in the straw and delivered five healthy kittens in the barn. I can't believe you or Seth didn't notice she was pregnant."

"Six cats?"

"We don't have to keep all of them. And they don't have to be indoor cats. But yeah, we have pets."

Uncle Pete chuckled, then covered his mouth and pretended it was a cough. Cat leaned back into her chair. The house was filling up quickly. And now they had pets. No, she corrected herself. Their home was filling up quickly.

She went back to eating and asked her uncle how his girlfriend Shirley was doing. Home and family was nothing if not messy and uncomfortable at times. But it was also the best way to live. This was the second time in two days she'd thought about home and what it meant.

Cat had lived two lives in this house. The one with Michael. and now this one. And she thought even if she had seven more lives like a normal cat, this one might just be her favorite.

One of Shauna's favorite things to do is bake with huckleberries. If you're from the Western mountain areas, you know the joy of going huckleberry picking in early June. But if you're out of your stash, or you don't live in Colorado, here's a way to substitute blueberries. And with using the yogurt instead of the sour cream, you make it diet food. Well, almost.

Lynn

## EASY BLUEBERRY COFFEE CAKE

½ cup butter or margarine
1 cup sugar
3 eggs, slightly beaten
½ teaspoon vanilla
1 teaspoon baking powder
1 teaspoon baking soda
¼ teaspoon salt
2 cups flour
1 cup sour cream or vanilla yogurt
2 cups blueberries (fresh or frozen)
1 cup brown sugar
¼ cup butter
¼ cup flour

Preheat the oven to 350°F.

Cream ½ cup of butter and sugar. Add next five ingredients. Add 2 cups of flour and sour cream (or yogurt) alternately to egg mixture, mixing with a spoon. Fold in blueberries. Pour mixture into greased 9"x13" baking pan. In a separate bowl, cream brown sugar and ¼ cup butter. Add ¼ cup flour to get a semi-dry mixture. Spread on top of batter. Bake in 350° oven for 30 minutes.

# Connect with

## Us

Visit us online at
**KensingtonBooks.com**
to read more from your favorite authors, see books
by series, view reading group guides, and more.

Join us on social media

for sneak peeks, chances to win books and prize packs,
and to share your thoughts with other readers.

**facebook.com/kensingtonpublishing**
**twitter.com/kensingtonbooks**

## *Tell us what you think!*

To share your thoughts, submit a review,
or sign up for our eNewsletters, please visit:
**KensingtonBooks.com/TellUs.**